Paul Ashford Harris was born and educated in New Zealand before completing an MA at Cambridge University. He has lived with his family in Sydney since 1969 and is the author of three books and two plays plus five children's books based on Australian native animals.

LOVE, OIL
AND THE
FORTUNES
OF WAR

PAUL ASHFORD HARRIS

LOVE, OIL
AND THE
FORTUNES
OF WAR

VENTURA
PRESS

VENTURA
PRESS

First published in 2023 by Ventura Press
PO Box 780, Edgecliff NSW 2027 AUSTRALIA
www.venturapress.com.au

A catalogue record for this book is available from the National Library of Australia

Love, Oil and the Fortunes of War
ISBN 978-0-645497-21-2 (print book)
ISBN 978-0-6454972-0-5 (ebook)

Cover and internal design: Deborah Parry Graphics
Managing editor: Amanda Hemmings
Printed and bound in Australia by Griffin Press

Ventura Press acknowledges the Traditional Owners of the country on which we work, the Gadigal people of the Eora nation and recognises their continuing connection to the land, waters and culture. We pay our respects to their Elders past, present and emerging.

AUTHOR'S NOTE

T HIS BOOK is about three remarkable people, Gertrude Bell, William Knox D'Arcy and Admiral 'Jacky' Fisher. The story of their lives is essentially true as are the interactions between them, although it's not certain that Gertrude Bell met Jacky Fisher but given the family interrelationship it is highly likely. The conversations are of course not true and many of the meetings are invented. This is not supposed to be a factual account and sometimes the dates have been shuffled, especially to account for the fact that Gertrude is much younger than the other two. Nevertheless, it does shine a light on a dramatic period mostly within the first decade of the twentieth century, and hopefully it does justice to the powerful personalities of each of them and some remarkable events that arguably influenced the outcome of the First World War. There are of course endless sources behind the book, but I must pay tribute to Barbara W. Tuchman and *The Guns of August*, Jan Morris' portrait of Jacky Fisher, *Fisher's Face, A History of the Burmah Oil Company* by T.A.B. Corley, the fascinating portrait of the Savoy Hotel in Edwardian times in *The Secret Life of the Savoy* by Olivia Williams, and the extremely comprehensive biography of Gertrude Bell's life, *Queen of the Desert, Shaper of Nations* by Georgina Howell.

PROLOGUE
Gertie, D'Arcy and the Admiral

~

QUEEN VICTORIA died at 6.30 pm on Tuesday 22 January 1901. Beside her bed were her son Edward VII and eldest grandson Emperor Wilhelm II. Her favourite Pomeranian, Turi, was laying on her deathbed as a last request. Her funeral was conducted strictly according to her request. It was to be a military affair and she would be dressed in white rather than the customary black. An assortment of mementos mostly acknowledging members of her family were laid in the coffin. One of Albert's dressing gowns was placed by her side, with a plaster cast of his hand, while a lock of her mysterious 'servant' John Brown's hair, along with a picture of him, was placed in her left hand, concealed from the view of onlookers and family by a huge but carefully positioned bunch of lilies. Items of jewellery included the wedding ring of John Brown's mother, given to her by Brown in 1883. Her funeral was held on Saturday 2 February in St George's Chapel, Windsor Castle. She was interred alongside Albert in the Royal Mausoleum.

Victoria's reign lasted sixty-three years but now it was the beginning of the Edwardian era. Great hopes were held for a bright future for Britain, heralded in part by the comforting sight of the son (English) and grandson (Prussian) standing side by side over Victoria's coffin.

The citizens of England and indeed of Great Britain and Europe and the United States all to some degree were participants in the end of Empire event. Among the assembled heads of Europe, military commanders, lords and ladies, the mighty and the ordinary people of London, were three special observers. Gertrude Bell, back from the deserts of Mesopotamia, had come specially from Yorkshire to attend and had joined her half-sister Elsa and a group of her Oxford friends to view the spectacle. On another part of the funeral route, on the balcony of his club, Australian millionaire William Knox D'Arcy was basking in the prestige that surrounded him from his known friendship with the new king, Edward VII. They shared a consummate passion for horse racing, fine dining and women. The third participant, watching with several of his naval colleagues, was the Commander of the Mediterranean Fleet and Rear Admiral. The striking but diminutive figure of Jacky Fisher, uniform glistening with medals, saluted as the coffin passed. With his head held high and a fixed expression on his remarkable countenance, he attracted his own share of attention from the crowds pressing the boundaries of the funeral route.

All three observers felt that they were in a new century and a new era. They all had great expectations, a hope shared by most of their fellow citizens, that the relationships between Germany and England could only be better. It would now be a family affair, a century of peace.

CHAPTER 1
London

A FULL FORTY YEARS before Victoria's funeral, on 30 September 1862, a formidable figure, Otto Eduard Leopold, Prince of Bismarck, known to history as the 'Iron Chancellor', addressed the Prussian Chamber of Deputies. In his address he stated, 'Prussia must concentrate and maintain its power for the favourable moment which has already slipped by several times. Prussia's boundaries according to the Vienna treaties are not favourable to a healthy state life. The great questions of the time will not be resolved by speeches and majority decisions; but by Iron and Blood.' 'Iron and Blood' was a powerful warning.

Nobody listened.

Well, a few listened but did not hear.

It was in May 1870 that George William Frederick Villiers, 4th Earl of Clarendon and English Secretary of State for Foreign Affairs, was strolling down Parliament Street from 10 Downing Street deep in conversation with Prime Minister William Gladstone. They were on their way to the Houses of Parliament. They walked slowly, enjoying the spring sunshine and the leaves breaking out on the trees that lined the way. Passers-by recognised the Prime Minister and doffed their hats or wished them a good morning. Villiers was shuffling along, his hands grasped behind his back.

Gladstone bent forward to ask him a question. 'Tell me, George, what's your opinion? Should we be worried by Bismarck and this Prussian skulduggery?'

Villiers chuckled. 'Not a bit, I assure you. First, they have no navy to speak of and no ports of significance, and secondly, Bismarck is entirely absorbed in throwing his weight about in Europe, keeping Russia out of it whilst he deals with France. He has the Austrians where he wants them, but he is a devout and highly conservative Lutheran, and he also needs to manage strong Catholic opposition in Austria and southern Europe. In the meantime, Field Marshal Moltke, on Bismarck's orders, is busily dismembering France. Napoleon III thinks he is Bonaparte, but he is sadly mistaken.'

Gladstone pondered this for a minute. 'I thank God for the English Channel.'

Villiers stopped and turned to face Gladstone. 'I am afraid you will need all your energy trying to tame the Irish question.'

Gladstone could not but agree. Disestablishing the Irish churches, both the Catholic and Protestant, had, with some difficulty, been achieved but there was a bigger issue. He put a hand on Villiers' arm. 'You're right. Getting the damn English landlords out of Ireland is proving dashed difficult. I despair.'

Villiers, who was rather partial to collecting rent himself, chose to ignore this sally.

One month later, on 27 June 1870, Villiers, after an excellent lunch of spatchcock accompanied by a fine burgundy, dropped dead. Three months later Generalfeldmarschall Helmuth von Moltke smashed France at Sedan. Napoleon III was captured. By 1871 Paris and France had surrendered. Wilhelm was proclaimed German Emperor in the Hall of Mirrors in Versailles. To rub salt in the already gaping wound, Prussia occupied Alsace Lorraine, the area between the French and Prussian borders, opening a sore which would run for decades. England watched from the sidelines. Gladstone was still busy with Ireland.

CHAPTER 2
Persia, 1907

⌐

T HE RIGS POINTED skywards out of the surrounding sands like some alien structure from another planet. Nothing else of human construction stood in the mighty expanse of desert. The sand stretched away uninterrupted to the horizon. Apart from the drilling team the only human activity in the vast area came from the Bakhtiaris tribesmen, who sat at a distance on their camels watching this strange activity that had invaded their land. The tribesmen had received nothing, but the arrival of the drilling team had disturbed their life. They were not in the least content to have these strangers in their midst doing whatever they wished. The camels were motionless until upon some unheard command they turned their heads and camels and riders vanished into the foothills behind.

George Reynolds leaned against the ladder at the foot of the drilling rig, slowly dragging on his cigarette and listening to the steady thump, thump of the engine driving the rig bit inch by painful inch to its designated depth. He could feel the rig gently vibrating. Maybe one more day would do it. He didn't really think they would find anything at this late stage in the drilling program. The whole fiasco had been going on for nearly two years with nothing to show for it, but orders were orders.

It was late in the afternoon, the sun a great red ball low in the sky. God, it was hot. Hot and humid, flies in swarms and mosquitoes at night. What a hellhole this godforsaken corner of the desert had turned out to be. Still, the money was good, and he needed money and had not the least desire to return to England. There was nothing there for him.

Back home they were all enjoying the uninhibited gaiety of Edwardian London. Still, drilling was his life and oil was the goal and there was no doubt in his mind, if not in his overlords' minds in Britain, that the oil was somewhere in the area. He lifted the brim of his hat, wiped the sweat dribbling down his forehead with the back of his sleeve, and spat some tobacco on the sand. 'Cheap local cigarettes,' he thought. 'Rubbish.'

He was readjusting the hat when he noticed in the distance a cloud of dust, a vehicle coming towards them over the rough track that was the only access. As it drew closer, he could see it was one of the company trucks. It was another ten minutes before the beaten-up old vehicle finally arrived and the driver, dressed in hard-worn overalls, hopped out. Seeing George as the only person apparently visible, he approached him. He had a leather case slung over his shoulder which he opened to extract an envelope.

'Would you be George Reynolds?' George acknowledged he was. 'This is for you. Express delivery. Marked urgent.' George took the envelope, signed a form to confirm he had received it and tucked it in his shirt pocket.

George was a small man of no apparent significance. He was dressed in a worn-out army shirt and trousers with an incongruously large hat. Even though the broad brim provided him with the maximum shade possible, his face was still creased with wrinkles from too much sun and disfigured by a large mole on his left cheek.

His most arresting feature was a huge bushy moustache, drooping each side of his mouth and rather too sizeable for its surroundings. In spite of it all, he somehow managed to project an aura of command to his small retinue of workers. They knew well on no account to cross him.

Of course, he knew what would be in the envelope. Another dreary missive from head office in Edinburgh, or else that bastard D'Arcy, complaining about the cost of everything and the failure to discover any oil at all worth talking about. He had heard it all before. This could be the final instruction to close the project down after all the blood, sweat and tears that had been shed. What then for him? Back to England? He would never do that. For all the sand and heat and disappointment he had no desire to plead his case in Scotland or London. He knew his bosses: D'Arcy in London, and the directors of the Burmah Oil Company, mainly living in Edinburgh. He could imagine them seated in their leather armchairs in the club, replete after a damn decent lunch, cigars lit, complaining to each other about him; asking themselves what on earth he could possibly be doing. At least they never came here, and letters took weeks. For most of the time he did things his way and nobody argued. If he had to go, he would rather be in Burma, where Burmah Oil's main activities were situated, than England. He decided the letter could wait. It would not be good news. He would open it later.

A couple of the workers who maintained the rigs were close by. Sitting on a cart having a smoke, they'd witnessed the delivery, and had seen George put it away unopened. Who sent letters to this hellhole, they wondered?

'Go on boss, open it,' one said.

'I don't think I will, actually,' said George. 'And if you want to keep your job, then the longer I don't open it the better, is my opinion.'

CHAPTER 3
Ceylon

⌒

I N 1841 A BABY WAS BORN on the Wavendon Estate
in Ramboda, Ceylon, the eldest of eleven children, only seven
of whom survived infancy. Although christened John Fisher,
throughout his life he would be called 'Jacky'. His father was Captain
William Fisher, his mother Sophie. William was a British Army
officer in the 78th Highlanders, serving as a staff officer at Kandy.
He had previously been aide-de-camp to the former Governor of
Ceylon, Sir Robert Wilmot-Horton, but when Sir Robert died he
was forced to find an alternative activity.

The year Jacky was born his father sold his commission and
became a coffee planter (and later Chief Superintendent of Police),
but it transpired that coffee was not such an easy business. Jacky's
father struggled to pay back the money he had borrowed and to
maintain his large family.

At the age of six, against the heartfelt protests of his wife,
William Fisher decided Jacky, as the oldest child, needed to be sent
to England. Sophie argued but to no avail. William replied, 'My
mind's set. If the child is to receive a proper education, he must go
to England. He must! That is my final word.'

When he left Ceylon, Jacky was just old enough to be mortified to leave his mother. Sophie wept unconsolably on the dockside. Stamping his foot, Jacky turned on his father and shouted, 'I don't want to go. Don't make me!' Jacky pushed back tears as his mother hugged him. His father had to prise him away and they finally shook hands awkwardly as his desolate young son was taken by a young sailor up the gangplank. Back to Britain Jacky went, to live with his maternal grandfather Charles Lambe, a wine merchant, at his home at 149 New Bond Street, London.

Charles Lambe, it transpired, also had money difficulties and the family survived by renting out rooms in their house. Despite being as thin as a waif, Jacky was a scarcely welcome additional mouth to feed: food was in short supply, and his diet consisted of boiled rice, brown sugar and occasionally some bread and dripping. Jacky was quickly sent off to Coventry to one of the lesser boarding schools; as usual for the time it was a repository of harsh discipline, brutality and sexual degradation. His only good fortune was that his godmother, Anne Beatrix Wilmot-Horton, widow of the late Sir Robert, a most elegant lady, lived not far away in a country estate called Catton Hall. He was invited for his holidays and suddenly he was in the 'other' England, experiencing the leisurely enjoyment of all that the good life could offer to the upper classes, now basking in the fruits of Empire.

After observing Jacky for a few weeks, Anne felt she was getting to know the child and began to perceive that there was something rather special about the young man. She wrote a long letter to Jacky's parents. She ended her letter by saying, 'I must tell you that young Jacky is an intriguing child. He is most lively and curious, and I am forming the impression he may be very clever. There was a discussion the other day in which some matters of the orbit of the moon around the Earth and the positions of the stars took place and Jacky sat and listened. In the evening he bombarded me with a series of questions on the subject which, I am sorry to say, I was quite unable to answer. It was clear that not only had he listened, but he had also recalled in detail everything that was said.'

For someone as smart as Jacky it would not have taken long to work out that if he were forced to choose between the life of Lady Anne Beatrix Wilmot-Horton and his poverty-wracked grandfather's existence, the choice was crystal clear.

There was another thing. Jacky had discovered a poem displayed in a frame in the study. It was by Lord Byron, who was first cousin to Anne's deceased husband Sir Robert, and it was dedicated to Anne.

She walks in beauty like the night
Of cloudless climes and starry skies;
And all that's best of dark and bright
Meet in her aspect and her eyes:
Thus mellowed to that tender light
Which heaven to gaudy day denies.

Jacky studied it carefully but found it hard to comprehend. It seemed to praise the beauty of his godmother. Yes, he thought, if that was its purpose, it was exactly true.

CHAPTER 4
London

I T WAS TOWARDS the end of the Michaelmas term in 1865, twenty-eight years into Victoria's reign, and William Knox D'Arcy was in the classroom waiting for the start of the day's first lesson. He was amusing himself, busy wrestling with a compatriot. Solidly built, he was big for his age, with straight dark hair combed sideways across his head. He was just administering a headlock when the door opened, and a prefect stepped in.

'D'Arcy?' he said.

William let go of his smaller adversary. 'Yes?'

'The headmaster wants to see you in his study. Now.'

William tidied himself up, tucked his shirt back in and set off. He knocked firmly on the door to the headmaster's study and waited.

'Who is it?'

'D'Arcy, sir.'

'Intro.'

D'Arcy stepped inside to find the headmaster seated at his huge desk behind a neatly stacked pile of papers, busily reading. He glanced at D'Arcy over his glasses.

'Sit down, D'Arcy. Now, I need to inform you that your pater is on the way to school to pick you up and take you home. You will need to go and pack up all your belongings and be ready by midday to depart. Do not forget anything and have your trunk in the vestibule for his arrival.'

'But why, sir? It's not end of term, and can't I leave some things here for when I return?'

The headmaster cleared his throat. 'D'Arcy, you will not in fact be returning and therefore you must take everything with you. Your pater will explain the circumstances to you.'

He glanced down at a sheet of paper, which clearly contained details of D'Arcy's short stay at the school.

'I see you have made some commendable contributions in sport, in particular rowing. Ah, and I am sorry you have not retained the gold sovereign as a memento.'

D'Arcy did not respond but he knew what the headmaster referred to.

Westminster School has a tradition, called 'The Greaze', dating back to at least 1753. On Shrove Tuesday, the school's head cook tosses an enormous horsehair-reinforced pancake over a high bar. The bar has been used since the sixteenth century, to curtain off the Under School from the Great School. The junior boys fight over the pancake, watched by the Dean and headmaster, dignitaries (occasionally including royalty) and senior school members. The pupil who grabs the largest piece after one minute wins, and receives a gold coin which he must return for the award the following year. The bar is quite high and, in D'Arcy's time, if the cook failed to get the pancake over the bar after three attempts, he would be pelted by the boys with Latin primers. At the end of the Greaze, the Dean begs a half-holiday for the whole school.

D'Arcy was the most recent winner and was immensely proud of his achievement.

'It will be a great memory for you to take away,' said the headmaster. 'Now, off you go. You have a lot to do.'

D'Arcy rose, then hesitated, not sure if that really was all. The headmaster had returned to his papers, but he looked up. 'We hope you have learned some lessons at Westminster that will stand you in good stead through life, D'Arcy. We believe any young man who adheres to the abiding principles taught at our school will have an infallible roadmap for the life ahead. I wish you good luck in whatever endeavours you pursue. Dismissed.'

D'Arcy still hesitated, his usual ebullience deflated by this earth-shattering news. He wondered if the headmaster would say more but he had again returned to his papers. The interview was terminated.

Westminster School, situated in the precincts of Westminster Abbey, is derived from a charity school founded by the Benedictine monks before the Norman Conquest in 1066. It prides itself on its academic excellence and its strong record of entrances to the Oxbridge colleges. The school motto, *Dat Deus Incrementum*, is a quote from Corinthians 3:6: 'I planted the seed ... but God made it grow.' The school dates itself to its foundation by Elizabeth I in 1560. The school has good reason to expect that its graduates will do their duty: they will rule England, through the army or as naval officers, as bishops, as headmasters and, of course, through politics. Westminster has provided England with six prime ministers.

William's father, also called William, picked him up in his carriage. William senior had married Elizabeth Baker (née Bradford) and the young William was born on 11 October 1849 at Highweek, Newton Abbey, Devon. His father was directly descended from Lord D'Arcy of Knayth, Lord Justice and Chief Justice of Ireland in the fourteenth century and founder of a prominent Anglo-Norman family. Proud of his heritage and disdainful of the Catholics from Ireland, William senior was somewhat dismayed to find his heritage meant for little in London. In his more expansive moments he would clap William junior on the shoulder and exclaim, 'You must always remember you are a D'Arcy of Knayth, William. Do not forget your heritage.'

His father stayed in the carriage while the cabin trunk was stowed. William junior climbed in and sat facing his father as the carriage set off. His father coughed and then explained. 'The headmaster has clearly told you that you are leaving Westminster. I am sorry but circumstances are such that this is the best decision for all of us. I trust you will understand.'

'But where will I go instead? I don't want to move, Father; I have my chums and I might make the rowing eight next year.'

His father contemplated his reply. 'It's somewhat complicated, William. We will explain what will be happening tonight with your mother. Please be patient. But I can assure you it will be an adventure and I know you like adventures.'

No more was said, and William sat quietly wondering what on earth could be happening. He looked out at the passing streets, the day still shrouded in pea-soup fog, with no wind to lift it. Passers-by appeared, barrow boys, women with shopping bags and men striding along on some unknown mission. It was near freezing. He huddled in his cape and pulled the collar of his jacket up around his ears then copied his father, putting his handkerchief over his nose and mouth.

The fog grew worse, swirling around them and enveloping the street so they could see no more than the veiled shapes of pedestrians. The coachman was forced to keep stopping the carriage and get out to feel his way tentatively through the fog in his search for the street signs. Every now and then a recognisable monument or building appeared and then disappeared. Eventually they found themselves in Trafalgar Square, but only the very bottom of Nelson's statue could be seen. It took over an hour to finally reach home.

William's mind was elsewhere. Could it have been something he had done? He tried to remember but could think of nothing that would have required more than a couple of strokes of the cane. It seemed his father was in no mood for questions. The steady sound of the horse's hooves on the paved streets was oddly soothing but William was no more comforted by the end of the journey than he had been at the beginning.

Dinner was served promptly as always at 6 pm but William was astonished to find that the maid, Mary, was not present, and his mother performed the duty of serving the meal. The first course was eaten almost in silence apart from some desultory chatter about the food and the horrible weather. William was busting to ask what exactly was going on but knew that it was not his place to do so. Finally, his mother, Elizabeth, decided to take the lead. She was a handsome woman, with a strong face emphasised by her hair scraped back, parted in the middle, and tied up in a neat bun. She patted her bun, and absentmindedly adjusted the hairpin.

'William, you need to understand that your father has run into some difficulties with his business interests and is the victim of some very vicious behaviour by people that he once thought were friends. As a result, he has been forced to close down his ventures in London. We cannot remain here under the circumstances. The situation is so dire that we have taken the huge step of leaving England.'

His father interrupted. 'It is unconscionable; they have attacked me, and I have found no way to defend myself. I never would have believed that such perfidious behaviour could happen. They refuse to listen to reason. Now they throw my Irish background in my face, as if that ever mattered in the past.'

William stared in incomprehension. 'Leave England? Just leave – and go where? Where are we going?'

His mother stepped in. 'In the circumstances, we have decided there is a great future for us and the family in Australia. We have booked places on a ship and our final destination will be a place called Rockhampton, in the state of Queensland.'

'Australia? Rockhampton? What are you talking about? I don't understand.'

Like most boys of his age, he knew nothing of Australia. All he could think of were the faraway city of Sydney, those strange creatures called kangaroos, and Captain Cook.

After dinner William's father rose from the table and went straight to his study, slamming the door behind him.

His mother sighed. 'Well, I'm sure they won't have fog.'

William stared back in silence.

'Son, I don't expect you to understand, but suddenly we have no money, and your father has debts he cannot possibly meet. We will be totally humiliated as this disaster seeps out into society. Our friends will snub us, and we will be living in penury. Even if you were to go back to school your friends and teachers would treat you terribly. I want you to understand: we have no alternative.'

CHAPTER 5
New South Wales

FREDERICK MORGAN was born in either Essex or London in 1807 – nobody seemed to care which. His family were poor, dirt poor; like many, barely able to make it through the week. It was no surprise at all when, aged seventeen, Frederick was arrested for stealing a length of cloth from a tailor's shop in Islington. What could he have thought to do with it? The results were catastrophic. The teenager was tried before Mr Justice Park in London's Old Bailey.

The judge was in a foul mood. He'd had a hurried breakfast and had exchanged words with his harridan of a wife. He was looking forward to lunch at his club and was heartily sick of the procession of thieving urchins that passed before him. Frederick was dressed in the best clothes his parents could manage. They borrowed a shirt from a neighbour, and washed and ironed a small cloth cap. His shoes had holes in them, but his mother had cleaned them as best she could, weeping silently as she worked.

It was a very brief trial. The offence was not denied; Frederick had been caught with the goods in hand. Frederick watched, his heart in his mouth, as the judge prepared to give his sentence.

Justice Park pushed his glasses up on his nose, peered briefly at a few cursory notes, and nodded to the bailiff. He then reached out for his black cap. Frederick's world collapsed around him. He was sentenced to death by hanging; but then someone mentioned that his parents were industrious. The judge considered this for some time. *Industrious* – that was a word he rarely heard. He grunted, and then commuted the sentence to life imprisonment and transportation to Australia, banged his gavel and departed for lunch.

In 1825 Frederick was transported to the colony of New South Wales on the *Marquis of Hastings*, arriving at Sydney Heads on 3 January 1826.

In Sydney he was assigned as a convict to a tailor for two years, and found he had some modest talent for that trade. It was up to convicts to find their own lodgings, and before long Frederick had found somewhere to sleep, he could feed himself each day and even manage to buy himself a beer at the local pub. He had grown fond of the warm sunshine, the sparkle of the harbour on a summer day and even had one or two friends, men like himself, transported but slowly struggling into some sort of life.

The latter was fortuitous. In 1836 he met Emma Martha Woodward and their first child, Frederick Augustus Morgan, was born on 2 June 1837. Emma had arrived as a free settler with her mother and two brothers in 1827. Frederick remained quietly in his employment until 'removed by authorities' in 1838. This allowed him to move about more freely and accept work offered to him. Frederick and Emma then headed across the Blue Mountains to the small country town of Bathurst. He received his 'Ticket of Leave' in 1839 which bore the endorsement 'allowed to remain in the District of Bathurst'. The ticket of leave was a recognition of Frederick's good behaviour, and meant that although he remained a convict he could work for himself, and it did allow him to marry.

Wedlock was not uppermost in their minds, but finally they were married on 24 April 1851, four months after their eighth child was born. By the time they had finished procreating they had managed sixteen children. Their ability to afford such a family must have stemmed from Frederick's decision to cease tailoring and become a publican, first at the Spread Eagle Inn in Bathurst, and then the George Inn in Tenterfield in 1856.

He had received a 'conditional' pardon, approved by Queen Victoria, on 12 August 1846. Clearly recognising that this (now not so young) man was of bad blood, the pardon was attached with the words: 'Never to return to England'.

CHAPTER 6
The British Navy

⌒

IN 1854 JACKY'S PARENTS were still living in Ceylon, but when Jacky was fifteen his father was killed in a riding accident. The question arose as to what to do with three of the Fisher boys. At this stage, the British Navy was continuously expanding to protect the assets of the growing British Empire, which now stretched around the world. New recruits were needed, and age was no great barrier.

The three boys joined the navy. The younger, Frederick, eventually reached the rank of admiral and the youngest, Philip, became a lieutenant before being drowned in a storm in 1880. Jacky found the requirements for being accepted less than arduous: being able to recite 'The Lord's Prayer' and jumping naked over a chair. Upon joining he was assigned first to HMS *Victory* at Portsmouth and then to HMS *Calcutta*, an old ship built in 1831 of wood with muzzle loaders and propelled by sail. Discipline was extreme. All young sailors were used to harsh discipline, but when Jacky first saw eight men flogged with a cat-o'-nine-tails he fainted.

Fisher's background would have made him an outsider by the traditions of the British Navy, or at least that was how he must have seemed to others on first meeting. Unlike his father, who was six feet two inches, Jacky was five feet seven inches tall; and worse, his skin was quite dusky. This, together with his birthplace, persuaded many that he had Indian blood. In fact, the colouration was caused by early bouts of dysentery and malaria. However, Jacky had three advantages that would far outweigh any tendency to be patronised by his fellow sailors: he had no regard for anyone's class, he was anything but shy and retiring and, as his godmother had realised, he was remarkably intelligent.

Jacky's next few years fulfilled the naval saying, 'Join the navy and see the world'. After participating on board *Calcutta* in the blockade of Russian ships in the Gulf of Finland, he was posted to HMS *Agamemnon* in Constantinople; after promotion to midshipman, he joined the 21-gun corvette HMS *Highflyer*, part of the Royal Navy's China Station, and saw action in the second Opium War. The *Highflyer's* captain, Charles Shadwell, was an expert on naval astronomy, and recognised the talents of his young recruit. He taught a receptive Fisher everything he could about navigation.

When Jacky was due to leave the ship, Shadwell called Fisher to his office. 'Well, young man,' he said. 'You have done very well on this voyage. If you can maintain your enthusiasm, you will go a very long way in the navy. I venture to say, the new navy will need you. I am going to give you a present which I hope you will find you will use. Every time you do, I hope you will remember me and fulfill your great promise.'

The captain handed Fisher a small box. Inside sat a pair of studs engraved with Shadwell's family motto: *'Loyal au Mort'*. Fisher was taken aback. He muttered a few words of thanks, but he never forgot this act of unexpected generosity and encouragement.

After passing his exams in 1860, Fisher qualified as a lieutenant and was awarded the rank of midshipman. He was then transferred to HMS *Chesapeake*. Shortly after, he was given his first command of the paddle gunboat HMS *Coromandel*, the 'yacht' of the China Station's admiral, taking her on his first voyage from Hong Kong to Canton. He was nineteen. Not many young sailors stayed on any ship for very long in the nineteenth century, and Fisher was soon off to join HMS *Furious*, a paddle sloop.

Arriving at the top of the gangplank, small bag in hand, he found himself confronted by what was clearly the captain, screaming at a cowering young sailor. 'Take him to the brig. And give him a good thrashing.' He was purple in the face with rage. 'Spilled food on the deck. I will not have it. I will not!' Turning, he glared at Jacky. 'Who the hell are you?'

'Fisher, sir. Reporting for duty, sir.'

The captain uttered a disdainful grunt and stormed off.

Captain Oliver Jones was a martinet. Jones terrorised the crew and disobeyed orders from the Admiralty. Within two weeks of Fisher's arrival there was a mutiny. Notwithstanding all this, even Jones reluctantly conceded that this lad Fisher was something special. He had to admit that young Fisher was better at navigation than he was.

In 1861 Fisher sat his First Lieutenant's examination in navigation at Portsmouth and passed with flying colours. He had already received top grades in seamanship and gunnery, with a mark of 963 out of 1000 in navigation, and achieved the highest score then attained under the recently introduced five-year scheme. For this he received the Beaufort Testimonial, an annual prize of books and instruments. Without doubt the navy had unearthed a new talent.

As he waited patiently for his new appointment, a letter arrived. It was from Captain Shadwell. 'Congratulations, young man,' it read. 'This is a remarkable achievement. You have certainly fulfilled your promise, but you must keep going and keep your eyes on the top of the mountain. I will accept nothing less than seeing you an admiral one day.'

Fisher folded the letter carefully. It stayed with him for the rest of his career.

CHAPTER 7
England

T AROUND THE TIME the Morgans were thinking of moving to Rockhampton and Jacky Fisher was on his way to command a ship of the line – a powerful warship – a baby was born in 1868 near County Durham, England. A granddaughter of one of the wealthiest men in Britain, she could hardly have had a more auspicious arrival than to be born into such a family, reckoned the sixth wealthiest in Britain.

Her grandfather was Sir Isaac Lowthian Bell. Educated first as an engineer, he studied at Edinburgh University and then at the Sorbonne, and in Denmark and the south of France. He became a metallurgical chemist and England's foremost industrialist. Manufacturing steel on a huge scale, he eventually was to produce one-third of the steel used in Britain. Author of the steel industry bible, *The Chemical Phenomena of Iron Smelting*, he was looked upon as the high priest of British metallurgy. At various times he was Lord Mayor of Newcastle, the Liberal member for Hartlepool, and High Sheriff of County Durham. A friend of Charles Darwin, Thomas Huxley, William Morris and John Ruskin, he was at the heart of a period of seminal advances in evolution, science, art, architecture and social reform. With his two brothers he owned collieries, quarries and iron mines. The furnaces from his foundries darkened the skies over northern England twenty-four hours a day.

Despite his wealth, Sir Lowthian's wife, Margaret Pattison, ensured he refrained from outdoing some of the ancestral piles owned by the aristocracy of England. His main residence, Washington New Hall, was not quite a mansion, and his second house, Rounton Grange, was not quite a stately home. Margaret was born of a no-nonsense family of shopkeepers and scientists and possessed the northern contempt for undue flamboyance. A house was to be lived in; it was not to be entered in a competition for extravagance.

The baby's name was Gertrude Bell and her parents, Hugh and Mary, lived quite modestly considering their wealth. She was born at Red Barns, their home near the fishing village of Redcar on the Yorkshire Coast, not far from County Durham. Hugh was of a gentler and kindlier manner than the formidable grandfather, whose children and grandchildren revered but feared more than loved. Sir Lowthian's scientific and business skills would not have taken him to such an exalted position without an iron will to succeed and a strong ruthless streak.

Gertrude's mother, Mary Shield, was a local girl, the daughter of a prominent Newcastle merchant.

Gertrude's parents enjoyed the relative peace of their own home, away from the domineering Lowthian. The Yorkshire coast runs between the estuaries of two rivers, the Tees and the Humber. The cliffs at Boulby are the highest on the east coast and behind them lie the Yorkshire moors. It was a wild place with extremes of weather, alternatively with sunny, inviting beaches, or the moors swept by snow and wild winds blowing in across the Channel from the east. It was a wonderful place for such a spirit as Gertrude. She grew up, often alone, among the people of Yorkshire, tough and resilient folk, who respected you for what you were and not the station into which you were born.

Three years after Gertrude's birth, her brother Maurice was born in 1871. Mary, beautiful but delicate, succumbed to some unrecorded malady and three weeks after Maurice's birth she died. Hugh was devastated and tried to keep his anguish at bay by concentrating on his work and his numerous other responsibilities. Gertrude was left alone to deal with her grief, communing with the beautiful but inhospitable countryside to which she found a lifelong bond.

CHAPTER 8
New South Wales and Queensland

FREDERICK MORGAN JUNIOR must have been one of the most enterprising of the sixteen Morgan children sired by Frederick senior and Emma. As the oldest, it is fair to assume his parents had more to do than worry about his upbringing. He had gone his own way. While nominally a butcher in Tenterfield he had seen the money that could be made from mining if you kept your nose to the ground and just had a stroke of luck. He set up a company mining for tin and then a small gold mine. He must have made some money, and with his father to advise, he took a licence for the Criterion Hotel in Warwick in southern Queensland. He eventually managed to set up a racing stable, racing being a highly popular pastime in country Australia, and helpful background for running a pub. His moment of triumph arrived when he won the Glen Innis Cup in 1877; he had become yet another convert to the great Australian pastime of betting on the nags.

One afternoon he was behind the bar in the hotel, keeping a good eye on the few patrons passing the time slumped over one flat glass of beer. There was a huge storm outside. Lightning flashed across the sky, accompanied by rolling booms of thunder. The rain slashed down and ran in rivulets off the roof. The gutters quickly overflowed, and water gushed back into the roof cavity, then began dripping through the ceiling in the entrance way. 'Something else to fix,' thought Fred.

Two fit-looking young fellas pushed through the swing doors into the bar. The new arrivals were soaked, their coats saturated and water dripping off the brim of their hats. Fred wondered if they were over twenty-one. His wife Mary Jane Wheatly – the daughter of a local innkeeper and an old hand at pub-keeping – fetched some towels. They got chatting. Fred asked where they were from; it turned out to be Rockhampton, way up north. As it happened, the last time they had been in Warwick they'd made a few bob on one of Fred's horses, so they knew who the publican was. The chat continued as the beers flowed. The young fellas revealed that they were making plenty out of working for the miners who'd arrived in Rockhampton in droves after some gold shows. Not only that, but a rumour was circulating that one of the local pubs was for sale. The landlord had died, and the two visitors reckoned it was a great opportunity. Rockhampton was growing fast. They were thinking that being a publican would be a good sort of a game. 'Wish we had the money. Those bloody miners sure can drink,' was their opinion.

Fred and Mary Jane talked it over. Warwick was about as exciting as watching grass grow and the pub was only breaking even. A lot of work for not much, as Mary Jane complained, and she was sick of breaking up brawls while Fred was off on his mining escapades or checking on his horses.

Fred came back from an afternoon at the stables to find Mary Jane standing in the bar with her hands on her hips. She exploded.

'For Christ's sake, Fred, while you've been having fun with your bloody horses, I've had a full-scale brawl to deal with. The scum from the abattoir. The police came and we'll probably get fined. I'm bloody sick of it. Look at all that broken glass. Beer all over the floor. It's like a bloody battlefield.' She took her apron off, rolled it in a ball and threw it at him. 'I'm off. It's your pub. You can get behind the bar. I'll see you later.' She marched out and slammed the swing doors behind her.

A week later they had made up their mind. Fred liked the mining opportunities: 'Where the real money is,' as he said. They headed up to Rockhampton. They liked the feel of it as soon as they arrived, apart from the heat. It was on the coast, had beaches, a great river and dramatic hinterland with forest and hills running away to the west. Most of all they liked the buzz generated by the citizens who were there to make a life, many starry-eyed about the gold that awaited them. Fred could see that what the young lads in Warwick had told him was true. There were plenty of thirsty men in this town and not too many places to spend your money. Fred took on the licence for the pub, the Bush Inn, but, like the rest of the population, his heart remained in the gold-mining opportunities which were continuing to prosper and fuel the population growth in Rockhampton.

True to his dream, Fred managed to acquire the lease on the Cawarral goldfield for the new Galawa mine. Up on Mt Wheeler, it enjoyed great views over the coast and a number of small leases pegged across the face of the mountain. He called his brother Edwin (Ned) and talked him into helping him manage the mine. Ned had a hard look around. He reckoned there were good gold shows, but it would require some better machinery for extraction, and the use of cyanide on the tailings. It was going to cost money, that was for sure.

Next, Fred's brother Tom agreed to help with the pub. Six months was all it took for Tom to find an opportunity to run a pub of his own. He took up a licence for the European Hotel. As he said when Fred frowned at the thought of competition: 'Plenty of drinkers for all of us, Fred. This town's a pub-owner's paradise.'

Fred wandered down to the European to catch up with Tom for a natter. They were having a beer in a corner of the bar when the subject of the Galawa mine came up. Tom wanted to know how Ned was going.

Fred frowned. 'It's okay, but he reckons it's a strange place. No one talks to anyone. Haunted or something; all rubbish really.'

'What happened?'

'Don't know. No one talks but the story has it that some mad officer in the Native Police, a white bloke of course, drove a whole lot of Aborigines off the cliff on the mountain. Lot of deaths.'

Tom took a sip of his beer. 'So, is it true?'

'Don't know. Just more bloody violence up here. We just need to do what we do. And keep out of it, I reckon.'

~∘

In around 1870 William McKinlay, a stockman in Rockhampton who dabbled in the mining industry like everyone else, had happened upon what, he was pretty sure, was a significant gold-bearing area on the side of Ironstone Mountain. Ironstone Mountain was more a spur from the main range than a mountain. It stood only 1276 feet above sea level, but it did contain ironstone outcrops and a little alluvial gold in the gullies. McKinlay tried to keep it secret while he organised money and what was needed to peg the claim. He told only his family, and ordered them to keep it quiet, but his daughter was a chatterbox and just had to tell her boyfriend Sandy, who worked on a nearby property. A few months later Sandy went to work for the Morgan brothers. One evening they were sitting outside after a hard day in the fields. There was a fire and a couple of cases of beer. As the beer flowed the chat became more outlandish, full of tall tales, bad jokes. Fred Morgan and his brothers began talking about the gold prospecting. They had done a heck of a lot of prospecting but had only a few small finds to show for it.

Fred spoke up. 'Don't reckon we'll ever find much. How much longer are we going to go on? I'm wearing out my patience and my boots.'

Sandy helped himself to another beer and waved the bottle around. 'You don't know where to look; there's gold there for sure, but no one knows where.'

'Bullshit,' was all Fred could say. 'How the hell would you know?'

His brother Tom joined in. 'Yeah, you know what, Sandy? You're full of it.'

Sandy rose unsteadily to his feet and, still holding his bottle, shook his fist at them. 'Bullshit, is it. Bullshit?' And out it came. What he'd heard from McKinlay. The secret chat about the big find.

Fred quickly changed the subject, but he'd only had a couple of beers, and he'd been listening.

To see if there was any truth in what Sandy had told them in his cups, the Morgans put in three days prospecting. That was all it took for them to find that this was something special, and McKinlay hadn't pegged it.

In 1882, while McKinlay was still messing about, he discovered that the Morgan brothers, Fred, Tom and Ned, had pegged the site and registered a claim. William was beside himself; he was out with nothing.

He never spoke to his daughter and her now husband Sandy again.

CHAPTER 9
Rockhampton, Queensland

ROCKHAMPTON had been proclaimed as a city in 1858. Its existence followed the discovery of the Fitzroy River by the Archer brothers in 1853. The river, when not in flood from tropical downpours or cyclones, flows amiably into the southern end of the Great Barrier Reef. It is quite wide enough for commercial traffic. In recognition that the river provided great opportunity for both commerce and farming, the Archers set up a holding there in 1855, followed soon by more settlers, enticed by the fertile valleys on each side of the river. Within a year gold was found, which inevitably led to the first north Australian gold rush and an influx of the usual chancers and reprobates eager to get rich. These migrants quickly transformed Rockhampton into Queensland's second largest port and led to it being nicknamed the City of the Three S's: 'Sin, Sweat and Sorrow'.

William's parents had concluded that Rockhampton was sufficiently remote – no one would care where or why the D'Arcys had chosen to come there. They would blend in with the locals, many of whose past lives would not have stood up to too much examination. William's father could set up as a solicitor, and should the worst happen and he eventually be struck off in London, who would ever know?

Arriving in Rockhampton, they managed to find themselves a modest house. Well-situated, it was on one of the wide boulevards copied from the Melbourne design, and which were to help make Rockhampton something more than just another country town.

The first experience was what seemed to the family to be extreme heat. Rockhampton is only twenty-three degrees south of the equator. Winters are mild but summers are roasting, the relentless sunshine only relieved by tropical downpours and the occasional cyclone. The family hated it – especially William's father, who tried to maintain some decorum by wearing his London suits, including his waistcoat.

His mother complained to her husband. 'This is too much. I feel I cannot breathe! I perspire constantly and my clothes are ruined and need washing every day. Surely we do not have to endure this?'

William senior patted her shoulder. 'I know, I feel it too, Elizabeth, but I've been talking to some of the men at the club. They all say the same. You will adjust. A few months and it will not feel so bad. In any case, winter is coming, and they said winter is a marvellous time. No more chilblains for you, my dear! I must also say there is plenty of opportunity for a solicitor. I have never come across such a disputatious bunch. They argue and fight over everything. My services are certainly in demand. We shall have a nice house with a cool verandah, mark my word.'

'Perhaps if we wait a little, we could return to England?' She wiped the sweat from her forehead with her handkerchief. 'I don't believe I will ever get used to this place.'

William nodded. He felt for now it would be better if she kept some hope that this could happen. He knew very well it would not, but this was not the time to say so.

The D'Arcys had realised that Australia would be full of Irish.

William's father had mixed feelings about this Irish diaspora. With their Anglo-Irish heritage he thought himself above it all and kept well clear of joining anything that looked like an Irish society. He especially stayed away from the powerful influence of the Catholic Church in Australia. The family would construct their own story.

William went briefly to the local school which he hated almost as much as his parents hated the weather. He had been at school with the cream of English society, with sons of the gentry, of dukes and the occasional earl. As the son of an Irish solicitor, he had suffered plenty of condescension from these children born to rule. Here he now was in the middle of nowhere, saddled with a plummy English accent and surrounded with what he regarded as the offspring of rogues and scoundrels. Fights were plentiful and insults and abuse constant.

One afternoon he was late leaving school and found himself walking home alone through the back streets. As he passed the local park, two of his classmates stepped in his way. One of them, Kieran Reilly, a large, freckled lout with bright red hair grabbed his shirt.

'You're scum, that's what you are.' He spat in William's face. 'Pommy scum.'

The other lad, a taciturn dark-haired youth, nearly as broad as he was high, grabbed him from behind and tried to pin his arms back. Reilly delivered a belt to the nose and followed up with a fist in the stomach.

'We don't want you bastards here,' he growled.

William suffered another belt in the stomach. But he was tougher than he looked, and managed to get one fist free to deliver a whack at his opponent's head. There was more scuffling until some spectators appeared. The assailants ran off jeering and whistling.

William's parents soon squeezed out of him what had happened. His mother went to the headmaster, and the headmaster sent her to see the boy's teacher, a Catholic priest called Patrick Houlihan.

Houlihan was immensely tall and thin. His heavily pock-marked face showed signs of sunburn from which his pasty pale skin was totally unprotected. He listened briefly, his face registering just a trace of a smirk. He then announced that he had considered the matter but as it had taken place out of school premises it was not the school's responsibility.

Elizabeth persisted but Houlihan was having none of it. In a thick Irish accent Elizabeth could hardly understand he announced, 'I questioned the boys. They know nothing about it. Must have been some miners on the way home from the pub. Good afternoon.' Elizabeth was shown out.

One of the teachers, an austere Irish lady called Briana Savage had come across the aftermath of the fight as she was walking home. Briana was head of the English department. Equipped with an encyclopaedic knowledge of English literature, she also had sharp eyes and a tongue to match. The headmaster asked what she might be able to add. She just shrugged. 'Nothing. It was over when I arrived. That's what boys do.' As far as the school was concerned the case was closed.

D'Arcy senior and young William had found themselves socialising at the Rowing Club down on the banks of the Fitzroy River. It wasn't long before some of the members learned that William had done a bit of rowing at school. He had even had proper coaching. He soon found himself on the river and next thing in a four with a plan to row in the upcoming Head of the River regatta. He was delighted at the prospect of being back on the water, but slightly taken aback when he found his fellow crew were three Irish boys from the local Catholic school. Not only that, David Clarke, the coach, was a history teacher, and also Irish. D'Arcy junior shrugged; they seemed to be good rowers and the coach a fine fellow who knew what he was doing. He was put in the three seat, with a bow side oar; the 'powerhouse', the coach said. There was plenty of banter between the other three and D'Arcy, most but not all of it good-natured. One afternoon the coach took them aside. They sat on the grass and listened.

'Boys,' he said, 'I have to tell you this is like no other sport. Rowing is the ultimate team sport. There are no heroes and no villains. No one hits a winning run or scores the winning try. You will win or lose together as one, so there can be no dissension among you, in or out of the boat. Do you understand?'

As well as picking up a bit of the backchat in the boat, David Clarke had heard about the scrap D'Arcy had been involved in; hence his little lecture. But he thought he might try going a little further.

One afternoon he collared D'Arcy and sat him down on a bench by the river.

'I know what happened with the fight, William, and I have a feeling you might be a bit contemptuous of these Irish lads. Perhaps you need to understand where this is coming from. You won't know, but for the last fifty-odd years there has been a potato famine in Ireland. Now, potatoes are most of what the Irish eat. In the fifties it was terrible. No one really knows, but they think maybe a million died and a million fled. The population dropped nearly twenty-five per cent. Many came to Australia. Forty-odd thousand were convicts, sent for stealing a loaf of bread. Many more assisted to emigrate. What made the famine and poverty far worse is that most of the land in Ireland is owned by absentee English landlords. The landlords sent the bailiffs to collect the rents. The bailiffs beat up the tenants and evicted the thousands who couldn't pay – fifty thousand of them. They say the landlords took six million pounds out of the land they owned there. Many of those bastards have never even been to Ireland.'

D'Arcy shifted uneasily on his seat. His father had told him plenty about the family connection to Ireland. He didn't know if he really wanted to hear this but there was no escape. He sat quietly and listened.

David continued. 'My father, before he came here, was part of the "Three Fs" campaign, a campaign for "Free sale, fixity of tenure, and fair rent". Then he was badly beaten up by some thugs sent by the bailiff when he paid short rent. He and Mam emigrated as soon as they could get on a boat. The vast majority of Irish here are Catholic, so it didn't help that the landlords back home were English protestants. They have carried the wounds with them. I'm telling you this so you know where this anger is coming from, but we all need to remember that we're in a new country. We need to forget it and start again but we, and you, need to understand the past before that can ever happen. Now, that's enough; the Head of the River regatta's in three weeks.' He took D'Arcy by the shoulder. 'I reckon we're good enough. We can win it, but only as a team. Fair enough?'

D'Arcy looked up. 'Yep. Fair enough.'

The coach smiled. 'Good man.'

On the race day, David pulled the boys together before they climbed into the boat.

'It's a bit windy down the course, boys, so short strokes. At the start go half, half, three-quarter, three-quarter, fifth stroke a full stroke. You've done it plenty of times. So go hard and good luck.'

The boys picked up the boat, swung it over their heads in unison and carried it to the river, then lowered it carefully into the shallow water and climbed in and set their foot straps. D'Arcy looked around. A good turnout, with crowds of spectators on both sides of the river. His mother and father had brought a hamper and chairs and were in the crowd somewhere.

The cox took them gently out to the start line, and they surveyed the seven other boats that were the competition. They could see the boat from Aloysius school, last year's winner and the hated opposition, that was their main threat; next to them was a boat from New South Wales. D'Arcy could feel his nerves, but he forced himself to sit still, stay calm. As they lined up the starter's boat patrolled up and down ensuring they were straight, before calling them for the countdown for the start.

D'Arcy straightened his back and fixed his eyes on the neck of the stroke. There was a crisp crack of the starting gun. They were away. The stroke took the boat out fast but it remained controlled and smooth, its oars hitting the water as one, the puddles nice and even. By the mile mark they had a half-length lead.

D'Arcy broke all the rules and stole a glance out of the boat. 'Eyes in the boat, Three,' snapped the cox. The cox stepped up the rating, the number of strokes per minute, and then called for a set of ten extra hard. Then another ten. As the finish loomed he called for one more effort. 'Twenty more lads, to get us home.' He shouted them out: 'One, two, three, four …' They crossed the finishing line and slumped, exhausted, over their oars.

For a few seconds none of the rowers could speak. The cox let them know. 'By Christ, we won!'

The boys won by a length. 'Monstered the opposition' as the local paper excitedly put it. The boys were ecstatic. They danced on the bank hugging each other and celebrated by throwing the coach and then the cox, who had never learned to swim, in the river. Then they all jumped in. In all the excitement, the big crocs that sat watching on the riverbank, downstream, were forgotten.

One of D'Arcy's greatest treasures was a small silver cup, not much bigger than an egg cup, with the club crest, and a record of the victory inscribed on it along with the names of each of the crew plus the cox. At the presentation dinner they wrapped their arms around each other and drank tiny toasts out of the cups they had strived so hard to win.

David Clarke, sitting close by, nudged his wife. 'Look at that.

Young D'Arcy – friends for life with the Irish boys. We had two wins today.'

It was Easter when the Rowing Club had a gala cocktail party and included the rowers in the invitation, especially their trophy-winning four. The hot, still day had brought out a selection of flying creatures: midges, sandflies, gnats and even houseflies. The worst were mosquitoes, blood-engorged from feasting on the surfeit of soft pink skin. Every now and then a sharp crack echoed as men slapped at them and the ladies tried to swat them away with ivory-handled fans.

Most of the prominent social set in Rockhampton were in attendance, including the Mayor and Lady Mayoress. As the afternoon grew hotter the Lady Mayoress, rather rotund, broke into a sweat, or 'perspired' as she preferred to call it. Little trickles of damp ran down the lines in her cheeks.

In a corner a group of ladies discussed the general situation around Rockhampton. 'Lives are in danger …,' 'Not safe in our houses …' they declared. A nattily dressed young man joined in. 'Don't know why they don't just shoot them all.'

The men were busy discussing whether Big Baby would win the steeplechase at the races on Saturday.

D'Arcy, bored with the chatter, wandered down to the place where they had launched the four and found himself with the bow oar, Liam. The river was in a benign mood, running lazily along with a few eddies and only the occasional ripple to suggest a light gust of wind or a small fish. Liam, tall and stringy, still looked fit from the racing. He stood holding a beer glass and greeted D'Arcy with a big grin. 'Hello Bill,' he said. 'Just reminiscing. A great day.'

The boys all called D'Arcy 'Bill'. At first he had disliked it, but now he saw it as a sign of friendship and acceptance. Liam's sandy hair was standing up in untidy sprouts, as if cut by a vengeful sister. He ran his fingers through it in an unsuccessful effort to tidy himself up a bit. Liam was never going to be tidy. They chatted a little and D'Arcy asked him how the family had found themselves in Rockhampton.

Liam shrugged. 'We lived in a tiny village in County Clare, surrounded by a huge estate owned by this rich English fellow. He lived in Oxford and hardly ever came to see the estate even though it had a magnificent house and ten thousand acres of land. A lot of it was just forest, wild country east of the Atlantic coast. The village was starving; potatoes had failed again. Da took up poaching on the estate, rabbits, hares, pheasants, quails, and pike or trout from the streams. He fed half the village. The estate was run by the gamekeeper, a brutal toe-rag from Yorkshire. He knew what was happening but couldn't catch Da. Da was a master of poaching. Finally, he bribed one of the villagers and Da was caught. He was lucky not to be hanged but sentenced to transportation to New South Wales.'

D'Arcy nodded. He knew the Anglo-Irish story well enough. 'What was the English owner's name?' he asked. 'Do you remember?'

'Remember? How could I forget! It was Sir Evelyn Bowater-Higginson.' Liam pronounced the name with a faux English accent. 'Baronet, of course,' he spat.

D'Arcy just nodded.

There was a silence, then Liam asked D'Arcy how he had ended up in Rockhampton. D'Arcy was vague in his reply. He changed the subject by asking Liam how they liked living there. Liam laughed.

'Oh, we love it. Da's animal skills and the fact that he's a good handyman means he's never short of work. We built the little row of houses we live in. Best thing of all is the fact that there's no shortage of food. Even the native stuff. Kangaroo stew or better still, endless types of fish. The Aborigines told Da about barramundi; it's delicious and we can get prawns from the river any time. Have you ever been starving?' He shook his head. 'It's horrible. You can't think of anything else. It becomes a total obsession. Funny, we eat so well now we're all twice the size of Da.' He took a mouthful of beer. 'Better still, in Rockhampton we don't doff our cap to anyone. Mam particularly loves being here. She started her life in Ireland as a penniless servant, bullied and abused. "Yes sir, no sir, three bags full sir." Kiss my arse,' he grumbled. 'Her devotion to the church got her through. She's very religious. She thinks that her prayers have led us on a path to paradise. Funny eh: paradise!'

D'Arcy laughed. 'Paradise! Well, I'm pretty sure that's not what my mother thinks.'

When D'Arcy got home, he called to his mother. 'You won't believe it, Mother. Liam, the bow oar – you've met him. Well, his family were transported for poaching on the Burren Estate in County Clare. It was owned by Sir Evelyn Bowater-Higginson. The thing is, one of his sons was in my class at Westminster. Funny little guy with a lisp. A bit wet. His father insisted he play Eton Fives, but Westminster didn't have a court, so he had to disappear for half a day to play. We called him "Twinkle". How about that?'

His mother smiled. 'Not all that unlikely, I suppose.'

D'Arcy nodded. 'I suppose not, but we better keep that one quiet. By the way Liam's mother thinks Rockhampton's paradise.'

His mother shook her head. 'It's a long way from paradise but I'm getting used to it.'

As soon as he could, William left the local school to work with his father, and after receiving his legal qualifications joined the practice.

One part of the business that developed fast involved disputes over the pegging of mining claims, inevitably overlapping and subject to skulduggery and lies. Claimants drove pegs into the ground to identify their claims, pegs were mysteriously moved, fights broke out and, if serious enough, litigation followed. All in all, a fortuitous set of circumstances for a firm of solicitors. William's father soon gave William the responsibility for the disputes about pegging. William's pugnacious personality allowed him to stand up to some of the outrageous, and often totally unbelievable, demands.

～⊙

The Morgan boys, meanwhile, had continued to explore the mining titles they had so deviously acquired. After posting some good results, they changed the name of the Iron Mountain claim to Mount Morgan and went to see the bank manager, offering half the shares in the mine to anyone who would invest £1200 in the venture. The bank manager sent them to see D'Arcy.

D'Arcy sat quietly behind his desk and listened to the Morgans' pitch. He'd heard plenty of these pitches before, most of them outrageous nonsense which he could quickly dismiss. D'Arcy asked a number of questions, but he didn't throw them out. He thought about it overnight, made some enquiries and a few days later took himself off to see a shrewd old bloke he had been doing some work for and who knew his way around Rockhampton better than D'Arcy did. A long conversation took place over a beer at William Patterson's grazing property.

'What do you think, Bill?' D'Arcy asked. 'We've heard all the blowhard stories but these are some pretty impressive shows. I've checked them out. They're real, in my belief.'

Patterson laughed. 'Morgan's the name, is it? Not related to "Mad Dog" the bushranger, I hope.' Mad Dog had died in a hail of bullets in Victoria. The *Moreton Bay Courier* had published the story on the front page, calling him a 'bloodthirsty villain'. He had plenty of blood on his hands and a few people around Rocky liked to reckon that the Morgan boys were related. *Just another bunch of bushrangers* was the opinion on the grapevine.

D'Arcy smiled and shook his head. Patterson had had a

particularly good year. Cattle prices were strong and so had been the buyers for wheat. He scratched his head reflectively. 'Go for the Morgans. Why not, eh?'

The two men stood up and shook hands. D'Arcy returned to town and called Fred Morgan. Another chat ended with D'Arcy and William Patterson investing £2000 and installing Fred's brother Ned to manage the new Mount Morgan mine. They were now the Morgan boys' partners, on board with the 'bushrangers', as Patterson liked to call them.

CHAPTER 10
Mexico and Queensland

❦

MEANWHILE, a little out of town, yet another interesting immigrant family had set themselves up. From 1864 Samuel Birkbeck and his wife Damiana lived with their large family at Glenmore Station on the banks of the Fitzroy River.

Nearly fifty years earlier Samuel's father and family had travelled to the US from England. His father had purchased a farm in Illinois which he ran with the help of young Samuel. On graduating from high school Samuel left the farm and qualified as an engineer. In 1827 he moved to Mexico in the silver boom, having been appointed to manage a newly opened silver mine. Although the Birkbecks were descended from an English Quaker family, Samuel married a local Catholic girl of Spanish-Mexican descent, Damiana de Barre Valdez. Damiana's parents had been a little disappointed that she would marry someone outside the church but, then again, Samuel had an excellent job and was well respected in the community. They were sure he would be a good husband and father to their only daughter. He had agreed that any children would be brought up in the faith.

The marriage took place back in 1839 in the cathedral at

Zacatecas. Every seat was taken. The ceremony was rather overwhelmed by the choir's magnificent rendition of the extract from the Ninth symphony, 'Ode to Joy'. The guests, together with the crowd which had assembled outside, exploded in applause. Damiana was just seventeen. As she listened tears trickled down her cheeks and splattered her white lace wedding dress.

Samuel and Damiana subsequently had nine children and Elena, born in 1840, was their only daughter. As promised, the children were diligently educated by the local Catholic clergy.

High in the central mountain chains of Mexico, Zacatecas was the centre of the silver trade and the source of much of the silver that had enriched the Spanish throne. It was also the centre of Samuel's job overseeing the silver mine. The War of the Reform had broken out in Mexico in 1856 and was ongoing in 1861. Young men were being conscripted into the army and, as in most civil wars, the fighting was particularly savage. One evening Samuel came back from the mine to find his street barricaded by a pile of wooden carts. Men in a variety of costumes were firing rifles over the top. He grabbed a spectator.

'What's happening? I need to get to my home.'

It's the conservatives,' said the spectator. 'They're down the street trying to break into a house. We don't know why.'

A body lay at a grotesque angle on the roadway. Samuel could see the front of his house at the other end of the street; it seemed as if all was quiet outside. He looked around. Behind him was a wooden cart on which vegetables and melons were stacked high. The cart's owner, a woman, crouched behind it, her head down. Beside her knelt a priest in black robes clutching a large wooden cross. Samuel noticed it was upside down. The priest seemed to be muttering Hail Marys. A volley of shots rang out and Samuel could hear the sound of bullets tearing through wood. A sharp pain pierced his face; he reached up to feel a wood splinter lodged in his cheek. Blood from the wound covered his fingers.

Damiana and Elena were hiding in the house in a little room they had designated a chapel. They were on their knees, holding their rosaries and reciting the Lord's Prayer, accompanied by the sounds of gunshots in the street.

That night, safely back in his house, Samuel decided enough was enough; it was time to find a safer shore for his young family. He particularly worried about Elena: shy, pious, she was made nervous by the constant fighting. He gathered the family together around the dining room table.

'It's time to leave,' he announced. 'Whichever side we support, this is a horrible war and we want no part of it. Tomorrow we pack up what we can. We lock the house up. Nina can look after it for us. Perhaps, one day, we will return. Damiana, I know you will not want to leave, but for now we must be gone.'

The eleven members of the family took ship to New York and then to England, where they stayed for a year and the children learned English, before sailing to Melbourne. There, one of the Archer family members from Rockhampton persuaded Samuel that the future lay in the north – Rockhampton to be precise.

When the Birkbecks arrived in Rockhampton they went straight to a hotel in the city centre. Unloading their luggage, they moved it inside with the help of hotel staff, keen to escape the baking heat outside. Just as they were shifting the last of the bags, they were distracted by the approach of a funeral cortege. The mourners, dressed in black, were following a black coach led by black horses clip-clopping slowly through the street. The attendants too wore black, as did the family following in the coach behind, the faces of the women covered by black veils. Faintly in the distance could be heard the 'Dead March' from *Saul*, played by a few stringed instruments, and interrupted by the occasional wrong note. The coach carried a coffin, so small they thought perhaps it contained a child. They stood respectfully at attention until it had passed.

That evening at the dinner table Samuel asked the head waiter what it had all been about.

A dour, moustachioed Hungarian in a dinner jacket, he carefully explained. 'It is the funeral of a young boy, the youngest son of a wealthy local pastoralist. It is very sad; he was only eight years old.'

Samuel asked how he had died so young. The head waiter explained that it had been a hot day even by summer standards in Rockhampton. The young boy had got himself to a nearby beach and taken to the water. He had ignored an instruction from his family, learned from the local Aborigines, not to swim in the ocean in summer, especially on a rising tide. The boy had run screaming from the water, writhing in agony, and had rapidly had a cardiac arrest. He was dead in a few minutes.

'How awful!' Damiana said. 'What could have caused such a tragedy?'

'Madam, this we are only just discovering. It is a jellyfish, quite large, that resides in the local seas in summer. They call it the "box jellyfish". The scientist at the hospital has examined its tentacles. They apparently carry a venom that he believes is one of the most poisonous he has ever encountered. The Aboriginals know this, and so do many of our locals. I advise you – do not on any account swim in the sea, at least in summer. In winter it is supposed to be safe, but why would you risk it?'

Damiana was aghast. 'Well, I hate swimming. But still, what a creature!'

Samuel shook his head. 'My god, I knew of sharks and crocodiles, but deadly jellyfish? I never heard of such a thing.'

Elena sat silent. Her face had gone crimson and her eyes bulged in horror at what she had just heard. She grasped the silver crucifix her mother had given her and which she wore on a gold chain around her neck.

At first they found the heat stifling. They tried not to go out in the middle of the day and to stay in the shade if possible. They welcomed the sudden downpours of cascading water and thunderstorms and the near cyclonic winds that came from nowhere. Those winds at least cooled things down. The locals laughed, told them to alter their European dress for the tropics, and assured them that in a matter of months they would adjust, and it would all seem quite normal.

After exploring for a few weeks, Samuel purchased a pastoral run of 127 square miles running down to the Fitzroy River. Initially they ran sheep, but soon realised that this was cattle country. For housing, Birkbeck bought a large slab building and re-erected it near the river. It had been originally built in 1858 as a hotel at Parkhurst but was transported to Glenmore in 1861. They were joined by a Mexican builder, Dennis Cifuentes, whom they'd helped emigrate from Mexico. Cifuentes assisted with the reassembling and the construction of a limestone brick cottage. It was much more suitable for tropical Queensland than some of the English cottages that had grown up in the town.

It had taken a few months to settle down, but Samuel had begun to get used to a lifestyle so utterly different to what he and the family had experienced. Prices were reasonable, he felt confident that they could make a good living, and there was plenty of demand for his mining experience. Yes, on the whole it had been a fair choice.

The river ran quietly past the front of the house. Samuel could sit in his chair on the verandah in the evening and watch the water birds feeding. Great clouds of parrots might suddenly appear; sometimes the beautiful black cockatoos, screeching belligerently, made a leisurely flyover, a wombat appeared on the lawn or a small wallaby hopped out to graze on the grass. He could smell the Mexican food Damiana was cooking on the stove inside. Damiana had not taken to European food and now had a whole array of vegetables and spices growing in her garden, including red and green chillies, garlic, onion, oregano and cumin. When they had visitors from town, he had to ask her to put the chillies away.

Samuel lifted his glass of wine and swirled it around. What about this fellow D'Arcy who seemed to be showing an interest in his daughter? Sure, he was very polite to Samuel, but Samuel detected a hard streak. He knew from town gossip that D'Arcy didn't mind a fight, physical or legal. Still, he reflected, the pickings were pretty slim in Rockhampton, and young D'Arcy and his father had a healthy business.

Elena waited until her father was out and her mother was in the kitchen before approaching her. 'Mama,' she said. 'Did you know that Mr D'Arcy has approached Papa to ask if he might marry his daughter? D'Arcy has not actually asked me.'

Damiana looked up. 'Yes dear, I know. But he also knows that he must get your father's permission first, otherwise nothing can happen.'

'But father has said "yes"! Mama, I don't really want to marry him. He is quite nice, quite good-looking, but I don't really know him.'

Damiana continued chopping the vegetables. 'Elena, you need to be married. Look at Rockhampton. How many eligible men are living here? Most of them are scoundrels or drunks with no money. He can provide well for you, and I am sure you want babies, and we need some little feet to fill our lives. You will grow to love him and if you are clever, you will learn how to manage him. I will help you.'

'But he is not even a Catholic! What will the bishop say?'

'He has agreed to be married in the Church. That alone is a concession since we know he has had a few incidents with the Catholic boys he was at school with. He will become a son of the faith. You will see how it happens.'

Elena hesitated. 'What about the, um, the "thing"?'

Damiana was flummoxed for a minute. 'Ah, yes. The thing. You must just be patient. Play your part. It is part of marriage. You can comfort yourself that you will add to Jesus' flock.'

On 23 October 1872 the young William D'Arcy married Maria Colletta Elena Birkbeck. It was at her mother's insistence that the couple were married in a Catholic Church, the grandest she could find. She settled on St Patrick's Cathedral, 930 miles away in Parramatta, Sydney, for the ceremony.

It was indeed a grand affair. Who would have known that the happy couple had such a great number of friends, if not relatives? Several prominent Rockhampton citizens, including the mayor and his wife, had made the long journey south to attend. The members of the rowing four, dressed in their splendid blazers, were all in attendance including cox and coach. David Clarke gave him a reassuring pat on the shoulders. 'Making friends with the Catholic boys is one thing: but marrying into the church! Well, for once I'm speechless. I wish you both every happiness.'

One hundred and twenty guests crowded into the cathedral to hear the young couple give their vows. The organ boomed, the bishop spoke inspiring words on life and the sanctity of marriage, and the primacy of the Catholic church. D'Arcy behaved impeccably, making polite conversation with people he would normally not bother to speak to. Eventually, though, it was all too much, and he slipped outside behind the stained-glass windows of the cathedral's presbytery. He was quietly puffing on a cigar when an exceptionally well-dressed gentleman wearing a perfectly knotted bow tie quietly walked up beside him. He took out a gold monogrammed cigarette case, tapped out a cigarette and lit up. D'Arcy vaguely remembered they had briefly met at the beginning of the service but needed a reminder.

'Inchcape. Ashley Inchcape,' the stranger said.

They chatted about the proceedings. D'Arcy picked up from his accent that he was a stranger, with a little Scottish and a slight

American burr. Ashley confirmed that he was originally Scottish, had lived in America for a time and now resided in Sydney.

'And what keeps you here?' inquired D'Arcy.

'A number of things. But just now I'm busy as a representative of Standard Oil in the US. I'm their eyes and ears in the Pacific. I'm on the lookout for oil, so I thought I might just ask you to remember me when you go back to Rockhampton. If anything that even looks or smells like oil turns up, just let me know.'

D'Arcy was surprised, but he'd heard about Standard Oil. Who hadn't?

'Gold and copper are my thing. Never heard anyone mention oil.'

'You will, you will. Do yourself a favour and keep your eyes open. The automobile age is coming, the age of oil-fired engines. Oil is black gold. Black gold! Remember where you heard it.' He stubbed his cigarette out and they both headed back to join the other guests.

Black gold, D'Arcy thought to himself. For some things he had a prodigious memory, and black gold would be one of them.

With a highly disputatious community the services of the D'Arcy legal practice were in demand. They soon did well enough to move to a new house, Ellen Vanin, a comfortable home in Rockhampton's Wandal district, which helped cement their place in local Rockhampton society. It wasn't long before Damiana's wish for grandchildren was amply fulfilled with the birth of two sons and three daughters.

CHAPTER 11
England

I N 1869, at the remarkably early age of twenty-eight, Jacky
Fisher was made a commander. He had married in 1866 while
stationed at Portsmouth. His wife, Frances Katherine Josepha
Broughton, known to all as 'Kitty', was the attractive young daughter
of a clergyman, the Reverend Thomas Delves Broughton. Kitty
understood Fisher: his exuberance, his eccentricities, but also his
genius. She was quite sure he would rise to the top of the tree. Her
two brothers were also naval officers, so Kitty knew well that she
would spend many months separated from Jacky as his career took
him away. As a naval wife she would often be alone but somehow,
through all that would follow, they stayed together, happy until her
death in 1918.

Not long after the marriage Fisher received a sad letter from
his mother, Sophie, still in Ceylon. Of course she missed this
extravagant child she had not been able to raise, and she would like
to come to England to see him. He was so often in her thoughts,
her last memory of him being that wrenching departure on the
quayside in Ceylon. She really had no idea what he had become
as a person whatever the occasional dribs and drabs of information

she managed to glean about his life as a naval officer.

But Fisher was having none of it. He wrote to Kitty, 'I hate the very thought of it and really, I don't want to see her. I don't see why I should as I haven't the slightest recollection of her.' Although he did provide her with financial support, he never did see her.

As a sort of strange alternative, Fisher found solace in the admiration he received from older women, and enjoyed a childlike relationship, almost certainly platonic, with some. Anne Beatrix Wilmot-Horton was Jacky's godmother. Good-natured, clever and rich, during one of the visits he made over the early years from his boarding school she introduced him to Admiral Parker, who helped find him his cadetship.

Then there was Mrs Edmund Warden, wife of the P&O manager in Hong Kong, whom he actually addressed as 'Mams'. He wrote to her constantly. They were strange letters: 'Hurrah! Well done, Mams. You are a real, jolly, good, good, good old party.'

Much later was a time when he lived with the Duchess of Hamilton, without, it appears, particularly disturbing Kitty.

These women were his mother substitutes; Sophie died in 1895 in obscure poverty, unlamented by Jacky.

His first posting was second-in-command of HMS *Donegal*, serving under a Captain Hewitt, a Crimean War veteran and Victoria Cross holder. Donegal plied between Portsmouth and the Far East. It was mostly uneventful, and Fisher took the time to finish a treatise on torpedoes.

He was transferred to HMS *Ocean* and while there installed the first electrical system allowing all guns to be fired simultaneously. It was no surprise when he was returned to England to head up the torpedo and mine training school.

Fisher had arranged a test run on HMS *Lightning*, a small attack boat. Barely ninety feet long, it was built by Thornycroft, and armed with the new Whitehead torpedoes. He pestered the officer in command about them.

'How accurate is this thing?' he asked.

'Needs improvement, but very accurate,' the OIC replied. 'You know the boat's speed and direction and same for the enemy's. You also know the speed and depth of your torpedo, so it is a simple mathematical calculation to arrive at your fire position.'

'Theoretically?'

'Yes, but the theory is right. We just have to improve the practice and the product.'

Fisher agreed. He had seen for himself how, if you could get better control of the speed and directional stability, a single cheap torpedo could sink a battleship. Fisher's concern was growing; torpedoes and submarines could be lethal.

Later, he paced up and down in the park outside his house, muttering to himself. He loved battleships, but could this turn the whole theory of naval warfare upside down? The trouble was it bloody-well could! What's more, you could build fifty torpedo boats for one battleship and afford to lose half of them. You couldn't afford to lose battleships.

Being back home in England was fortuitous, allowing him to spend more time with his wife but also to indulge in his other two great passions: his devotion to ballroom dancing and to the Church of England, particularly the Old Testament. Being Fisher, he was extremely adept in both areas. No doubt he whispered the merits of the torpedo into the ear of his dancing partner if she seemed a little disinterested or, if that didn't work, the merits of the Old Testament. Since he was also a particularly adept flirt, perhaps she didn't mind.

In a society where one's accident of birth was a sentence to a place in society that could not be changed, Fisher, whose background was anything but aristocratic, was an anomaly. It is a credit to the Royal Navy that even the most died-in-the-wool admirals were forced, one-by-one, to acknowledge that they had in their midst an obsessive nautical genius.

For the next ten years Fisher passed from ship to ship, each time earning a small promotion, and serving in numerous foreign stations. His background had made him a demanding commander of both his seamen and his officers; demanding but also fair. A midshipman who later became an admiral wrote: 'Fisher was a very exacting master and I had at times long and arduous duties, long hours at the engine room telegraphs in cold and fog, and the least inattention was punished. It was, I think, his way of improving us, for he always rewarded us in some way when an extra hard bit of work was over.'

In recognition of Fisher's clearly exceptional knowledge of the potential for torpedoes, in 1869 he was chosen by the Admiralty to attend the opening of the new German naval base at Wilhelmshaven. Prussia had concluded a treaty with the Grand Duchy of Oldenburg to cede an area on the Jade Bight, a bay of the North Sea, sufficient to build a dockyard and naval base. Fisher put on his civilian clothes and wandered about observing what was taking place. There was no doubt in his eyes; this was a serious facility. It was clear enough that Prussia was intent on building a navy.

At the opening Fisher briefly met Bismarck, Moltke and King William of Prussia, soon to become Emperor of Germany. Wilhelmshaven faced England's east coast directly across the North Sea. Fisher absorbed all he could about Prussia's or Germany's intentions from those in attendance. No one much bothered with this rather junior English naval officer. Fisher particularly took notice when he heard Count Helmuth Moltke quote his uncle, Helmuth von Moltke, Field Marshall and chief of the Prussian general staff: 'Eternal peace is a dream, and not even a pleasant one; and war is an integral part of the way God has ordered the world ... Without war, the world would sink in a mire of materialism.'

Fisher was no shrinking violet. He was steeped in the Old and New Testament, particularly Matthew 11, verse 12: 'The Kingdom of Heaven has suffered violence, and the violent take it by force.' He thought of Jehovah, the war god whose values he identified most closely with. He had paid close attention to the events at Wilhelmshaven. He felt he had been a witness to a warning.

On returning to Portsmouth Fisher was pulled into the officers' mess. What had he learned in Germany? he was asked.

Drink in one hand, Fisher did not mince his word. 'They are set on expansion, especially outside Europe, to allow colonies in Africa. To do it they think they need a navy to compete with us. Believe me when I say that their ship-building design and capacity to build is impressive. Admiral von Tirpitz is clear-eyed about the objectives.'

The inevitable question was how should England react to this? Fisher had no doubts. 'We must renew our fleet. We have too many old ships and too many slow ships. We need large capital ships, and they will need to be much faster. *Much* faster.'

Most of his senior officers nodded and returned to their drinks and by the time the mess closed had largely forgotten the impassioned words of their junior officer. This Fisher was an odd cove; clever though, very clever.

Fisher imposed his own frenetic activity on all those around him. In 1879, as flag captain on the *Northampton* he had the crew carry out 150 torpedo runs in a fortnight. The rest of the navy performed 200 in a year. Some of his officers complained in the wardroom. 'He never lets up. What on earth is it with him? It's as if he's demented. Just as I'm settling down for a snooze, in he marches, and off we go again.'

Most of the other officers muttered their agreement. He was a tiresome fellow, but a young lieutenant had a different view.

'No, you're wrong. Look at the results of the torpedo runs. We have improved. We are quicker and much more accurate. The other thing is, he's exceptionally bright. Don't get into an argument with him because you'll lose. It's not because he's arrogant, it's because he gets it. If we must fire a torpedo in anger, I know who I would rather be serving with.'

It was in the same year that Fisher's brother, Philip, was lost when his ship went down in a fierce gale. Fisher was disconsolate, but his spirits were revived by his appointment to the new ironclad battleship HMS *Inflexible*. *Inflexible* had the largest guns and the thickest armour in the navy, but in some arcane nod to tradition, it also had masts and sails. Fisher walked up the gangplank, looked about, fixed his gaze on the masts and furled sails, and remarked to the officers greeting him, 'Those have got to go.'

Inflexible joined the Mediterranean Fleet and was assigned to the protection of Queen Victoria during her visit to Menton, in southern France. *Inflexible* then moved to Egypt and took part in the bombardment of Alexandria. The British, with support from France, had sent fifteen ironclad battleships to support the sultan, Khedive Tewfik Pasha, against the Urabi uprising, which was backed by the Ottoman Turks. Fisher was appointed the commander of a landing party which was quartered in the Khedive's palace, in the abandoned harem at Ras el-Tin. The troops were receiving a battering from the Urabi forces. They could not access Cairo to protect the European settlements. Fisher realised that he could use the railway to take troops inland to Cairo, but he needed to protect them.

'Damn it, we'll turn the train into an ironclad' was his solution. He requisitioned an elderly steam locomotive, fitted armour to the outside and set up gun platforms with firing ranges on each side of the train. He protected them with sandbags and armour plate. Bristling with weapons, including a Nordenfelt machine gun, two Gatling guns, two 9-pounders and a 40-pounder. Fisher was confident the 'armoured' train was impervious to attack from the Khedive's camel corps.

When it set out on its first trip up the line Fisher waited anxiously for the result. He was pacing up and down in the officers' mess when the door burst open and the officer in charge of the train stormed in.

'Perfect, perfect,' said the officer. 'They attacked on camels from both sides as we passed through the sand dunes, firing their guns and howling threats and insults. The lads kept calm. I waited until they were only a few hundred yards away and then the machine gun and Gatling guns opened fire. Carnage! Camels and bodies everywhere. What was left of them fled into the hills. We had one wounded.'

Fisher clapped him on the shoulder. 'Wonderful! I hoped, but you never know. Gentlemen, the bar is open and drinks are on me.' He perched on the edge of the table, and clinked glasses with the men who had carried out the operation so effectively. He clapped one young soldier on the back. 'What's your name, lad?'

The boy looked about sixteen. 'Alfred, sir.'

'First time in action then?'

'Yes sir.'

'So how was it then?'

'Crikey sir, I nearly pooed myself.'

Jacky roared with laughter. 'That'll scare off the Gypos.'

The evening continued with much raucous laughter, jokes of many complexions and good-natured ribbing, all of which Jacky joined in with great gusto.

Back on the *Inflexible* the captain was holding a more sober celebration, with a solemn round of hand-shaking and jolly well done. But Jacky preferred his 'lads'.

On-the-spot innovation was a very rare commodity at the time, so Fisher found himself with a surprising degree of fame. To his amazement he also found himself befriended by the future King Edward VII and Queen Alexandra. In 1882 he was appointed Companion of the Bath.

Fisher's dedication to his task caused him a serious problem. He had a recurrence of malaria plus dysentery and, refusing to take sick leave, became so ill he was ordered home by Lord Northbrook who commented, 'The Admiralty could build another *Inflexible* but not another Fisher.'

In 1890 he was appointed aide-de-camp to the Queen and promoted to rear admiral. The timing could not have been more propitious for Britain.

Fisher was at home with Kitty, gradually recovering his health after his return from Egypt when a letter arrived in an envelope marked HMS *Inflexible*. Fisher tore it open.

> Sir,
>
> We the ship's company of HMS *Inflexible* take the earliest opportunity of expressing to you our deep sorrow and sympathy on this sad occasion of your sickness, and it is our whole wish that you may speedily recover and be amongst us again, who are so proud of serving under you. Sir, we are all aware of the responsible duties you had to perform, and the great number of men you had to see to during your long stay on shore in Alexandria, which must have brought the strongest man to a bed of sickness; but we trust shortly to see you again amongst us and on the field of active service, where you are as much at home as on your own grand ship, and at the end may you receive your share of rewards and laurels, and your ship's company will then feel proud and prouder than if it was bestowed on themselves.
>
> Sir, trusting that you will overlook the liberty we have taken in sending this to you, we beg to remain, your faithful and sympathising ship's company,
>
> INFLEXIBLE

Fisher was showered with medals and recognition all his career but, as he said when he had finished reading the letter to Kitty, 'No reward I shall ever receive will mean more to me than this.'

His background allowed him to move between social classes without discomfort. In a hurry to get back to England from Turkey he jumped a tramp ship leaving Istanbul. The master looked him up and down. 'There's only one bunk, and when I ain't in it the mate is, and we ain't got no cook.'

Fisher just laughed. 'Don't need a bunk and don't need a cook. Just need to get there.' From then on everyone got on famously.

In fact, Fisher had always been comfortable with people of all classes. It was as if he hadn't noticed, but of course he was all too aware of the rigidity of the distinctions in English society, replicated in the navy. His highly unusual background gave him entrée at any level of society but, like everyone else, he knew just how contemptuous the English establishment could be to those not born to rule.

CHAPTER 12
England

ERTRUDE'S FATHER, Hugh, for a while was
inconsolable about the death of his wife. But with young
Gertrude's help, and dedicating himself to the business,
gradually his life returned to some sort of normality. Young, wealthy
and with an engagingly open personality he was never destined to
be alone for long. His sisters Maisie and Ada were keeping their
eyes open. Through a shared interest in music, it was not long before
they felt they had found a perfect match.

Twenty-two-year-old Florence Eveleen Eleanore Olliffe was
studying at the Royal College of Music and singing in the Bach
choir. She was tall and slim with dark hair and compelling eyes.
As a result of a stint in Paris she spoke English with an irresistible
French accent. The sisters contrived some fortuitous meetings, but
Hugh seemed not much interested. Florence at first resisted the very
idea of any involvement with an Englishman and Hugh refused to
countenance any attachments, burying himself in his work. In any
event, for Florence, who loved Parisian charm and sophistication,
the possibility of ending up in Redcar, buffeted by the gale-force
winds off the North Sea and surrounded by industrial cities belching

fumes and covering the countryside in soot and grime, would have been less than compelling.

Maisie feared that she and Ada were mistaken. The match was not destined to happen. Ada disagreed. 'For two people so disinterested they spent a lot of time together after Florence's concert last week,' she mused. Hugh's sisters would not give up and one evening they inveigled him to an opera, *Bluebeard*, which Florence had written and in which they were both singing. Afterwards Hugh took Florence home, and strode into the drawing room to confront her parents.

'I have brought your daughter home,' he announced. 'And I have come to ask if I may take her away again?'

Lady Olliffe burst into tears. In truth, Florence was perfect for Hugh, since underneath she really loved children and domesticity above the sophistication she had absorbed growing up. On 10 August they were married in a small church in Sloane Street.

The presence of a new stepmother from such a different background could have proved disastrous for Gertrude's relationship, especially given the ongoing strong affection between Hugh and Gertrude which Florence might easily have resented. Instead, Florence gained Gertrude's affection, which was to last a lifetime. Although a stickler for manners and behaviour Florence was both talented and fun. Modesty prevented her putting her name to the many publications she authored: she wrote music, opera, plays and books for adults and for children, which helped to entertain both Gertrude and Maurice and later her own children.

The intellectual milieu must have been quite demanding. Over her life Florence was friends with numerous intellectuals and artists, including Charles Dickens, Virginia Woolf and Sybil Thorndike. She remembered her parents' friend, William Makepeace Thackeray, visiting, and their great sadness when he died. She was just twelve at the time. Her ideas on education were strongly influenced by Maria Montessori, but curiously she had not crossed the divide that prevented women from studying the male preserves of such things as maths, the sciences and of course engineering.

Gertrude on the other hand was strong-willed, clever and athletic. She rode a horse like a wild thing, not side-saddle but like a man. She climbed on everything – the walls surrounding the property, the walls of the house, the roof and the biggest of the numerous trees around the estate. Often she dragged Maurice with her. Maurice was younger and far less assured; he fell off whatever they climbed or refused to join in. On one occasion he toppled through the glasshouse's roof. The various governesses came and went, unable to keep up with Gertrude physically, and wilting under her argumentative nature and her ability to absorb an encyclopaedic store of data from all that she read or heard.

Gertrude's love of riding led her to adventure further out across the moors. She rode from early dawn until the sun went down, exploring on her own. There was so much to engage her. She began to learn that life on the moors went back 8000 years, through the Mesolithic and Neolithic periods and the Bronze and Iron Ages. Then came the Romans, building their roads, the remains still poking through the long grass. She loved the heather, the vivid purple blossoms of ling or bell, the latter rich in nectar. The heather sprouted everywhere, growing up to three feet tall and turning the country lavender in spring, often covered with clouds of bees. She learned that if you knew where to look the archaeological remnants of the ancient occupations could be found. She gradually collected a few small relics which she cleaned and stored in her room, sometimes showing them to Hugh or Florence.

The railways across the moors were still being built, including the line to Whitby, originally designed by George Stephenson himself for horse-drawn carriages, but now converted to steam.

Gertrude made it a rule to avoid anything that looked like people. She rode to the iron ore mine at Rosedale, scanned it from afar, and turned away. She was more curious than usual because she knew her grandfather was involved in the mine. As she trotted away through the moors, pheasants and quail would leap from under the horse's hooves, and sometimes an adder would wriggle away.

One afternoon she stopped to rest on a bench overlooking a small lake, full of squabbling waterfowl. As she sat quietly her pony ambled down to the lake to drink. Around the bend came an older man, dressed in the attire of a country gentleman, with a neatly trimmed goatee beard and a Tyrolean hat, a pheasant feather sticking out at a jaunty angle. He was walking a fine English setter that ran up to Gertrude, furiously wagging its tail, to say hello. The gentleman doffed his hat, tapped out his pipe, and stopped to talk. At first Gertrude thought, from his hat, he might be German, but he had a fine Yorkshire accent. He introduced himself as Mr Armitage and lived in the village about a mile down the track.

Gertrude had noticed a lichen-covered stone memorial poking from the grass and had tried but been unable to decipher the words carved on its face, other than the date, 1769. She asked him if he knew its origin. It was then she was introduced to the legend of the 'Martyr of the Moors', the Blessed Nicholas Postgate; in folklore, the 'Good Samaritan' of the moors.

Waving his empty pipe for emphasis, her new companion explained: 'In 1678 Titus Oates had falsely spread the story that the Catholics were plotting to kill the King, Charles II. As a result, Catholic priests were detained everywhere. Nicholas Postgate was one of them, arrested by an agent, a psychopathic ruffian called Reeves.' He sucked at his pipe, forgetting he had failed to light it. 'In 1679 Postgate was hung, drawn and quartered; one of eighty-five Catholic martyrs. It was said that Reeves had later committed suicide for what he had done. A good riddance too.'

Gertrude thanked her new acquaintance, patted his dog and collected her pony.

Back at home Gertrude cornered Hugh. 'What does "hung, drawn and quartered" actually mean, Father?'

She had to explain her morning's encounter when he asked why she wanted to know. He coughed, and decided there was no alternative but to answer. 'Well, as I understand it, "drawn" means the convicted prisoner was drawn through the street behind a horse tied to a piece of timber. "Hung" of course means hanged from a gibbet until nearly but not actually dead, and "quartered" means that after having his head chopped off, he's then cut into four quarters.'

Gertrude stared at him in silence. 'Oh, my god. For what possible crime?'

'High treason, I believe. Then they would stick the heads on the pylons on London Bridge, *pour décourager les autres*. Effective, I would think.' He paused as she glared at him accusingly. 'Of course, you know we don't do it now.'

She frowned. 'Actually, it should be drawn, hung and quartered then.'

A few weeks later, she quietly took herself on a pilgrimage to the place near Whitby where Postgate was arrested.

Gertrude left for London a short time after her pilgrimage, but she soon returned, grateful to escape the noise and competitive tension of life in the capital. She was relaxing reading a local magazine when she came across an article on Whitby Abbey, a place she hadn't seen since she was a small child. She read the article quickly and then, her interest piqued, again more carefully.

It seemed the Abbey began as a Christian monastery in the seventh century, built by Oswy, the King of Northumbria who appointed Lady Hilda, Abbess of Hartlepool, as the founding Abbess. In 664 the Synod of Whitby took place in the monastery and agreed, at King Oswy's insistence, to adopt 'Roman' practice.

It then became a Benedictine abbey. It was built high on a cliff above Whitby with commanding views of the North Sea, inviting numerous raids by marauding Vikings in their longships. Eventually the abbey and its priceless possessions were confiscated by Henry VIII during the dissolution of the monasteries, about 100 years before the havoc wreaked by Titus Oates as commemorated on the headstone she had not long ago been examining up on the moor with her new friend. The towering ruins were still there, used as a landmark by sailors.

Gertrude decided she must investigate, so a few days later she saddled up and in the late afternoon headed to East Cliff. She tethered her horse and set off to wander the deserted ruins. The sun was sinking, and the light glowed through the apertures that had been the windows. The peak of the roof still stood five or six storeys above her, but the roof itself was long gone. What remained was lit in a golden halo as the sun sank from sight. Gertrude sat cross-legged on the chapel floor in silence. As her horse picked its way home in the gathering darkness, she rode quietly in the saddle.

Through all this Hugh and Florence were busy tending their business and especially, and rarely for the time, caring for their workforce. They understood what it took to alleviate the atrocious conditions that poverty-stricken families could endure if even the smallest setback occurred. It was only a short time later when Florence walked into the kitchen where Gertrude was making coffee.

Gertrude looked up. 'Good god, Florence, what's happened?'

Florence's dress was dishevelled, and Gertrude could see spots of blood.

Florence sadly shook her head. 'Just another woman with bruises and a badly cut lip. Poor thing, just a girl. She gave the food to her children. Her husband arrived home roaring drunk. There was nothing to eat so he slammed her against the wall and punched her head. When I arrived he swore at me and stormed out. I tried to patch up the cut and gave the unlucky woman a few pennies – it was hardly anything, but it was as if I had given her a fortune.'

Often it was only small acts of generosity like this that kept families out of the poor house.

For a long time, Florence had dedicated what time she had to some of the charities created to assist the poor and sick in the community. In 1918 she would be made a Dame of the British Empire for her charity work, particularly her work for the Red Cross, an honour richly deserved.

CHAPTER 13
Queensland

THE MORGAN BROTHERS were pretty pleased with themselves; and why not? Ironstone Mountain was proving to be as rich as its early promise had showed. They were well in front on their investment, but still they all knew how risky mining could be. The pubs of Rocky were full of men who had failed after thinking they had struck the mother lode. Edwin was least happy, so Fred rolled his eyes and bought him out. It was not much later when the brothers were sitting around the table talking about the mine, as usual. Edwin was stirring the pot.

'Thanks for buying me out, Fred – you did me a favour. You all know what's gonna happen. It's always the same up here. The surface results are good. Then the deeper drilling starts. It gets more expensive and as the bit sinks the grades go down. Seen it all before.' He grinned. 'Don't say I didn't warn you.'

Fred, sipping his beer, didn't respond, but Thomas laughed. 'You sold to Fred too cheap, ya mug. He's already well ahead.'

Grunting, Fred rose and left the room, but in his mind he was wondering. Edwin was partly right. There had been so many false starts, and if you looked around the area not much had happened of any consequence. Ironstone Mountain was already the biggest. The early grades had been a bonanza, several times what the miners were getting down south in Ballarat and Bendigo. The syndicate was making money all right, but how long would something as rich as this last?

A few days later Fred was in D'Arcy's office. He was a seller, and he was prepared to give D'Arcy first offer, but he wasn't going to mess around. 'Buy me out for £63,000,' he said, 'but decide by five pm tomorrow or it'll be open to all comers.'

D'Arcy just nodded, but when Fred returned the following day, he had his sale. It was six months later when Thomas decided he too wanted out. He was the last brother left, and he didn't want to look like a goose. In 1863 the D'Arcy syndicate bought him out, too.

The Morgan brothers were not really stayers, in racehorse parlance. By 1884 they had sold all their shares and Edwin and Tom had disappeared from Rockhampton and the mine that bore their name. They had timed their sale perfectly badly. Still, Fred was philosophical. He had done well anyway, and he stayed in Rockhampton, invested in local businesses, bought the Canal Creek and Targinie runs, and built a meatworks and jetty. By 1891 he was mayor of Rockhampton. Still, he knew what he had missed.

As it happened the mine lasted ninety-nine years and produced 225,000 kilograms of gold, 50,000 kilograms of silver, and 360,000 tonnes of copper. Ironstone Mountain became a huge hole, 325 metres deep. It also became one of the most polluted mine sites in Australia, with the Dee River a contaminated indictment on the dark side of the mining industry. Today there are no swimming, no recreational activities, and no drinking the water.

⤙

As always, the biggest threat to Mount Morgan were the claim jumpers and itinerant would-be miners who by now knew how much gold was sitting in Mount Morgan, but D'Arcy had the energy and legal knowledge to fight them all off. Mount Morgan also had the money. The fights were not just local contests: in the early 1880s two of the lawsuits reached the highest point in the legal chain, the Privy Council in London.

As a result of his efforts and those of his fellow directors and shareholders plus the continuing good results, the shares moved from their original £1 to nearly £18. D'Arcy by then must have been the wealthiest man in Rockhampton.

One of the largest of the eight founding shareholder groups was Walter Russell Hall and his young brother Thomas, who happened to be the Rockhampton manager of the Queensland National Bank. Walter was born in Hertfordshire in 1831 and together with his family migrated to Sydney in 1852 with scarcely a shilling, but at least he was a free settler. He quickly headed for the Victorian goldfields but like most found little reward, so then joined the growing transport service of Cobb & Co. Founded by an American, Cobb & Co had grown rapidly, eventually becoming another part of Australian folklore. It provided a service carrying passengers and mail to a widening selection of destinations around the country. By 1857 Walter was a partner. By 1874 he had accumulated significant wealth and served for a time in the Victorian parliament. When Thomas approached him to join the syndicate the timing was fortuitous.

Mount Morgan was indeed a bonanza. Walter was very unlike D'Arcy – modest and careful with his money, yet very aware of the needs of others. He used his growing wealth to support the local children and their education. In 1874 he married Eliza Kirk. Eliza shared Walter's social conscience and together they quietly continued with their charitable contributions.

D'Arcy received a message that it looked like some funny business was going on, with more illegal claims pegging around Mount Morgan. He decided he should go and see who might be infringing on the mountain that was providing him, Walter and the other shareholders with such largesse. He arranged for one of the stockmen who knew every rock and gully around the pegged areas to take him there. He invited Walter along, but Walter was going to be out of town and was happy to rely on D'Arcy's report.

Even though it was late afternoon and the sun was low in the sky it was hot and still. D'Arcy wore a broad-brimmed bush hat but still the sweat ran down his face and armpits, and the shoulders of his shirt were similarly stained. He stood glancing about. The steep hillside was covered in sandy shale, rocks jutted out at odd angles and bushes and low trees dotted the landscape, their leaves limp in the still evening air. The countryside shimmered in the heat and away in the distance stretched the ocean, glistening like a sapphire shot through with sunlight.

The stockman, a laconic local named Flynn with a fierce ginger beard, stood quietly beside him. 'Doesn't look much, eh.'

D'Arcy grunted.

Suddenly Flynn spat out, 'Don't move an inch!'

D'Arcy followed his gaze. At the base of a rock a few feet away he could see a large snake. It was a good six feet long, with honey-coloured scales, a yellow belly and a small skull. It raised its head and contemplated D'Arcy, who was closer than Flynn. Its tongue flicked in and out and it swayed its head slightly.

'Don't move,' Flynn whispered again. 'It's an inland taipan. It's deadly. If it strikes, you're dead.'

D'Arcy froze, holding his breath, forcing himself to ignore the cloud of small bush flies buzzing around him. For what seemed like a lifetime the stand-off continued. Finally the snake lowered its head, slowly uncurled and slithered away, disappearing among the rocks. D'Arcy let out his breath, and felt his body relax.

Flynn led him to the trunk of a dead tree lying sideways on the ground. It was shaded by a couple of big old gum trees. He sat D'Arcy down and gave him some water. D'Arcy, for once in his life, appeared quite distressed. He didn't say a word but sat silent with his head hanging, his hands on his knees, staring at the red earth surrounding them, blind to a colony of bull ants trailing past his feet.

They were about to move when, from above, there sounded a piercing shrieking and cackling, like Macbeth's three witches had descended on Rockhampton. They looked up and in the tops of the gum trees saw a flock of white cockatoos had arrived, swooping and diving above the treetops. Some sat among the foliage, their sulphur crests extended as they waddled along the branches or picked at a seed in their claws. Flynn laughed. 'They can see the funny side, all right. Having a good laugh at you, I reckon. Even cockies don't like taipans.'

D'Arcy lumbered to his feet. 'For Christ's sake, let's get out of here. Shit, what a country! Crocs and snakes and heat and flies, and bloody screaming parrots. Jesus.'

Flynn laughed. 'Think yourself lucky, mate. If the taipan strikes at one of our steers, it's dead before it hits the ground.'

Back in town D'Arcy had a quick beer with Flynn. They were about to depart when he remembered he had forgotten to check for the pegs. He would have to go back. He cursed. Flynn clapped his shoulder. 'Don't worry, I'll do it.'

D'Arcy couldn't wait to get home. Elena gaped at him with her eyes wide as she listened to the story of the encounter with the taipan. She shook her head and crossed herself. 'What a country,' she cried. 'It's the devil's backyard!' She had only just recovered from removing a spider, the size of her fist, from the curtains in her bedroom. One of the hands had told her it was a huntsman, not dangerous, but Elena found all these hostile creatures horrifying.

It was as if God had cursed this land.

When she was alone Elena fell to her knees and, holding her rosary, she prayed. 'Dear Lord, after all that has come about us for our evil deeds, and for our great trespasses; seeing that thou our God has punished us less than our iniquities deserve, and given us such deliverance as to save my husband from this evil creature, oh please Lord, also deliver us from this cursed land where thou hast cast all the evil creatures of the world.'

Elena's world had been shaken a few weeks earlier when, leaving D'Arcy in town, she had stayed for a few days with her parents at Glenmore Station. They were out and she was alone in the house when she had heard a strange sound faintly in the distance: a wailing coupled with a rhythmic resonance, as if someone was playing an unusual wind instrument; a hollow booming; and, she thought, human chanting.

She ventured from the rear of the house towards the scrub-covered hills at the end of their property. The noise grew louder, and she could see the flicker of a fire. Then through the trees she could make out the figures of the local Aborigines – Darumbal, she believed they were called. She startled some kangaroos that had been feeding on the grass in the back paddock. They bounded away into the distance. Peering into the fading light, she discerned a sort of ritual taking place. As she crept closer she saw dark figures dancing, stamping their feet, their bodies covered in white stripes, chanting, clapping with the sun disappearing behind them. She edged behind a rocky outcrop and peeked around it, and immediately jumped back.

Staring back at her was an Aboriginal man, eyes wide, as shocked as she was. He gaped at her and then his face split into a huge smile. It was Ed, the Aboriginal man who worked on the property. 'Hello Missy,' he grinned.

She hesitated, smiled uncertainly, turned, and fled down the hill.

Elena realised she knew nothing of these people; only that some years ago there had been a dreadful fight at Glenmore Station. Native troops had ambushed a Darumbal ceremonial corroboree not far from where she had just seen the gathering. They shot dead eighteen Aborigines and then collected the bodies and burned them all on a great funeral pyre. It was not to be spoken of. No one went to the place.

Her mind was in a turmoil. She felt as if she was at an intersection between heaven and hell; as if Satan had chosen this place, judged it to be devoid of God, and claimed it as his own. It was not like Europe or Mexico, where the churches played a central role in the life of everyday citizens, where people were respectful of the role of the church, of its teaching, whether Catholic or Protestant; respectful of the story of Jesus, where everywhere colossal buildings towered over towns and cities attesting to the greatness of God. Here she could look around her and see nothing but endless trees and scrub, sand and scabby hillsides where little grew. Nothing as far as one could see to the horizon – perhaps a few wild creatures, but no signs of the presence of either man or God. She crossed herself. Of course, sometimes in the distance she glimpsed the native people, Aborigines, but what were they doing? Perhaps they had been sent by the devil to help him take this place? What could their purpose be?

In England an elderly lay Catholic preacher had taught Elena the story of Dante's *Inferno*, of Dante's journey through Hell. Of the nine concentric circles within the Earth leading to its centre, where Satan is held in bondage. Of the nine circles of bondage, corresponding to each of the great sins. She tried to remember the nine. The first was limbo, which she had never understood, then came lust, gluttony, greed, anger, heresy, violence, fraud and treachery. She had also been shown a book containing the drawings of Botticelli illustrating the Inferno. She recalled the drawing of Lucifer and the 'Map of Hell'.

When she returned home, she opened the old Bible her mother had given her for her Confirmation. It was printed in Spanish, and elaborately illustrated. Her mother had written inside the cover: 'Submit yourself then to God. Resist the devil, and he will flee from you.' Elena thought again of Dante's nine sins. Certainly, she had been guilty of some of them, and she must pray for forgiveness; if she did, she could be saved from Hell. Only by prayer and repentance could she instead be sent to Purgatory where she might labour to be free of her sins.

She retired to bed and tossed and turned before falling into a deep sleep. A dream came to her of Botticelli's frightful portrait of Lucifer, with three heads and four dead eyes, hair like scimitars, and struggling human bodies hanging from his mouth, blood oozing from their limbs.

At first light she was awakened by a chorus of derisive cackling, as if directed at her; a cacophony of abuse. It was the kookaburras greeting the dawn, the first red streaks of the rising sun, a feathery jury perched in the gum trees.

The next evening D'Arcy came early to the house to stay the night before they returned to town the next day. He sat in his favourite chair on the verandah, drink in hand, watching the sun slide away below a blood-orange horizon. Elena was right. 'What a country!' he thought again. Every creature in and out of the water could kill you; the climate was ferocious, at least in the summer; there was no culture at all (not that he cared much for that); and you spent your time surrounded by chancers and crooks, dregs sifted from around the world to be dumped as far away from civilisation as possible. He took a sip and idly watched a large goanna stroll across the lawn. As far as he was concerned, the people and the country deserved each other.

A few weeks later Elena was having lunch with her friend Briana, the head of the English department at the same Catholic school

William D'Arcy had attended. They had met at a ladies' circle that Elena had joined recently. Briana was rather stern, but Elena had found she was a good companion, although a little brusque. No one seemed to know anything about her except she was Irish and had an extraordinary knowledge of English literature. It was as if she had just appeared in Rockhampton, another piece of unidentified human flotsam, her personal history buried.

Briana asked Elena how she liked Father Houlihan at the school.

Elena sighed. 'So different from my priest at home in Mexico. He was Father Bartolomeo de Moya Velasquez. Such a sensitive man. I was quite a nervous child and when I got upset, he would massage my back and shoulders. He called me his little Rosca. It's a little cake you know, *Rosca de Reyes*, sometimes topped with a model of the baby Jesus, *Niño Dios*. I remember one day he persuaded the Cardinal to visit the town. It was like royalty. Such a gentleman and,' she giggled, 'so handsome, like one of those actors in the theatre.'

She sighed and took a sip of her coffee and a tiny slice of chocolate cake.

The talk somehow moved to Elena's brush with the Darumbal tribe at Glenmore, which had so alarmed her. Elena wanted to know if she was right to be alarmed.

Briana put down her tea. She patted her bun, adjusted her glasses. 'I might as well tell you. You should know since you are living in the country. There have been some terrible things. Killings; whites against blacks and vice versa. It is always happening.' Elena sat quietly.

'A few years ago,' Briana continued, 'away out west of Rockhampton, the owner of Cullin-la-ringo station, Tom Wills, was killed by the local blacks along with eighteen others, some women and children. It was revenge for the poisoning and shooting of Aborigines up at Kairi Kairi, actually by Tom Wills' neighbour. Anyway. It didn't take long before the native police with their white bosses were ordered to exact revenge. The Aborigines tried to escape. They headed for Mount Wandoo, but the native police caught up. The local tribesmen and their families were slaughtered. Maybe over 300 were killed. The ground was stained crimson, so they say. Dingoes and crows savaged the bodies that were left to rot in the sun.

'The worst was the so-called "Leap Massacre", up near Mackay.' Briana sighed. 'Two hundred-odd men, women and children from north of the Pioneer River were chased by the native police, led by a savage thug, an Inspector Johnstone. The Aborigines were camping on the Balnagowan pastoral lease. Some cattle had been speared and machinery stolen so Johnstone, his troops and some local farmers pursued them up towards the top of Mount Mandarana. They hid in some caves, but Johnstone and the troops chased them out and forced them down to a cliff, then over nearly a thousand feet of vertical rock face. Over two hundred died they think, including children. No one was counting.'

Elena shuffled in her seat, still silently listening.

'There was one astonishing outcome,' said Briana. 'An Aboriginal girl, Kowaha, leapt off clutching her baby in a shawl. Somehow the baby ended up caught in a bush. A local farm lad, who had been drafted in to help, saw what had happened. When the others had gone, he somehow scrambled down the cliff, and he brought the baby back home to his parents who took it into their care. Eventually it was adopted by a kindly English couple called Ready. The little girl grew up in a loving atmosphere and was recently baptised. The strange thing is her baptismal name is Johanna Hazeldene. Oh, there are plenty of other stories, plenty, but I will not burden you with them.'

'I thought there had been a killing of Aborigines out near Glenmore?'

'That happened too, but there are murderous little fights all the time. You would know they use the native police. A white officer and then Aborigines from a remote tribe from another region who do not care for the other tribes. Between them they are viciously effective.'

There was silence. Elena sat stock still, her face flushed. She gathered her belongings, muttered a farewell, and stood up.

Briana put a hand on her arm. '"In the middle of the journey of our life I found myself within a dark woods where the straight way was lost." I know you know your Dante's *Inferno*, Elena, but don't be overwhelmed. This does not lie on your head, or mine. We also need to remember that "the path to paradise begins in Hell."'

In the morning over breakfast Elena turned to D'Arcy. 'William, I couldn't sleep last night. I was visited by all these horrible creatures. This is a terrible place. Did you know of this killing of the Aborigines? It's bestial.'

D'Arcy sighed. 'Of course, I know. Everyone knows but no one speaks, and neither should you. Forget everything about it. Do you understand?'

'I will pray for all the souls lost, whosoever souls they are.' Elena nodded. 'I will seek forgiveness from my confessor. But you know him, he is that Irish priest. I cannot understand a word. What sort of confession is that? William, I would like to leave – go home, go anywhere, but go.'

D'Arcy looked at her. 'Home to where? To Mexico? I don't think so, my dear. There's nothing for me in Mexico. But perhaps England – yes, England might indeed be a good option for us. It has occurred to me.'

Elena clapped her hands. 'Yes, England. I'm sure I would like to return to England. It is full of apostates but still, they are much more refined than these heathens.'

᠆ᡂ

D'Arcy had finished in his office. It was time to go home and enjoy whatever Elena had prepared for the evening. She was certainly a good cook and he had grown to like the spicy Mexican food which she had learned from her mother. But then again. He pushed back his chair and loosened his tie, then opened his top drawer and removed a glass and a bottle of whiskey and poured himself a decent draft. Elena; she was becoming more religious by the day. Muttering Hail Marys, humming tuneless hymns, fiddling with her rosary. And then she had taken up fasting during Lent and tried to persuade him to join her. Fasting? One of the worst ideas he had ever come across. He took a large swig of whiskey. She would be better in England. There would surely be more diverse attractions for her to bury her head in than the Catechism.

~

Apart from Mount Morgan, D'Arcy and his partner Walter Hall had one other underlying passion. They both loved horse racing. Walter was a committee member of the Australian Jockey Club from 1871. In the 1880s his horses won the Sires' Produce Stakes, the Doncaster and the Champagne Stakes. D'Arcy, with probably one of his few good memories of Westminster School being rowing and his success in the local competitions, became president of the local Rockhampton Rowing Club and joined the committee of the Rockhampton Jockey Club. They each owned several horses, which raced in their respective local derbies. If they tired of talking about the mine, horses were their second love.

The first horses came to Australia with the First Fleet in 1788. The military and the governor and his staff brought the industry with them from England. Breeding, hunting and racing were soon taking place and before long the races had become an established part of Australian life, along with the gambling.

The next Saturday was a race day in Rockhampton. Well after the racing was over Walter, visiting from Sydney, and D'Arcy found themselves the last remaining guests in the Members' Enclosure at the racecourse. D'Arcy swirled the whiskey in his crystal glass and looked at Walter speculatively.

'So, Walter, we've made some money. Significant money. All very satisfactory, but what now?'

Walter was surprised. 'Well, continue as we are, I suppose. The mine's well run, the gold price is strong. Why change anything? The dividends are rolling in. What could we change?'

For good reason, no one in Rockhampton knew anything significant about D'Arcy's background. D'Arcy was not the sort of man who would welcome unwanted questions. They certainly did not appreciate that D'Arcy was driven by a burning sense of humiliation. To be thrown out of Westminster School in front of teachers and pupils alike, some of them from the most aristocratic families in England, was a shame he woke up with every morning. What was worse, he was surrounded by some of the wickedest scoundrels imaginable, chancers and rogues, thieves who had the temerity to try to steal his gold. Even though his ancestry was Anglo-Irish D'Arcy thought of himself as English establishment. The Irish ex-convicts, swarming about the town bent on making money any way they could, were a constant affront. He took a sip of his whiskey.

'I'm going back. I have the money to do what I like. I'm going back to England, and we will see who's top dog, my God we will. I know those aristocrats. Most have barely a shilling. They will bend their knees to anyone who offers them a passable glass of champagne.'

Walter was astonished. 'Back to England?'

D'Arcy laughed. 'I can't stand another summer or the heat, humidity and tropical cyclones trying to flatten our town. I long to see snow again. Then there are these constant fights with the Blacks. I can't see how that ends well.'

'But you've made a great life here. A most respected citizen of Rockhampton. You're part of the town.'

D'Arcy gazed across the racecourse. 'You know, I went bush to see Mount Morgan. We had an encounter with a snake. A taipan. Deadly, Flynn said.'

'He's right about that, that's for sure.'

'I prefer pheasants and foxes myself. Taipans.' He shook his head. 'You couldn't make them up.'

Walter was an established member of Australian society; he could not imagine leaving. But D'Arcy was not joking. He was a millionaire in 1880s' pounds. Some industrious bean counter had worked out that the shares had risen 200,000 per cent in ten years. Now was the time to move. So in 1886 he sold his legal practice and began the slow journey back to England in considerably more comfort than his arrival.

The D'Arcys' departure was delayed, what with selling the house and the interest in the legal practice, not to mention organising the next twelve months' work schedule for Mount Morgan. They were almost ready to go when D'Arcy received a message from his father-in-law out at Glenmore. William had had a warning from one of the blackfellas on his property of a severe storm.

Samuel had been home when there was a knock at the door. He opened it to find an old blackfella standing there. It was Ed, as everyone called him, an irreverent nod to Prince Edward. Samuel did not know his real name. He was a worker on the farm, doing odd jobs; sometimes there, sometimes not. Samuel was taken aback; what did he want?

'Heh Boss, I tell you. Watch out,' said Ed. 'Big storm coming. Plenty big. Big wind, big rain, flooding.' Samuel asked him how he knew. 'We know, Boss. We feel it coming. You take cover. Okay?'

He turned and was gone.

Samuel called D'Arcy and warned him, but D'Arcy reckoned it was all bullshit. 'Nothing wrong with the weather,' he declared.

Samuel went outside and stood by the river. It was hot, steamy hot. He glanced around. Where were the birds? He looked back towards the far-off chain of low hills. There a bank of black clouds was stacking up. He could hear thunder and see a few flashes of lightning.

When the storm hit it was vicious. Screaming wind, branches blown from trees, the wind tearing at the roof. It broke the wind vane in half and snapped a tree in the yard. It was followed by a lightning flash and a clap of thunder that sounded as if a thousand stock whips had been cracked over the roof. The whole house shook. Then the rain came, sluicing out of the sky in great pouring gouts, cascading off the roof in a waterfall and flooding the lawn and gardens. There was a crash and the sound of splinters and breaking glass. Samuel peered out. The roof on the shed had lifted, flapped feebly then blown off. It slammed into the wall of the house like a torpedo, smashing the window. Damiana was crouched down holding her rosary. She screamed. 'What's happening? The house is falling!'

Samuel put his arm around her. 'Come on, love.' He led her to the large sofa and lay her down covered with a blanket. 'Just stay there. You'll be fine. This will pass.' Three oil lamps effused a dim light on the corridor and sitting room. The rest of the house was in darkness.

In the morning the river had risen and was halfway across the lawn. The carriageway was flooded and there was no way out. They watched as the water inched up the lawn, reached the verandah and seeped towards the front door. Piling towels and old sheets behind the doors they managed to stop the full force of the water, but still a thin film oozed across the floor as they rushed to move the rugs and furniture where possible. At last it seemed to ease, but it was another day before they could get out.

When they caught up with D'Arcy and Elena they too had been flooded and the low-lying streets of Rockhampton had all been under water. There was a clean-up going on with all citizens involved in some way. Damiana, relieved to see Elena, hugged her tightly but Elena shook her head. 'The devil's country, this is. I cannot wait to go.'

CHAPTER 14
Rockhampton, Queensland

⌒

T HREE DAYS BEFORE D'Arcy and Elena were due to leave, Elena and Briana met for lunch at their favourite restaurant. Knowing their customers, the management sat them in a window booth where they would feel private. Briana arrived after Elena, a little breathless for she did not like to be late. Apologising, she took her seat and sat back to look at Elena. 'Well,' she said, 'I never thought it would happen. Not with your husband's mining interests and that lovely house.'

Elena could only repeat that she was glad to be going. Briana leaned forward and patted her hand. 'Well, I'm happy for you then,' she said.

It was then that Elena noticed she was wearing a silver chain with a cross, only it was unlike the crucifix that Elena often wore. This one was quite different. It had ten sides and a silver rim around a black centre, with a hole in the middle. 'Your cross, Briana,' she remarked. 'It's not a crucifix. What is it?'

'Ah, I should explain. I love this cross but hardly wear it lest it offends the school. It is a Chakana Peruvian Inca cross. It was given to me by a dear friend. He came from Yorkshire in England.' She paused, fondling the chain. 'It's made of silver and the black stone is something called "jet" from Whitby, an important port in Yorkshire. It's really a square surrounding a circle and has twelve points and a careful symmetry. Each part has great symbolic significance for the Inca people.'

She turned it over and showed Elena the other side which was made of intricately carved silver. Briana explained. 'You can see three creatures. The first, the puma, represents the world of the living, a world of wisdom and strength. The second, the snake, the world below – the world of the dead, the unlucky. The third, the condor, is wonderful, a great bird with the largest wingspan in the world. Condors soar above the Andes. They fly for hours observing all that happens below. Most importantly they transport the souls of the dead on their journey to the afterworld. The beliefs are a central part of life in Peru but as I expect you know the conquistadors wiped out the Aztecs and their religion in Mexico and very nearly did the same to the Incas in Peru. But in places like Machu Picchu those beliefs are still very much alive.'

Elena coloured. 'We brought them, those heathens, to the Church. We saved their souls!'

'Elena, the Incas are not alone. The Zoroastrians in Persia and in India leave the bodies for the vultures. It's the same concept, but the vulture is a very poor cousin of the condor. You know, around the world exists a constant bubbling cauldron of beliefs.' She shrugged. 'I know this is strange for me to say, but one must open one's eyes to the world.'

Elena sat back. 'Why do you talk this way? You cannot say such things. You are already in the gateway to Purgatory. You need to save your soul, not burn in Hell.'

Briana sighed. 'Elena, you should look more carefully at what is around you. This country also contains some wonderful creatures, tiny marsupials, gentle creatures, beautiful birds and small animals, fish of wondrous colours and an abundancy of life on the coral reefs. It is us that have threatened them with cats and dogs, the foxes we introduced, those great bullocks and the animals we farm; we have threatened them most of all with Man. We have invaded their space. If you have time before you leave, on a quiet night go outside and look up at the sky. A million times a million stars gaze down at us: the Milky Way, the heaven tree of stars. It is a sight to silence the arrogance of men.' She paused, lowered her head then stared up at Elena. 'Men, Elena, *men* are God's mistakes.'

Elena was flustered. She rose from the table and went to the toilets to recompose herself. When she came back, she looked hard at Briana. 'You must not say such things. It is blasphemy.'

Briana would not relent. 'Elena, we must learn to respect nature, to live with it and see it for what it is. The great chief of the Suquamish Red Indian tribe in North America, Chief Seattle, said what we should all know. It goes something like this: "The Earth does not belong to man; man belongs to the Earth. This we know. All things are connected like the blood that unites one family. Man did not weave the web of life. He is merely a strand in it. Whatever befalls the Earth befalls the sons of the Earth."'

Briana hesitated. 'Elena, I admire what you and D'Arcy have done here. D'Arcy's mine is a wonderful thing. It has made many people rich, but it has also created a terrible mess for nature. The river is poisoned, many fish are dead, the trees have all gone, the hills are eroded. There is a cost, but we ignore it.'

Elena sat stunned; what was she hearing? Briana continued. 'I know that telling you all this could well break our friendship, but it's imperative you are aware of such things. Have you heard of Charles Darwin, of his book *On the Origin of Species*? It has just come out. And it's created quite a disturbance. He claims that all creatures evolve over generations from adaptation to their natural surrounds; from what he calls 'natural selection', each evolves to suit the world that it, that we, live in.' She held her hands wide. 'Isn't that amazing?'

Elena stood up, breathless. 'I am lost for words. What are you trying to do? Why are you talking to me like this?'

There was a short silence then Briana shook her head. 'You are right. I am so sorry. It is not my place to say such things to a friend. Friendship is more important. I apologise.'

A few days later Elena arrived home to find a parcel had been delivered to her. In it was a beautifully bound little book. Its title was *The Marriage of Heaven and Hell* and it was written by someone called William Blake whom she had never heard of. It was accompanied by a note from Briana: 'I hope you find this of interest; it's an entry to another world. It is my first edition copy. Keep it as long as you want but, eventually, I would like to have it back. With best wishes, Briana.'

Opening it, Elena saw it was illustrated, and flicked through the images. She was horrified. They appeared to be made by Botticelli who had done some of the illustrations for the Inferno, but then she saw that Blake had created them himself. Regardless of the artist, she found the intense colours, the distorted creatures, gargoyles and devils, together with the flames and violent storms, grotesque. She opened a page at random and began to read. It seemed incomprehensible, troubling, a challenge to everything she believed. She was closing the book when she noticed a sheet of paper inside the back cover. On it was handwritten the words:

> *To see a world in a grain of sand,*
> *And a heaven in a wild flower*
> *Hold infinity in the palm of your hand*
> *And eternity in an hour.*

She hastily put the book down. What was Briana thinking; what was she trying to tell her? She decided to return to it later, but she never did.

~

In 1887 Walter and Eliza, also enjoying their wealth like D'Arcy, took a visit back to England. They met with D'Arcy who was beginning with considerable panache to lay about him with his financial resources. Returning to their hotel after being the beneficiaries of some of D'Arcy's sumptuous entertainment, Eliza looked at Walter and laughed.

'Well, who would have thought it? He's quite the country gent. Poor Elena. She looks totally out of place. All dressed up and not getting a word in, not that she probably wants to.'

Walter shook his head. 'Quite a story, but I'll wager she wishes she was back in Mexico with her own people, or even back in Rockhampton. I feel very sorry for her.'

'Her church is her consolation.'

'Hmm.'

Walter and Eliza were glad to get home to their house in Potts Point, not too far from the glistening waters of Sydney Harbour.

CHAPTER 15
England and Romania

⌒

IT HAD OCCURRED to Hugh and Florence that life up north was not nearly challenging enough for Gertrude, so in 1884 they packed her off to school at Queen's College, London to stay with her step-grandmother Lady Olliffe at 85 Sloane Street, an imposing but rather decrepit house. Gertrude enjoyed the more challenging school environment, but her quick mind meant she often jumped to conclusions, many of them highly critical, and was very forthright in expressing them. No wonder she made few friends amongst her fellow pupils. She developed something of a contempt for the secondary role that most women accepted without complaint as their lot in life. The fact remained though: she was extremely bright. She came first in English history (out of 88), second in grammar, third in geography and fourth in French. Shockingly she did badly in scripture and defended herself by loudly exclaiming, 'I don't believe a word of it.'

Her two history teachers believed she was brilliant, and persuaded her somewhat reluctant parents that she should apply for Lady Margaret Hall, one of two women's colleges at Oxford. The principal of the college, the first in fact, was Miss Elizabeth

Wordsworth, the grand-niece of the poet, but even she expressed the view that women were designed to be 'Adam's helpmate' and must develop the 'minor graces'. Gertrude was outraged at such a suggestion. Everywhere she looked women were being demeaned. She marched out of the college and ran straight into the senior tutor, rather a timorous soul, whom she then subjected to a torrent of her frustrations, to all of which he sagely agreed.

Fortunately for her more pious colleagues, Gertrude didn't attend chapel. If she had, she would have been treated to Dean John Burgon thundering, 'Inferior to us God made you, and our inferiors to the end of time you will remain.'

She could also have attended the lectures of the philosopher Herbert Spencer: 'The overtaxing of women's brains will lead to the deficiency of reproductive power.'

Ignoring all this, Gertrude polished off her course in two years instead of three, and became the first woman to obtain a first-class degree, having written a paper described as 'brilliant'. Since the very presence of women spread dismay in the university this was a stunning turn of events and very unwelcome to the male students. After all, Oxford did not admit women as full college members until 1919 and Cambridge not even then. It certainly didn't make Gertrude any less combative.

What might have made Gertrude even more unbearable to some students was her family money. For the Commemoration Ball Gertrude went to London and came back with an emerald silk gown and an enormous straw hat covered in cabbage roses. Some of her fellow female graduates looked on in silent fury.

The topic of the status of women was reignited when Hugh was elevated to the baronetcy, still being awarded, but actually a title dating back to James I in 1611, and only able to be inherited through the male line. It could not be inherited by bastards or women. Back at Red Barns, Hugh, Gertrude and Florence celebrated with a bottle of Cristal champagne. Her half-sisters Elsa and Mary made the journey to join the celebrations.

Gertrude challenged Hugh. 'Of course it's disgraceful. The baronetcy is handed down only through the male line. Some of the greatest idiots I've ever met have been some chinless dill, marching about and being addressed as Sir Something-or-other, or Something -or-other Baronet. Honestly, it's absurd.'

Hugh laughed. 'I agree. They should be for life only. I might have felt differently if it was going to you, but there we are. The mystery of the honours system.'

Gertrude raised her glass. 'And, may I ask, why are we drinking the Czar's champagne?'

Elsa giggled. 'Really Gertrude, you are such a prig. It's wonderful champagne and we are all so pleased for Papa. Really!'

Mary joined in, raising her glass. 'To you, Papa. Just enjoy the honour.'

Gertrude's outburst was tantamount to communism in the deeply class-riddled England of the late-nineteenth century.

Hugh and Florence rather enjoyed their combative daughter but one morning Hugh walked into the drawing room to find Gertrude deeply engaged in a book. He asked her to show him. It was a copy of *Das Kapital* and she was reading it in German, but Hugh knew exactly what it was. Engels had visited Manchester, where his father owned a textile factory in Salford, Lancashire. He had been appalled by the dire situation of working people and had invited his good friend from Germany, Karl Marx, to visit. *Das Kapital* was the result.

Hugh looked severely at Gertrude. 'You know very well we try to look after our workers. We understand the problems they face. But this is going too far, worse than communism. My God, revolution.'

He turned to leave, but Gertrude called out, 'I know what it is. I'm reading it, not preaching it! And by the way, Papa, I'm thinking of going to a rally in support of the movement for women's suffrage. Emmeline Pankhurst is speaking. Maybe I'll join the WSPU – the Women's Social and Political Union. You must know of them. The sisters are on the march! You and Mother should come too. I bet you would end up supporting Mrs Pankhurst.'

Hugh shook his head, and retreated to his study.

Hugh's next conversation with Florence was straightforward. They both agreed that it was time for Gertrude to do some travelling, as far away as possible. They could see Gertrude would ruffle a lot of feathers if she spent too much time in the social straitjacket of England. Hugh sighed. 'The fact is that our young lady is far too clever and far too outspoken to drift around in the social set in London. She is someone who definitely does not need to come out; in fact, she might take to hunger strikes and I'm sure she would just love prison. You're so close to her, Florence. Do you agree with me?'

Florence laughed. 'I have to agree. She is incredibly blunt with her comments and totally without a care who she delivers them too. She scandalised poor Reverend Armitage by shaking her head and declaring the Resurrection a "load of tosh". What are we going to do with her?'

Hugh paused, then nodded. 'I have an idea. You know that Aunt Mary, who Gertrude is very fond of, is off to eastern Europe. Mary has offered to have Gertrude travel with her on her way to Bucharest. The purpose of the trip is to make her way to Romania to join Sir Frank. He's just been appointed the British Minister to Romania. We'll set her on a task to track down the story of Dracula – "Vlad the Impaler", I believe he's called. That should be sufficiently bizarre to keep her occupied.'

Florence gave her blessing, and Gertrude was delighted with the idea.

It turned out to be a master stroke. It was Christmas and Bucharest, as a surprised Gertrude quickly discovered, was smart, socially active and far less stitched up than London, let alone the north of England. Even divorcees were admitted back into society. Gertrude had grown into an attractive woman, slim with wonderful auburn hair, her curls escaping from her hairpins. But should any man become carried away, she still had that penetrating stare and her sharp tongue.

Gertrude joined Bucharest's social set, became a comfortable friend of the young Queen, and danced the days away with a group of sophisticated young men both expatriates and locals. The 'young Queen' was Marie. The daughter of the Duke of Edinburgh and Grand Duchess Maria Alexandrovna of Russia, she'd been raised in Britain and later Malta where her father was commander-in-chief of the Mediterranean Fleet. She was attractive and fun-loving and bursting for entertaining company. Gertrude and Marie were made for each other.

Gertrude also became great friends with Valentine Ignatius Chirol, foreign correspondent to *The Times* and Charles Hardinge, later Viceroy of India. The former became her lifelong friend and correspondent, her dear 'Domnul', Romanian for 'gentleman'. With several languages and an intimate knowledge of foreign affairs and Britain's place in the world, he would be a mentor for years to come.

Reluctantly, after four months Gertrude returned with Aunt Mary to Britain. Florence, taking the chance to escape, left her in charge of the household at Red Barns, including the children, domestic affairs and also, importantly, the accounts. Gertrude managed these with ease, escaping to London whenever she could. In London she was a fully involved member of the social world but in truth, she missed the exotic freedom of Bucharest.

When Aunt Mary announced that Sir Frank Lascelles would be the British ambassador in Tehran, Gertrude was determined to be an early visitor. However, it would not do unless she became fluent in Persian. By the time she caught the train from Germany to Constantinople, Tiflis and then Baku around the Caspian Sea, she was reasonably fluent. Arrival in Tehran seemed almost like a homecoming, a sense of freedom and exoticism that Gertrude deeply needed. The surroundings had a magnetic appeal to her. She had been brought up in Yorkshire with summer rain, spring greenery, pink blossoms; in winter, icy snow-covered fields, the country crisscrossed with small paddocks bounded by moss-covered rock walls, low hills and grey skies. She was used to domestic animals, dogs and cats, or farm animals; cows chewing their cud and gazing softly upon her. Around Tehran ran desert, flat endless stretches of sand and rock stretching away to craggy mountains looming up darkly on the horizon; the sand was only peppered with stunted bushes, clumps of palms or intense patches of emerald-green, where water bubbled up out of nowhere. The country was mostly empty, with a few camels, donkeys and stray birds or hovering vultures. She had entered a new world.

Now in her early twenties, and yet to form any real romantic attachment, nothing could have been more natural than that she should fall hopelessly in love with the tall, thin and totally charming figure of a good-natured legation secretary, Henry Cadogan, the grandson of the third Earl Cadogan. Riding horses together away from Tehran in the mountains, they roamed unescorted wherever they wished. They were amazed by the mountain where stood the 'Citadel of the Dead' and the gleaming white Tower of Silence, where the Zoroastrians left their dead for their journey to the afterlife. The body was placed on the circular tower as part of an elaborate ritual to keep evil away. Picked clean by vultures and bleached by the sun, the souls passed through the seven gates of the planets on their way to the sacred fire of the sun.

The East had bewitched Gertrude. It was as if she had left one planet to arrive at another. Florence and Hugh were at home when a letter was delivered from Gertrude in Tehran. Florence read out bits and pieces to Hugh. 'Here that which is me, which is an empty jar that the passer-by fills at pleasure, is filled with such wine as in England I have never heard of.' She went on: 'How big the world is, how big and how wonderful. It comes to me as ridiculously presumptuous that I should dare to carry my little personality halfway across it.'

Hugh grunted. 'The novelty will wear off. She's born and bred Yorkshire. It never leaves you.' Florence was just pleased that Gertrude was happy.

The next letter had a different emphasis. Gertrude told Hugh and Florence of her encounter with Henry Cadogan. 'Tall and red and very thin,' she wrote. 'Intelligent, a great tennis player, a great billiards player, an enthusiast about Bezique, devoted to riding though he can't ride in the least … He's smart, clean, well dressed, and looks upon us as his special property to be looked after and amused.' Hugh read the letter and passed it to Florence without comment. Florence read it once and then again.

'Well,' she said. 'At least she's found someone qualified to act as her guide and mentor in Tehran. Aunt Mary hasn't said anything, so I suppose that's all to the good.'

Hugh lit a cigarette, took a long draw. 'All to the good. Yes, I suppose it is.'

Henry loved Sufi poetry and he would pull out a book and read to Gertrude the mystical poems of Hafiz. Gertrude was a contradiction. On the one hand supremely practical and incisive, able to digest complex issues quickly and unafraid to bluntly state her view. On the other a dreamy romantic who loved the mysticism of the East, the other worldly twilight zone that offered a contrary reality far from the humdrum practicality of life in England.

One evening, with a crescent moon rising above the mountains, and the sky alight with stars, Henry proposed to her. She accepted, writing excitedly home to tell Hugh and Florence. There was a long silence before she received a reply. It was not to be. Hugh had enquired and discovered that Henry came from a penniless family, had no money himself, and worse still a compulsion to gamble. The fortunes of the family business had suffered some setbacks, and Hugh had no desire to find himself responsible for the demands of a penniless son-in-law.

Gertrude wrote to tell her friend Chirol the whole sad story. 'I write sensibly about it, don't I? But I'm not sensible at all in my heart. It's all too desperate to cry over – there comes a moment in very evil days when times are too evil for anything but silence … It's easier to appear happy if no one knows you have any reason to be anything else. And I care so much … I'm forgetting how to be brave, which I always thought I was.'

Florence was worried about how Gertrude would recover from this stern prohibition, but she and Hugh had only really seen the strong, clever, practical side of Gertrude. 'She'll be over it in a jiffy,' was Hugh's view.

A year later Henry fell into a freezing river and died of pneumonia. Gertrude sunk into a state of melancholy and to help revive herself she dived into Hafiz poetry and perfecting her Persian and Arabic language skills. Finally, she published a book of the poetry of Hafiz. The greatest English authority on Persian literature, Edward G. Browne, pronounced it 'probably the finest and most truly poetical renderings of any Persian poet ever produced in the English language.'

CHAPTER 16
England

I N 1892 FISHER was appointed Admiral Superintendent of the dockyard at Portsmouth. For someone less frenetic this could have been a relaxed and undemanding post, but Fisher was not at all like that. He used his boundless energy to harass underlings and superiors alike in pursuit of improved performance. He had ships built in two years rather than three; changing a gun took two hours instead of two days. He welcomed ideas and suggestions no matter the source.

Fisher was acutely conscious that the French were building small, fast torpedo boats which posed a threat to the British battle fleet. The shipbuilders Thorneycroft & Yarrow came to him with a faster boat to defend them using a new type of gun, the precursor to the machine gun. Fisher approved the building of a number of these craft, which he christened 'Destroyers', but he then angered T&Y by seeking more competitive pricing from other boat builders. The disputes continued as Fisher relentlessly pursued modernisation. He championed water tube boilers which were clearly superior, but after a vigorous debate in the House of Commons he lost, even though he was soon proven correct.

One of the events of the year 1897 was the Naval Review for the Diamond Jubilee of Queen Victoria at Spithead on 26 June. The Prince of Wales, foreign dignitaries and the Lords of the Admiralty attended. The might of the British navy was lined up in two rows stretching as far as the eye could see. Among the enthusiastic crowd was Jacky Fisher striding about, chattering to all who would listen while watching events as closely as he could. There was a sudden gasp from the crowd. An unusual-looking steam launch, narrow, with one small funnel, an uninvited intrusion, appeared from nowhere and careered through the moored warships at high-speed, setting up quite a bow wave for such a small vessel. A navy picket was sent to arrest it but was easily outpaced. The launch streaked into the distance with a defiant hoot. The other admirals were disgusted but Fisher danced up and down like a competitor in the Fleet's hornpipe competition.

'Look at that!' he shouted at anyone who would listen. Before the crowd had dispersed, he had extracted the story. The vessel was the yacht *Turbinia*. It was the first ship to be powered by three axial flow steam turbines and was the personal vessel of Sir Charles Parsons. It had charged through the assembled naval vessels at the unheard-of speed of 34 knots. Apart from the turbines, the *Turbinia* had three propellor shafts, each driving three propellors. It was the fastest ship in the world.

Only someone with the immense self-confidence of Sir Charles Algernon Parsons OM, KCB, FRS and a graduate of Trinity College Dublin and St John's College Cambridge, not to mention him being a product of the Anglo-Irish aristocracy, would have had the effrontery to pull such a stunt. Little did he realise that one naval person was particularly impressed.

Fisher found Sir Charles at his suite at his hotel. He waited until he arrived in the foyer and then confronted him. 'I must speak with you, Sir Charles. Urgently.'

Sir Charles was accustomed to admirals who wanted to talk about Nelson and Trafalgar. He looked more closely at his protagonist. Short, a dusky complexion, his immediate conclusion was that this was a most unusual admiral, but such was his enthusiasm that he consented. 'You have ten minutes and then I must be off,' he said.

'My name is Admiral Fisher, and what I have seen is a potential revolution,' said Fisher quickly. 'The *Turbinia* does 34 knots. That is unheard of. Twenty-one is all we can get from our existing ships, but it is my opinion that speed is of the essence. It is the basis of naval supremacy. We must have our navy go much faster. Can we use your steam turbines? I want to know – would they work in a battleship?'

'They would work in any ship, Admiral Fisher. The size is not the issue.'

'You raise the steam with coal. The stokers can hardly keep up, I understand.'

'That's correct. Of course, we should use oil, or so my German friend Rudolf Diesel insists. It is far more thermally efficient. But there are some technical issues to overcome, and England has coal not oil so we must make do. Not only that, I have to solve inertial cavitation of the propellers, a significant challenge. Now if you excuse me.' He doffed his hat and stepped away.

Fisher followed him. 'We must persuade the navy. They must listen.'

Parsons stopped. 'Your enthusiasm is gratifying; extremely rare, I might add. I am happy to have persuaded you, but I doubt you will persuade those fossils around you. Most of them want me arrested. I wish you luck.'

Fisher was almost exploding with excitement. Thirty-four knots would outstrip any navy vessel he had ever heard of. But powering turbines with oil! He had never heard of such a thing.

In 1899 Fisher had been chosen to represent Britain at the first

Hague Peace Convention. The convention eventually agreed to ban dumdum bullets, poison gas and bombing from balloons. Fisher returned to be appointed commander-in-chief of the Mediterranean Fleet, the prime role in the navy. The German delegation watched all this and concluded correctly that British power depended on the navy and the British would reserve for themselves the right to use its superior fire power when and where they chose. Kaiser Wilhelm determined that Germany would not cede their place in the world to Britain.

Fisher was all too aware that the Germans had a substantial naval ship-building program in progress which was clearly meant to strengthen their options in the waters of the Baltic, North Sea and Atlantic. The Kiel Canal, the 60-mile canal linking Schleswig-Holstein to the North Sea, was about to be widened and deepened so it could take the bigger German dreadnoughts, thus cutting out the trip around the northern tip of Denmark, saving nearly 310 miles. Fletcher calculated this would bring the German ships into the North Sea directly opposite the coast of England at Newcastle. The threat was clear although completion of the building was still some years away.

Fisher saw one of his tasks was to make certain the high stakes that the navy was involved in, compared to the army, were understood. For the army, a loss of even a substantial number of men or territory could be recovered. Men could be moved, a retreat managed, reinforcements deployed. The loss of a capital ship, however, was a devastating blow in terms of military capacity, replacement options and hundreds of highly trained seamen, not to mention being a global propaganda coup. A dreadnought was a revolutionary development. The first HMS *Dreadnought*, launched in 1906, was built in a year and a day. It had huge guns (ten 12-inch guns), was 17,000 tons and 525-feet long and carried 800 men. The first battleship with steam turbines (a legacy of *Turbinia*), it could reach nearly 25 knots. As dreadnoughts were deployed around the world, they were meant to intimidate, and they did; but what Britain could build, Germany could too. Fisher had named the ships 'dreadnoughts', with more than a nod to his own personal motto: 'Fear God and dread nought.'

Fisher also understood, in a way that the majority of his fellow officers, rigid in their upbringing and outlook, did not, that to grow his resources as he deemed necessary, he would need to enlist support from non-naval sources. A ferocious and ruthless opponent, he also could turn on the charm, his warm humour combined with generous hospitality, whenever he needed. He cultivated statesmen and the press, making sure he could get his requirements understood whenever a barrier to his obsession with Britain's naval superiority arose. As he said, 'On the British fleet rests the British Empire.'

The most significant change that Fisher had in mind was a switch from driving the navy with coal to oil. The Italians had already shown this could be done, and already small destroyers were using oil. At the very least the navy could agree that spraying the coal with oil increased its effectiveness significantly. In 1902 he had written: 'It is a gospel fact that a fleet with oil fuel will have an overwhelming strategic advantage over a coal fleet,' but most of the senior naval officers were unimpressed.

In 1903 Fisher decided to stage a demonstration. He arranged for an oil-fired dreadnought, HMS *Hannibal*, to steam in front of the senior naval officers and selected politicians. Initially all went well. The ship was first driven by coal, but then it was switched to oil. The demonstration became a disaster. No sooner had the switch taken place than a faulty boiler exploded and stopped the ship, engulfing her in heavy smoke. Fisher's detractors guffawed to themselves, patted Fisher on the back and departed, nodding wisely that good Welsh coal would suffice. Fisher, purple in the face, was at the dockside when *Hannibal* finally returned.

'What went wrong?' he bellowed at the commanding officer as the ship docked.

'A faulty burner. Nothing to do with oil.'

Fisher stamped his foot in fury. 'My god, how will we persuade them now?' He hurled his cap on the ground and marched away, pursued by a scampering young rating who nervously returned the cap.

The first person Fisher saw after he had left Portsmouth was Herbert Richmond. Richmond was in an office at the officers' mess when Fisher stormed in. An excellent sailor, Richmond was clever, and a rising star in the navy. He was tall, straight-backed, handsome with his hair swept carefully off his forehead and he never (well, almost never) raised his voice.

Richmond calmed Fisher down and persuaded him to take a drink. Fisher slumped in his armchair.

'This is serious, Herbert,' he said. 'I felt we were making headway, if slowly. Now they've gone off to snigger with each other in the Army & Navy Club. How am I going to persuade them?'

Richmond was silent for a minute. 'Jacky, the fact is the merits of oil are indisputable. Eventually they will not be able to ignore it. You have more supporters in the navy than you know, and outside the navy just about every man of science or any engineer or naval architect worth his salt is on your side. We must use our friends in the press and in parliament, like Churchill. We will prevail, I know we will. But much more important, which fortunately they have not focused on, is the fact that we must have a coherent answer to the question, "Where is this oil to come from?". That at the moment is not clear. All we know is it could not possibly be Shell, for all that company's professed friendship, and it certainly could not be those thieves at Standard Oil.'

❧

Winston Churchill won his first seat in parliament in 1900 as one of two Members for Oldham, a constituency north-east of Manchester. When Fisher called in to congratulate him, they repaired to his study for a drink. Churchill was bursting with enthusiasm for all the things he might achieve, and Fisher was only too happy to encourage this young radical even though he knew very well that Winston would soon run into the solid wall of parliamentarians who thought that England was an example to the world, and clearly had not the slightest need to change anything.

Eventually Churchill turned to the navy, of which he knew relatively little.

Fisher sighed. 'Winston, you know only too well the rules of birth that apply to government apply to the navy. I love the men below decks. I want to give them a chance to make it to the top, as I did. The people's navy, as in Cromwell's day. The men are entitled, and many are worthy. With the switch from sails to power, from wood to steel, we need educated officers, not someone born to rule who cannot follow the mathematics of navigation. You know we now must have engineers on board. They are essential to the running of a modern ship and are by necessity most capable, but they cannot command. It is my wish that soon we shall glory in the day of engineer-admirals.'

Churchill could only agree. He was already colliding with the majority of his fellow Conservative Party politicians. He tapped his cigar on the ashtray. 'The army is the same, only worse. In war, leadership is everything. Hundreds of soldiers died in South Africa because of decisions by half-witted officers of mind-numbing stupidity.'

It would be a long battle. In 1910 on the dawn of war, the *Naval and Military Review* would trumpet, 'We should view with grave apprehension any attempt to officer the fleet with men of humble birth.' As one shocked aristocrat muttered to a former First Lord of the Admiralty, a quiet supporter of Fisher, 'What! Are you going to defend our officers going down the coal hole?'

CHAPTER 17
London

QUEEN VICTORIA's funeral should have been a family affair, a coming together of two great nations bound by interlocking relationships across Europe. There was no country in Europe more closely intertwined with England than Germany. On 10 February 1840 Victoria had married Albert, a prince of the German Duchy of Saxe-Coburg Gotha, a minor principality with little status. However, Victoria adored Albert so much that she managed to have nine children by him within ten years. His English was poor, so much of their conversation was in German.

The nine children were set up to extend the reach of the English royal family across Europe. The oldest, Victoria Adelaide, the Princess Royal, married Frederick William of Prussia, and was rewarded with the title of Empress of Germany. The third child, Alice, married Prince Louis of Hesse-Darmstadt on the Rhine and became a grand duchess, and to her mother's chagrin, a great champion of women's causes. The fourth, Alfred, was given the title of Duke of Saxe-Coburg and married a grand duchess of Russia. The fifth, Helena, married a German prince, Christian of

Schleswig-Holstein and was one of the four founders of the Red Cross. The sixth, Louisa, broke the mould by marrying a Scotsman, the Marquess of Lorne, later the Governor General of Canada, and reputedly gay. The seventh, Arthur, married Princess Louise Margaret of Prussia, and was the Canadian Commander-in-Chief in WWI. The eighth, Leopold, married Princess Helen of Waldeck-Pyrmont, a German principality, and died in a riding accident in Cannes two years later. So six of the children married what can loosely be described as German aristocracy. That left the second child, Albert Edward, Prince of Wales and heir to the throne.

Unknown to the royals, somehow princesses Alice and Beatrice carried the haemophilia gene, and it was passed through the male descendants over the years to the royal families of Spain, Germany and Russia.

Albert was a domineering husband despite his inferior credentials, and with Victoria more or less permanently pregnant he had no difficulty taking over much of the reins of office. He was assisted in his duties by his German advisors.

The second-born child, Edward Prince of Wales (the future Edward VII), was difficult to mould as his parents wished, so in 1861, aged nineteen, he was sent briefly to Ireland to the Curragh camp of the Grenadier Guards, a jolly bunch of 'good time Charlies' who welcome Edward to the officers' mess. They joshed the young newcomer, prince or not, slapped him on the back and promised him a grand time with a knowing wink. The next Saturday night they intended to get together with some spirited young ladies and Edward would be sure to find a delicate flower to delight him. As it transpired, the officers were regularly entertained by a group of young ladies called the 'Curragh Wrens'. After a little more probing, they discovered that their young friend was a virgin. Some careful consideration of this surprising information led to his fellow officers kindly arranging for the services of a comely Wren called Nellie Clifton to take him on a training exercise.

Most of the girls were orphans, victims of the Great Famine, and penniless, but Nellie was an English actress introduced by Edward's pal, Sir Charles Carrington, of Eton and Trinity College. Edward returned to the camp full of enthusiasm; he had enjoyed it so much that the exercise was to be repeated as soon as possible. Sir Charles and Edward stayed great friends and Sir Edward progressed as a viscount, an earl and a governor of NSW, and finally the Marquess of Lincolnshire. He was also a Grand Master of the Masonic Lodges. Nellie's relationship with Edward continued briefly back in London. Her career highlights are not recorded.

After Edward's return to England, he was sent up to Cambridge University in November 1861. Unfortunately, to their horror, Victoria and Albert discovered his escapades in Ireland and then London. An outraged Albert went straight up to Cambridge.

Albert met Edward outside the porter's office at his college, Trinity. Albert was tall, with a dark moustache and receding hairline, and an imposing air of authority. He insisted they walk together along the backs of the river, the grassy banks that face the back of a number of colleges. The weather was overcast but dry, but in the intensity of their meeting, neither of them had taken notice of the bank of heavy grey cloud rolling in over the town. Suddenly the temperature dropped. There was a lightning flash, a rumble of thunder. A few minutes later came a deluge. Rain poured down, dripping off the ancient spires, spilling over the gutters and running down the cobbled streets. Neither of them was dressed for the dreadful weather but Albert would not be deterred. At first, they walked in silence. Then the rain eased a little. Albert finally stopped as they strode across the Bridge of Sighs, built across the Cam outside St John's College. He turned on Edward.

'You are a disgrace to the royal family. You have betrayed all that we stand for.' He banged the walking stick he was carrying on the ground. 'Your mother cannot speak to you; she will not speak to you. If this becomes public knowledge we will be humiliated. What have you to say for yourself?'

His rage accentuated his strong German accent. Notwithstanding, Edward had no trouble following his father's words. He could think of nothing more to say than a few muttered apologies. He could hardly state that he'd enjoyed himself. Edward peered over the bridge to the river below. In the swirling grey water, a drake was busy violating a somewhat unwilling duck. The duck flapped its wings, squawking loudly in protest. Rather ironic, he thought to himself.

They recommenced their walk and Albert's anger only increased. He shouted at Edward. 'There will be consequences. When I get back to the palace, we will decide what to do with you.' The only thing that interrupted the stream of vitriol was a sudden outburst of furious sneezing. He stopped again. 'You have sinned grievously against God. Know your Bible: "Whoremongers and adulterers God will judge."'

He turned on his heels and marched away leaving Edward standing in the rain by himself. Edward was stunned. This was his father. Albert had only ever delivered him improving lectures, but this was much more. However, if they would not have him back, he would not be the least put out.

Edward strolled again along the backs of the river. He loved the old pedestrian bridges, the stately facades of the colleges and the willows drooping over the water. In better weather the punts would be out, meandering up and down, enjoying very much the experience of going nowhere.

He wondered who his friends really were, who might care about him; who might be more family than his family. Eight brothers and sisters had given him a full family, but they were not often left to be themselves. Their world was full of flunkies, clerks, valets, stewards and servants. Few were the occasions when they found time on their hands to play or do as they pleased. He had only a handful of contemporaries he knew well, having been schooled in the palace by a string of humourless tutors. Perhaps some of the officers he had met at the Guards would be his close friends, or even Nellie – she had seemed quite fond of him. He knew she was only sleeping with him because she liked the money; but still. He wondered what it must be like to have no money, to live each day foraging for the next meal, and realised that he actually knew no one like that. Not even one person whose name he knew fulfilled that description.

It dawned on Edward that perhaps he was just too intimidating for ordinary people. After all he was the future king, but was also the Duke of Cornwall and of Rothesay, Prince of Saxe-Coburg, Prince of Wales, Earl of Chester and Dublin, Knight of the Garter, and the Thistle. Most people called him 'Sir' or 'Your Royal Highness'. Only a few called him Edward, or more likely 'Bertie'.

Edward's academic endeavours to date had been poor. He'd found his tutors dull and paid little attention. But at Cambridge he was being taught by Charles Kingsley, Regis Professor of Modern History, but also a reformer, a novelist and a poet. Kingsley's enthusiasm for life, for his subject, bubbled up irresistibly. Suddenly Edward found that history was interesting, even fascinating, especially the history of Europe. His marks greatly improved. He had shown that he was not the dullard that many had thought.

So, he thought, life must continue, but for now he would keep as far away from Albert and his mother as he could. The showers were easing. He adjusted his jacket, pulled his cap more firmly on his head and set off back to college. Actually, when he considered it, many of his fellow students were thoroughly good chaps. His spirits lifted. He turned and headed to The Buttery, the small bar in the college, expecting an ale or two, a few jokes, rugger songs with the rugger team; a night on the town. Just the ticket! All in all, he thought, thank god for Cambridge.

Prince Albert was not well and was still soaked to the skin when he arrived back at his accommodation. He returned to the palace the next day but developed a fever. The doctors muttered and fussed over him, but he died two months later. It was 14 December; Christmas was coming, and Albert was forty-two years old. Victoria was devastated. She remained for the rest of her life dressed in black, in a state of ill-tempered mourning, supported by her mysterious servant, John Brown. Her relationship with all her children ranged from a chilly acknowledgement to active hostility. Victoria never forgave Edward; as she wrote later, 'I never can, and never will, look at him without a shudder.'

Edward eventually married Princess Alexandra of Denmark but never allowed his marriage to interfere with the task of having a jolly good time. It also did not prevent him from being proud of his Britain and his Empire, dedicated to his country, and much loved by his people.

Notwithstanding the strains of arranged marriages for Victoria's children, Fisher, D'Arcy and Gertrude would have been joined by most Englishmen in expecting a close and cooperative relationship with Germany, with which their country appeared joined at the hip.

CHAPTER 18
England

D'ARCY, together with his wife Elena and their five children, set up home in England in the expansive mansion of Stanmore Hall, Stanmore, in the borough of Harrow, one of the more elevated locations in London. The house was several storeys, with a variety of chimneys and buttresses built in the Gothic Tudor style. D'Arcy had both house and garden extended. A staircase, ceilings, fireplaces and mosaic floors were added. A spacious mansion by itself would not be sufficient to bring D'Arcy to the attention of the aristocracy. After all there were mansions everywhere.

D'Arcy then hired Edward Burne-Jones to create a series of six large tapestries depicting the legend of King Arthur and the search for the Holy Grail. When they were finished and installed D'Arcy stood back, admiring them. 'Rather appropriate. After all, I'm a King Arthur sort-of chap, don't you think?' he confided to Burne-Jones.

Burne-Jones was not exactly sure in what respect, but still he gravely agreed that indeed he was.

Of course, D'Arcy loved to entertain, ten to twenty at a time seated around the huge dining room table. Courses would come and go, each richer than the last, accompanied by champagne and wine. The table had a built-in silver port trolley, and at the end of the evening a bottle or two of the best Portuguese port from the Douro Valley would be carefully brought up from the cellar; the women were banished, the cigars lit, and D'Arcy would slide back in his chair and discuss the ways of the world according to D'Arcy.

To celebrate his new house and show off the tapestry (not to mention the paintings by two much-admired artists, Frank Dicksee and Frederick Goodall), D'Arcy held a small dinner party, inviting among others a couple he had met in the City and his wife, and the mayor of Stanmore, plus an elderly solicitor, the head of the only major legal practice in the area. The guests were suitably impressed as they entered through the capped pillars that held the gates to the house and then through the double oak front doors. They duly admired the tapestry hanging in the dining room. A fire burned in the large fireplace and silver candles decorated the table and the mantelpiece. The mayor sat next to Elena, and his wife beside D'Darcy. D'Arcy rose to his feet and made a short speech of welcome before Elena was invited to say grace.

> *Benedic, Domine, nos et donna tua,*
> *Quae de largitate tua sumus sumpturi*
> *Et concede, ut illis salubriter nutriti*
> *Tibi debitum obsequium praestare valeamus,*
> *Per Christum Dominum nostrum.*

There was a solemn chorus of 'Amen' before one of the other guests, a resident of Stanmore and a deacon of the Church of England, rather offended by being passed over to say grace, pronounced loudly, '*Te Deum laudamus.*'

D'Arcy's new French cook surpassed himself, and excellent wine flowed. D'Arcy entertained the mayor's wife and most of the table by telling tales of the dreadful creatures that abound in Australia, especially so in Rockhampton where they lived. She shuddered in horror as he told of his near escape from the taipan. 'Had it bitten me,' he said, 'I would have been dead before my body hit the ground. Even worse, they have a jellyfish that can kill you just as quickly. Imagine, a jellyfish! Just a clump of jelly, but deadly.'

'What a dreadful, dreadful place!' she exclaimed. 'How do people live in such a place? I'm sure you were jolly glad to leave.'

Elena had been quietly listening. Suddenly she spoke up 'And they have been killing the Aborigines in hundreds.'

The mayor looked sceptical. 'What are these "Aborigines" then?' he demanded. 'I have never heard the expression.'

Elena was about to explain when D'Arcy stepped in. 'Enough, Elena. We are not here to discuss that. We are here to have an enjoyable dinner.'

Elena glared at him. 'Rockhampton is the gateway to hell.'

D'Arcy banged the table. 'That's enough!'

The next course was being served, and D'Arcy quickly moved on to the skill of his chef. 'I hope you enjoy this, the speciality *de la maison*. Try it; what do you think? And I am sure the wine complements it excellently.'

There were muttered words of appreciation. Indeed, it was an excellent dish and an excellent wine.

The conversation returned to more domestic issues for a while, with Elena looking extremely cross at being interrupted. The mayor thought it prudent to return to a more general topic with Elena. He had struggled a little with her, not helped by her Spanish accent, but she was not to be deterred from her subject. She explained to him in a hushed voice how Australia was a godless place and that she was happy to return to civilisation in England. He nodded agreement. She acknowledged that her faith had been a great comfort to her. 'Be not afraid of sudden fear, neither of the desolation of the wicked when it cometh, for the Lord shall be thy confidence and shall keep thy foot from being taken.'

The mayor confessed to being unaware of this piece of scripture.

'Proverbs 3:25,' Elena explained.

The deacon looked mortified by this Catholic intervention.

After the guests had left D'Arcy confronted Elena. 'You will never do that again,' he thundered. 'The issue of Aborigines in Australia is not a subject for dinner-table conversation. Not a subject for conversation at all. Am I clear?' He paused. 'And by the way, will you stop that rubbish about Rockhampton being the gateway to hell; it's extremely embarrassing.'

Elena stood silent. She was holding a crystal champagne glass, one of a set that D'Arcy's interior decorator had acquired at great expense at a Christie's antique auction only a week ago. Elena hurled it to the floor then turned and walked away. As she exited, over her shoulder she declared, 'You will all answer before the Lord.' She slammed the door behind her.

It was a few days later when Elena received a parcel, stamped from Australia. She opened it and inside was a small velvet box. It contained a Chakana cross, and was accompanied by a short note.

My dearest Elena,

I have been conscious that our last conversation left you in some distress but hope that it has not disturbed our friendship too much. I managed to obtain another Chakana cross. I hope you like it and even if you are not inclined to wear it you will keep it as a reminder of our friendship. I also hope you are enjoying being in England and all the great experiences, so different to Australia, that it may bring.

With warmest best wishes,

Your friend, Briana.

Putting the note down, Elena noticed there was something written on the back. She turned it over, and read the words: 'Tread softly! All the earth is holy ground.'

Elena looked at her cross and admired the little carvings of the snake, the panther and the condor. She tucked it away with the letter in her cabinet but a few weeks later, when she was heading to London by herself, she carefully took it out and hung it around her neck. Thereafter she wore it more frequently. No one ever asked her what it was, and she took care not to wear it in front of D'Arcy.

~

Following his love of horse racing, D'Arcy had a brilliant idea to cement his place in the society that had rejected his family. He purchased one of only two stands at the Epsom Downs racecourse. The other stand was owned by King Edward VII, friend and supporter of Jacky Fisher, no less fanatical about horse racing than D'Arcy.

D'Arcy could no longer be ignored. Reinforcing his return to the good life and enjoying a little hunting and shooting, D'Arcy also rented Bylaugh Hall in Norfolk, although it is not clear whether this included the vast grounds, some 19,000 acres.

~

In 1895 his twenty-three-year marriage to Elena collapsed under all the bonhomie that surrounded the new life of D'Arcy. His conversion from a ruthless risktaker to an English squire was the game at hand. Elena simply could not keep up with his endless entertainment, not to mention his constant flirting or worse. Elena was dark, with jet-black hair swept back, and a strong accent. She longed to visit Mexico again and see the now large family that lived in her hometown. Neither the climate of England nor the people appealed to her, although it had at first been a relief after Rockhampton. She had raised D'Arcy's five children with little fatherly input. As she remarked to a friend, 'Flattery and success has turned his head.'

D'Arcy managed to convince the Church that one of the criteria of sacramental marriage had not been met. The marriage was annulled.

D'Arcy was hardly fazed by this little hiccup. Within two years he had met and married Nina Boucicault, daughter of the Irish-Australian newspaper magnate Arthur Boucicault and cousin of Nina, the celebrated Irish stage and later film actress. His new trophy wife loved the bright life as much as he did. Social life continued apace. D'Arcy purchased a town house conveniently located in Grosvenor Square. Entertainment included musical soirees by names such as Caruso and Melba. *The Times* breathlessly described Nina as a 'tall, slim, handsome woman with an abundance of pale golden hair. She is a good bridge player and a quite exceptionally graceful dancer.' D'Arcy had arrived.

As D'Arcy's extravagant lifestyle continued, the value of his shares in Mount Morgan began to decline. It was all very well to hold parties, balls, extravagant dinners and go about London ostentatiously displaying that you were a 'man of property', but where were those dividends that had paid for it all?

D'Arcy definitely needed another win; and a large one.

His social aspirations were about to pay off. He was approached by a new friend, the diplomat, Sir Henry Drummond Wolff, a former British minister to Tehran who happened to mention that he could possibly introduce him to an exciting prospect. For years it had been rumoured that oil existed underground in Persia; a meeting could be arranged with the Shah who was thought be a little hard up. A geologist, H.T. Burls, a Burmah Oil man, had discovered several surface traces, encouraging if not definitive. In May 1901 D'Arcy sent an envoy who returned to deliver the astonishing news that an exploration permit had been acquired for an exclusive right to search for oil over an area of some 480,000 square miles, good for some sixty years. The area was equivalent to the whole of Persia apart from the five northern provinces. It was no wonder the Majlis, or Persian parliament, was none too pleased with the Shah's 'deal'.

The most prospective areas according to Burls appeared to be Chiah Sourkh in the north-west and an area near Ahwaz in the south-west. It was essential to find an engineer to oversee the exploration. The man chosen was George B. Reynolds. In his late forties, Reynolds was employed by the Indian Public Works Department. He decided the first exploration efforts would be in the north at Chiah Sourkh, unsurprisingly a difficult site. The drilling equipment had to be shipped to Basra in the Persian Gulf, then 300 miles up the Tigris to Baghdad, then manhandled over the mountains to the site. It took until November 1902 before the first well was spudded in. Naturally, costs were already mounting.

It took until 1903 before the company, called the First Exploration Co Ltd, was set up, with D'Arcy having 350,000 of the 370,000 shares on issue but only having to pay £20,000 to the Persian government at this point, and grant them 20,000 shares and a vaguely defined sixteen per cent of net profits. D'Arcy was chairman and there were two other directors but an external expert on oil was desperately needed. The only choice was in the person of Dr (later Sir) Boverton Redwood, the leading oil consultant in Britain. When Boverton met D'Arcy, he (Boverton) was immaculately attired with an orchid in his buttonhole. He spoke in a slightly affected but impressive manner which was somewhat muted by his provincial accent. Boverton had out D'Arcied D'Arcy. There was no doubt that Boverton actually knew his stuff, and after some wary exchanges with the bluff D'Arcy they worked out a satisfactory modus operandi. D'Arcy's real problem was that he was overdrawn with his banks in London. He had lost money through the closure of the Queensland National Bank, and the value of his Mount Morgan shares had declined significantly.

In 1904 several good oil shows were struck at Chiah Sourkh. Seizing the moment, D'Arcy decided to sell; after all, who would not wish to be involved in such a prospective venture? Unfortunately, oil exploration had not yet yielded much apart from that found by the Russians or Standard Oil. By the time D'Arcy began to market his shares the strikes had proved yet again to be a false dawn, and he received a series of knock-backs.

Finally, he hit upon approaching the Paris branch of the Rothschilds who, he understood, had a one-third stake in Asiatic oil, and supplied kerosene to the Indian government. The meeting was testy from the beginning. D'Arcy, ever the horse trader, threw an outrageous offer on the table. The Rothschilds stared blandly back. One brother glanced at the other and raised his eyebrows. 'This fellow is a bounder, I think, not a chap we can deal with,' he said.

'Apparently he's from Australia, which I have enquired about from London. It's full of convicts.'

Fortunately, the conversation was conducted in Yiddish and D'Arcy could only watch. But even he could tell that the negotiation was at an end.

Desperate, D'Arcy returned to London, where he read an article in *The Times* debating the merits of oil over coal in driving ships. He wangled himself an interview with E.G. Pretyman, Parliamentary Secretary at the Admiralty. His goal was to obtain a loan.

In the background, discussions continued with a cautious Burmah Oil. It took until 1904, almost four years from the granting of the concession, to consummate the match between D'Arcy and Burmah Oil in London.

The new financial structure was called the 'concession syndicate' and D'Arcy's company became a subsidiary and D'Arcy a director, after transferring 85% of his shares to the new entity. After further discussions Burmah consented to bear the expense of proving up the oil and afterwards to undertake to raise £1 million of capital for development. Reynolds set the exploration budget at around £70,000. The agreement would lapse if no oil was found and D'Arcy would have to repay £25,000. If successful, a £2 million company would be formed, and Burmah would underwrite £800,000 of debentures.

CHAPTER 19
Austria, Sicily and England

⌒

THERE WAS NO DOUBTING Gertrude's intellectual capacity, but what was unexpected was her physical prowess. She threw herself into all sorts of demanding physical activity; the more demanding the better. She hunted, danced, bicycled, shot, fished, gardened and skated, and bit by bit discovered hiking and then climbing, beginning with slopes, hills and crags.

In 1897 the whole family set off to holiday in Massif des Écrins in the Dauphiné. Gertrude and Hugh had a wonderful time walking then scrambling up high hills and small rock faces. Finally, they roped themselves together and climbed a local peak. For Hugh this was sufficient, but Gertrude was bitten by the mountain bug, and she hired two local guides who introduced her to her first serious climb. She was elated.

In 1900 she was back, and this time she was determined to reunite with her guides and work her way towards an assault on the Barre des Écrins, a 13,000-foot peak involving the full climbing requirements of ropes, ice axes, boots and the best weather-resistant clothing that the locals could procure. Her adventure would be led by two local mountain guides, Mathon and Marius. No specific climbing equipment had been made for women, so Gertrude simply discarded her skirt and climbed in her undergarments, eventually cutting down a pair of men's trousers to fit. Now she was finally climbing in places where a slip could cost you your life: crevasses, rock faces, sheer cliffs, buttresses, and swinging by rope under overhanging rock walls. To provide enough time for long climbs they frequently left in the dark and slept overnight where they could, completing the climb the next day. Although it was summer there were blizzards, fog and snow showers. The more demanding it was the more Gertrude liked it. Her guides were astonished at her determination. They conquered the 13,000-foot Meije. Now the guides and the locals were beginning to take her seriously.

～

From 1900 to 1904 Gertrude travelled extensively, spending most of her summers climbing in Austria, but in 1903 she took a diversion. She made her way to Pergamon in Turkey and joined an archaeological dig, moving on to further explore Magnesia in Ionia and then Sardis, capital of the Lydian empire. She was heading eventually to the offices of the *Revue Archéologique* in Paris to present her essay on 'The Geometry of the Cruciform Structure' to Professor Salomon Reinach, the formidable editor, who was immersed in his own theories about Asia Minor being the origin of civilisation. She wondered about a subtitle: 'The presence of palindromes or inverted repeat sequences,' but decided perhaps not.

This promised to be a challenging interview so on a whim she stopped off for a few days of preparation at the little town of Santa Flavia on the Sicilian coast, about ten miles from Palermo. One of her companions, hearing of her plan, volunteered to give her an introduction to Winston Churchill, who had departed Britain to spend a little time painting in between his battle with the Conservative Party and his decision to join the Liberals. He had chosen Santa Flavia for that Mediterranean light so beloved of artists, not to mention Sicilian cuisine.

Churchill turned out to be a charming guide and escorted Gertrude around the small town standing over the Mediterranean. A pleasant southerly breeze kept the temperature down and Gertrude enjoyed the comfort after the heat of the desert archaeological sites. She followed Churchill about as they visited the ruins of the ancient town of Soluntum, a Phoenician settlement destroyed by marauding hordes of Saracens in the Middle Ages. They clambered happily over the ruins until they came to a large partially destroyed house with a peristyle, a continuous columned porch built around an inner courtyard. Churchill thought it had been a gymnasium and they bickered amicably about the possibility that it was a house of ill repute. Churchill was escorting her back to her hotel when they found the path blocked by a recalcitrant donkey which, laden with baskets of vegetables, was pulling one way while its master, a fierce Sicilian peasant, shouted curses and pulled ineffectually the other. Winston's misunderstood offer to assist was ignored. Gertrude stepped forward and said something loudly in Arabic. The donkey shook its head and moved away. Winston was astonished. 'What did you say to it?'

Gertrude laughed. 'I asked it if it would kindly move over.'

Winston shook his head. 'Amazing.'

'It's not amazing, Winston. It's coincidence.'

Hesitating at the hotel entrance (after all, she was six years older than him and rather challenging), he tentatively asked her if she would like to join him for dinner: 'Just a little local taverna, you understand.' Gertrude was pleased to accept. She dressed suitably for such an excursion, in plain white cotton and a Sicilian shawl she had purchased from the markets that day. He met her in the hotel lobby and they strolled through the cobbled streets down to the taverna. It was a tiny stone house with a garden lit by lamps and full of ancient olive trees and even more ancient clay pots, most of them broken. A grapevine dangled from a rickety trellis.

Winston ordered the local wine which came in a stone pot. There was no menu but a parade of local dishes: caponata, chopped and fried eggplant in an *agrodolce* sauce with a little octopus added. It was followed by *couscous al pesce*, using a freshly caught swordfish. Eventually the pièce de résistance arrived, a sort of cake carefully shaped like a woman's breast, which claimed to have been invented by the monks of the Monastery of the Virgins of Palermo. Winston was particularly taken with it, and he and Gertrude chattered happily about why Palermo might have had a high number of virgins and any connection between that and the invention of the cake. Gertrude watched as Winston demolished the dessert, pausing only to wave his spoon about while he made a point or took a slice or two of the local grapefruit. They walked happily back to her hotel where Winston doffed his hat, took her hand to his lips and wished her a safe onward journey. They promised to meet up in London whenever they might both find themselves there. She had badly neglected her research of the cruciform structures.

~o

As a warm-up to her passion for climbing, Gertrude climbed Mont Blanc; relatively straightforward given the many climbers that preceded her. She had now developed a close relationship with two experienced mountain guides, the Fuhrers, Heinrich and Ulrich. They soon realised that this slip of a woman was incredibly tough physically but, more importantly, mentally. The first assault was the Schreckhorn in Switzerland; its two peaks represent one of the more challenging climbs in Europe, the final 2000 feet to the summit being a sheer rock face. Mastering the Schreckhorn without any major incidents, Gertrude then conceived of a scheme to climb the unclimbed north-east face of the Finsteraarhorn. The Fuhrers insisted this would not happen until they had climbed the peaks of the Engelhorn range, in the Bernese Alps. The Engelhorn range is a long, narrow mountain chain with a series of peaks each a little higher than the one before. Two weeks of hard training took place and then, satisfied with her improved techniques and physical fitness, they were off. They climbed seven virgin peaks one of which, the Gertrudspitz, is still named after her.

Now it was time for the Finsteraarhorn itself, via the unclimbed north-east face. The first attempt took them into blizzard conditions; poor Heinrich lost his nerve and there was nothing for it but to leave him wedged in a rock face while they continued. Confronted by an overhanging rock face they managed it only by Gertrude standing precariously on Ulrich's shoulders. They managed to reach a high platform and catch glimpses of the peak, still 1000 feet above them. The way led up a narrow pass to a pinnacle, which they reached by crawling along the knife-edge of a col; but they were then confronted by an icy overhang penetrated by some brittle rocks. The time was passing and the weather much worse, with heavy falls of snow, mist and then fog. Only 300 feet from their objective they crawled to a halt, visibility rapidly dropping and blasts of snow hitting them horizontally in a freezing wind. They looked at each other. Ulrich nodded, and without a word they turned and inched their way down.

They tracked back to Heinrich in filthy weather, with snow and sleet slamming into them. For two nights they were stuck, and wedged themselves into cracks and crevasses in the mountain. All they had was two sacks to use. At one point all three of them had suffered falls and been saved by the ropes and ice axes. Gertrude had torn a muscle in her shoulder. Going down was no easier than going up and at one stage Heinrich and Gertrude tumbled head over heels down an ice field, saved only by Ulrich's ropes. Just when they thought it could not get worse, a thunderstorm exploded above them. One of the ice axe handles attracted a lightning strike and the whole mountain was briefly illuminated by the flash. Choosing the route down was hazardous, with the possibility of taking a wrong turn and being lost in freezing snow and no way to judge the next move. Should they head to the left or right, into a snow-filled gully or across a rock face? Gertrude could only trust Ulrich.

Somehow, in the grey light of dawn they staggered into the little village of Meiringen after fifty-seven hours on the mountain. The astonished villagers came out to help, even more astonished to find that, unwrapped from her mountain clothing, a woman was one of the survivors. After a hot bath and some food Gertrude slept for twenty-four hours. Her hands and feet were frostbitten. Her fingers recovered quickly but it was days before she could wear her shoes. Gertrude's astonishing ability not to give up and not to panic was explained in her own words. 'When things are as bad as they can ever be, you cease to mind them much. You set your teeth and battle with the fates. I know I never thought of the danger except once, and then quite calmly.'

Her strength was summed up in a few words by Ulrich Fuhrer: Of all the amateurs, men or women, that he had travelled with, he had seen but very few to surpass her in technical skill and none to equal her in coolness, bravery and judgement.

CHAPTER 20
England

⌐

FISHER STOOD BEHIND a throne-like gilt chair at the head of the boardroom table, his hands resting on the back. The door opened and five of his most trusted advisors trooped in and found themselves seats: an admiral, a rear admiral, the officer in charge of Portsmouth Dockyard, the chief constructor from Malta and the senior naval architect. One of the admirals was Herbert Richmond, Fisher's assistant and someone Fisher found he could rely on.

Fisher had little use for pleasantries. As usual he had no time for small talk when the future of his navy was a stake.

'Gentlemen,' he said. 'We all know why we're here. We are here because a decision must be made on the propulsion of our ships in the future. Do we stay with the current coal-fed power units, or do we make a huge leap into a future fuelled by oil? You have all been considering this issue for some time.' He turned to the rear admiral. 'So, why are we contemplating such a radical proposition?'

The rear admiral looked at the tightly packed sheet in front of him. 'There are a number of very clear advantages. I will list them as follows. One, coal is difficult to move from shore to ship, but we have discovered we can move oil from ship to ship quite easily, even in moderate seas. Two, coal is dirty and strenuous physical work is necessary to move it. Three, as stated it is impossible to refuel coal at sea. Four, oil has double the thermal content. Five, oil generates greater speed and no smoke to give your position away. Six, it removes the need for stokers thus resulting in smaller crews and less on-board space requirements. There are no significant disadvantages, and by the way, the Italians are already using it. Furthermore, a coal-fired submarine is impractical and despite the disdain of some of our number, submarines are the future.'

He remained standing but nodded to Richmond. 'Admiral Richmond, I believe you have some calculations that compare the two fuel sources.'

Richmond contemplated the paper in his hand. 'I do,' he said. 'We have calculated the following. A ton of coal takes five cubic feet of space less than a ton of oil. Its steaming efficiency is eighty per cent against sixty-five per cent. This works out at a forty per cent saving in bunker space. On a large ship, crew required is twenty-seven against 312. Ten to twenty per cent more mileage. Oil is cheaper and does not deteriorate as quickly. Finally, and not to be ignored, the engine room is twenty-five per cent cooler, mostly because there are no furnace doors to open.' He passed copies of the paper around and sat down.

There was a long silence.

'Does anyone disagree?' asked Fisher.

The head of Portsmouth Dockyard cleared his throat. 'Those points are all entirely valid and furthermore there has been plenty of practical testing to demonstrate the case. By the way, I'm not sure how many of you have spent time down in the engine rooms but a few years ago when I was still at sea, I had to go down to sort out a fight between a couple of young stokers. The conditions were atrocious; no fresh air and no daylight, the temperature could run as high as an asphyxiating sixty-five degrees Celcius, the stokers covered in slime and coal dust. On this battleship they were carrying 3000 tons of coal on board and shovelling twenty tons an hour, nearly a ton every three minutes, twenty-four hours a day when sailing.'

The room remained quiet. Then Rear Admiral Brockman spoke. 'I think we all know what the real issue is. We have abundant coal here and in Wales. It's right alongside us, but we have no oil. We should indeed make the change, but where are we going to get the oil from?'

'I have been investigating this issue for some time,' said Fisher. 'The problem is that, at the moment, most of the world's oil is either controlled by Standard Oil of America, or to a much lesser extent by Shell. The only alternative is the Russians. These sources are completely unacceptable to the navy. Standard Oil are totally ruthless and would cut us off for a dollar. Deterding, who runs Shell, is sadly the same, and after all Shell is Dutch not English. As much as he says he loves the English, Deterding would cut us off for a florin. We have limited leverage. As for the Russians, I need comment no further.'

Fisher scanned the room. 'If those are the choices, they are indeed unacceptable.'

Brockman put a hand up. 'There may just be a way out. We understand there are strong possibilities of finding quantities of oil in southern Persia in a concession, thank goodness owned by British investors. Furthermore, the current exploration area is only one hundred-odd miles from the port of Abadan in the Gulf. If it is proven, and if security can be ensured, we could build a refinery there. It is quite well situated for India and the East and for the Mediterranean and the Atlantic through the canal. I think Burmah Oil may be involved but we need to find out more. Burmah we could probably deal with, but right now they are based mainly in Burma and are concentrated on kerosene.'

Fisher nodded. 'We have work to do. I need to talk to Gordon Miller, and the Oil Fuel Committee. We must ensure supply. It is the key to this decision. We cannot trust Shell or Standard Oil. "Those who trust the Lord will find new strength, they will soar high on wings like eagles"; but we still need more earthly commitment.'

The meeting was about to break up when Fisher held his hand up. 'One other matter. The politics of this are important. The politicians will be concerned about how it will play in Wales and how it will appear to the public – those politicians that care, I suppose – but we must manage it. Any ideas?'

There was silence. Then Richmond interjected. 'I actually have been wondering about that and do have a few ideas.' He asked the assembled officers how they had got there this morning if coming from London. A couple muttered that they had had a terrible drive. London was shrouded in a foul-smelling fog. Visibility was minimal and the fog got into their lungs and made them cough and splutter. Richmond went on. 'Yes, fog. The scourge of London and all our cities. May I read you something from a book by the wonderful Charles Dickens, one of his most popular? *Bleak House*, it is called. I recommend it. Has anyone read it?' Not a hand was raised.

Richmond pulled out a sheet of paper and carefully read from it. '"Fog everywhere. Fog up the river, where it flows among green aits and meadows; fog down the river, where it rolls defiled among the tiers of shipping and the waterside pollutions of a great (and dirty) city … Fog on the Essex marshes, fog on the Kentish heights … Fog in the eyes and throats of ancient Greenwich pensioners, wheezing by the firesides of their wards … Chance people on the bridges peeping over the parapets into a nether sky of fog, with fog all around them."

'What causes the terrible fog?' he continued. 'I can tell you every house and building in London, in all our great cities, heats itself using coal fires. There is no other way, but it is filthy. Our job is to persuade the politicians that we can get rid of the damage wrought by the coal fires and replace them with oil burners.'

The men glanced at each other, nodding. Fisher sat back. 'My god, Richmond. Brilliant. Even the socialists will get that one.' There was a round of applause. 'Well, gentlemen, when the time comes, we will be contacting every politician – Conservative, Labour or Bolshevik.'

~

Fisher was in his office when his aid poked his head around the door. 'Admiral Atwell Peregrine Macleod Lake to see you, sir. He has no appointment but seems most anxious to have a word.'

Fisher sighed, tidied some papers. 'Show him in. If he's not out in fifteen minutes come and tell me Mr Churchill needs to talk to me urgently.'

The door opened and a bent-over figure holding a cane shuffled in. He was dressed in his admiral's uniform and an impressive row of medals jostled as he hobbled over to Fisher's desk and sat himself down. Fisher looked at him in silence without moving; he really did not need this. Eventually the admiral spoke out. 'Fisher, what the hell's going on?'

'I beg your pardon?'

'I hear you're removing 150 ships from service effective immediately. Including my old beauty. Is this correct?'

'Those are my instructions. Is there anything else?'

'They're damn fine ships, don't you know? Damn fine!'

'You are aware that some of them, including your last vessel, still have masts and sails?'

'So they should. Nothing wrong with a sail when there's a good breeze on the quarter. What are you going to replace them with, eh?'

'Dreadnoughts. Now I hope you will excuse me; I am very busy for reasons that I assume are obvious.' Fisher rose to his feet and taking the admiral by his elbow escorted him to the door.

Admiral Lake exited, banging his cane on the wooden floor. 'Damn fine ships, that's what they are.'

Fisher sighed and quietly closed the door behind him. He had no sooner sat down than the door reopened and the admiral's head peered around. 'I hear a rumour about moving to oil, eh,' he barked. 'Damn fool nonsense.' The door slammed.

~⌒~

D'Arcy's conversation with E.G. Pretyman, whose roles included Chair of the Admiralty Oil Fuel Committee, seemed like grounds for optimism. At last, perhaps he was getting somewhere. Pretyman referred him to the Admiralty. Bureaucracy then took full flight. The Admiralty referred him to the Foreign Office, the F.O. referred him to Treasury, Treasury to the Chancellor of the Exchequer, Austen Chamberlain, and Chamberlain via his staff, to a junior of the Indian Office.

The Indian Office wallah sat languidly back in his chair. 'Who is this D'Arcy fellah, anyway?'

The Treasury official explained that he was an Australian millionaire.

'Really! A convict then? Do you expect me to take this seriously?'

The Treasury official explained that actually he was Anglo-Irish and had been educated at Westminster school.

'Ah, I see.'

Fortunately, someone in the India Office thought to cable Lord Curzon, the Viceroy of India. Lord Curzon, Marquess Curzon of Kedleston, educated at Eton and Balliol College, Oxford, was a scion of the establishment. He regarded India as the jewel of the Empire and his personal fiefdom. His preoccupation was protecting the British rule and his greatest threat he deemed to be Russia. He discovered there was a chance of finding significant oil in Persia and that Britain could control it, and furthermore that if they didn't, the Russians would. Nasty rumours had reached him that Sergei Witte, the Russian Minister of Finance, was bribing various members of the Majlis in Tehran. Were Persia to fall to the Russians, then Mesopotamia might be next, and that opened the gateway to India. He sprang into action.

Still, Curzon was an extremely cautious individual, and he made a note to himself to converse on the subject with Sir Arthur Hardinge, British minister in Tehran. Sir Arthur knew very well that the Persian government was very hard up. This was good news in terms of striking a deal but bad news in the sense that anything from Russian Minister of Finance Witte would be very positively received. Hardinge had pleasure in pointing out to Curzon that the Russian banks in Tehran would gladly finance a pipeline down to the Persian Gulf, thus providing a gateway to India. This was a possibility not to be contemplated.

It was about this time that D'Arcy had another of the strokes of luck that seemed to come to him when most needed. D'Arcy had accumulated some health problems, not surprisingly given his lifestyle. To be more precise he had become extraordinarily rotund. Someone advised him he should visit the spa town of Marienbad in Czechoslovakia and take the waters.

The main town of Marienbad only really grew in the eighteenth and nineteenth centuries on the back of the 100-odd mineral springs and their reputation for recuperative benefits. The town is surrounded by green hills and mountains; small streams run everywhere. On the mosaic of pathways and gardens a series of noble nineteenth-century houses were built along with luxury hotels for the famous visitors. The fame of its waters attracted an eclectic selection of the rich and famous: Edward VII, the man born to be king, Czar Nicholas of Russia, the Emperor Franz Joseph visited; but also Goethe, Chopin, Wagner, Nobel, Nietzsche and even Thomas Edison. 1n 1905 Edward VII opened the golf course. By the turn of the century nearly one million bottles of spa water were being sold, mainly it seems as a laxative.

Arriving in Marienbad, D'Arcy found himself promenading up and down or sipping champagne with some of Europe's most prominent citizens, not excluding King Edward VII himself. There were women in feather hats and tiers of pearls, men in spats with fine side whiskers and trilby hats, displays of fashion in the parks and gardens and the bars and restaurants. Edward stayed at the Hotel Weimar, which stood in pre-eminent position above the Colonnade. He lavishly entertained other visiting dignitaries and was a setter of the fashion trend for the season. *Tout le monde* loved Edward. He was less successful in the pursuit of his particular stated goal, like D'Arcy, of losing weight. The two of them side-by-side resembled Lewis Carroll's illustrations of Tweedledum and Tweedledee.

D'Arcy was promenading in the Colonnade, the elegant glass-roofed construction that housed the main springs of the spa. He found himself alone with an unusual-looking gentleman, elegantly attired but with a dusky complexion. When this gentleman opened his mouth, it was clear he might be someone of significance, worth conversing with perhaps.

This charismatic stranger was Jacky Fisher in one of his favourite places, a place he visited year after year believing in the efficacy of taking the waters, and not averse to the charming company of the beautiful women promenading. Fisher and D'Arcy fell to chatting and the subject of D'Arcy's oil play soon came up. Fisher had a feeling this brusque Englishman (or was he Australian?) might be worth listening to and he curbed his loquacity while D'Arcy expanded on his successful history in exploration.

Fisher had made several visits to Marienbad, some accompanied by wife Kitty, and some when she chose not to join him. No matter. He had plenty of interesting people to converse with. On one occasion he was taking a morning stroll when he saw a small group of men striding towards him. In their midst he could see someone in full German naval uniform. He looked more closely. It was Grand Admiral Alfred von Tirpitz, eventually to become Secretary of State of the Imperial Naval Office and a grand advocate for the building of a great German naval fleet, a fleet to challenge Great Britain.

Fisher reflected on what D'Arcy had imparted about Persian oil. The man might be a charlatan but still he was clearly not without success, and if he was at all correct perhaps this represented a unique opportunity. In addition, it agreed with what his admirals had told him.

He decided on another chat with D'Arcy. Fisher suggested D'Arcy meet him at the new Rubezahl Marienbad Hotel, built in a fairytale style, which sits on the top of a hill surrounded by the Slavkovsky Forest and with sweeping views over the town below. In front of the hotel stands a statue of the gentle giant Rübezahl, the guardian of the mountain who can make wishes come true. Fisher had arranged a table in front of the fire.

The waitress arrived, dressed in a velvet uniform with elaborate gold embellishments and the hotel's name carefully stitched on the sleeves. She was a young statuesque blond, with large blue eyes, a voluminous bust and provocative decolletage. Both Fisher and D'Arcy were briefly silenced. Then Fisher asked, 'Do you happen to enjoy dancing?'

She stared at him. 'I can waltz, sir.'

'Would you consider partnering me at a tea dance, by any chance?'

'Certainly not! I'm a married woman.'

Fisher smiled gallantly. 'I meant no secondary intention, I assure you. I love to dance. I do apologise.'

They ordered cocktails. 'Good initiative,' D'Arcy smirked. The two had found a common interest other than oil.

Fisher wanted to find out if this D'Arcy could be taken seriously. He had D'Arcy tell him the story of Mount Morgan. It was hard not to be impressed.

'So, William – may I call you William?' said Fisher. 'Should you locate this oil in quantity, how will you manage the Persians?' Jacky knew well that the Persian Empire had been extremely successful. He knew about Cyrus the Great. Persia was not some African backwater where the colonials could do as they liked. What had been achieved once by Persia could be achieved again.

D'Arcy sat back and took a sip of his cocktail. 'I am used to dealing with these situations. There were any number of lying, duplicitous bastards in Australia, I can tell you. You have to let them know that, without any shadow of doubt, you will not back down. Pay them what it takes but never blink. You blink, you're dead. I have made some enquiries of my own. I have a feeling you and I might be cut from the same cloth.'

'In what way?'

'I take no prisoners.'

Fisher burst out laughing. Then, with a nod to the Persian connection, ordered a dish of beluga caviar and a second round of cocktails. A different waitress arrived.

'But I take it you have not spent any time in Persia?' asked Fisher. D'Arcy agreed. 'Can I suggest then,' Fisher continued, 'that you are going to need some help, someone who knows the Persians, how they work and how they think.'

'My man on the ground knows them well enough. If I need more help, I'll get it. There's plenty of eggheads from Oxford wandering about busy digging up stuff. Most of them couldn't find their way home. But if I need help, I'll get it. Maybe that's something you could think about?'

Fisher did think about it. 'Yes, maybe I could.'

On his return to England, he would further investigate. Such was Fisher's curiosity that he asked D'Arcy in 1904 for a weekend stay at the commander-in-chief's residence at Portsmouth. Gradually the pieces were coming together; but still the various parties prevaricated.

Most of the exploration had been at Chiah Sourkh. It seemed to an impatient D'Arcy it had been going on for years. There had of course been shows at Chiah Sourkh, but they had all petered out. D'Arcy had shown an optimistic face to Fisher, but his money was running low. Somehow D'Arcy struggled on.

In 1905 George Reynolds, after a short break, returned to Chiah Sourkh. He had to concede; it was no good, the oil they had found had come to nothing and it was time to try elsewhere. He plugged the wells and locked away the drilling machines. Now the job was to get forty tons of machinery, carts and camp equipment across the desert via Baghdad to the Tigris River, and then on whatever water transport he could find to Basra and across to the port of Khorramshahr. He found a launch to tow the barges downriver, and in the meantime twenty men slowly walked the 125 mules and horses down by land. That was the first challenge. The second was to persuade the Bakhtiari tribesmen that they should let this rabble drill in their land, given that the command of the Shah had no authority in their tribal lands. The main issue was to persuade them not to pilfer the equipment.

With the equipment available drilling was tediously slow, less than fifty feet a month. When no oil was discovered at the surface, they had to go deeper through gypsum beds and then rock. The first drilling was done with wooden plugs which led to the plugs becoming mangled. It was essential to replace them with steel which in turn had to be sent from England. In the appallingly hot weather behaviour deteriorated, and men wandered away or were sacked for unauthorised drinking. Fights broke out and pilfering continued.

With nothing much achieved Reynolds decided to move again. The destination was Masjid-i-Sulaiman. Reynolds needed another engineer, but the young Indian engineer chosen never made it past Karachi. Burmah gave in and sent one of their own technicians. W. G. Parsons hardly started on the right note by, on arrival, revealing to Reynolds that he was no surveyor but good at weightlifting. The result was predictably a mess and Parsons solved that problem by taking to the bottle. Eventually Reynolds booted him out whereupon he returned to Glasgow and wandered about bad-mouthing Reynolds. Reynolds was hardly surprised when he discovered that Parsons had confessed when in his cups that he was on the rebound after having been sent out of Burma for having shot a Burmese in a shoot-out while drunk.

No sooner was this over than an elderly driller with the unlikely name of Tinswood Slack was invalided home; he promptly complained to anyone who would listen that Reynolds was a brute and kept the men on harsh rations. The upheavals continued with more complaints, including one from a touchy camp doctor, Rustom Desai, moaning about inadequate medical supplies. All this was topped up by constant hectoring from head office. It's astonishing that Reynolds stayed the course, but somehow, he did.

Drilling was about to start at Masjid-i-Sulaiman and D'Arcy, who on the whole was a supreme optimist, was confident this would produce the results he needed. It had better!

It was then that D'Arcy and Reynolds at last had some luck. Reynolds was finally rewarded when a Doctor Young from Glasgow arrived, proved highly competent and ended up as Reynolds' staunch friend.

It was also then that Sir Boverton Redwood exerted his considerable influence. He introduced the chairman of Burmah Oil, Sir John T. Cargill, Bt, and director Charles Wallace to D'Arcy.

Sir John looked D'Arcy up and down. 'Be clear, D'Arcy,' he declared. 'We have a very methodical attitude to risk. We explore a lot of sites; we work out the probability of success and how much we are prepared to wager. When we reach our budget if there is no progress, we cut our losses. No tears. Understood?'

D'Arcy nodded agreement. Personally, he loved risk, especially if someone else was taking it.

Burmah became involved with the negotiations but had its own problems keeping Shell and Standard Oil out of its hair in Burma, let alone worrying about Persia. The Admiralty were still anxious that this exploration should take place, but of course they would not be financing it.

What to do? They hit on the idea of involving a group of wealthy and patriotic investors but to gain their trust a suitable figurehead would be needed, indubitably not D'Arcy. One of Fisher's more patrician admirals approached one of the wealthiest self-made men in Britain, Lord Strathcona. Then eighty-four, he had made a fortune in Canada and was their high commissioner in London.

Strathcona smiled cynically when approached. He asked only two questions: Was it in the country's interest that the project should go forward, and would his participation help?

The answer was an emphatic yes to both questions, so Lord Strathcona graciously consented to invest £50,000.

D'Arcy was quite satisfied with the progress being made, but good relations with the Burmah directors were essential. He was conscious that his assertion that major oil shows were imminent had not turned out to be true. He hit on the idea of asking Charles Wallace and his daughter to his box at the Epsom races, 'alongside the King', as he explained. Wallace was an accountant with a very tidy mind and a limited appetite for adventure. Born in Calcutta, the son of an East Indian merchant, he had large searching eyes, tight lips and invariably wore a high starched collar hiding his scrawny neck. He would not normally have been D'Arcy's idea of fun. Nevertheless, needs must.

The usual luxurious cuisine and champagne were provided and perhaps Wallace indulged well above his normal abstemious levels. In any event he began to feel quite ill and had to ask his daughter to help him back to his carriage. His health was not aided by losing £5 on one of D'Arcy's nags. D'Arcy helpfully suggested he double up on the next race. 'After all, when I lose, I always double up. My principle in life, you know.' Wallace did know.

CHAPTER 21
The Far East and England

⌒

IN 1903, Gertrude's parents decided that it would be immensely productive to send Gertrude, escorted by brother Hugo, on a grand world tour. The visit would be comprehensive, to places as diverse as Mexico and Canada, Afghanistan and the Himalayas but would extend particularly to the Far East, and include Japan, China, Burma, Hong Kong and Singapore.

It was while Gertrude was in Singapore that she naturally was introduced to Sir Frank Swettenham, the first Resident-general of the Malay states. Sir Frank was in the mould of most of the Colonial Service; a suave, upper-class English public-school boy doing his tour of duty. However, it turned out that Sir Frank was much more than just a seat filler for the Colonial Office. He had a passion for the arts; an amateur painter, photographer and antique collector, he had taken the trouble to learn the Malay language well enough to co-author a Malay dictionary, although stopping for some reason after reaching the letter 'G'. In 1877, while on leave in England, Swettenham had met and subsequently married Constance Sydney Holmes, the daughter of a housemaster at Harrow School. The marriage was not a success and appeared to have survived on a concerted effort from both parties to stay as far away from each other as possible. Much later Sir Frank was to divorce Constance on the grounds of 'insanity'. Someone more likely to appeal to Gertrude than the sophisticated Frank, especially with his knowledge of esoteric languages and cultures, it would be hard to find. By the time the two met, Gertrude had travelled extensively in the Middle East, visiting over a period Damascus, Baalbek, Jerusalem, Beirut, Smyrna and Athens, but spending extended time getting to understand the Druze and living in Jabal al-Druze, the elevated area in southern Syria built on the remains of a volcano. All the time she was improving her language skills: Arabic, Persian, Latin and French (of course), but now also the various Middle Eastern dialects at an advanced level. She also was fluent in German, Italian and some Ottoman languages. Her facility in language was truly extraordinary.

The British Empire was close to its peak, the ravages of the First World War still a decade away. Britain ruled the waves and the colonies, and an Englishman took his duty to the Crown and the Empire as an obligation conferred by God. One can imagine the pair meeting at the Tanglin Club in Singapore or perhaps the Selangor Club in Kuala Lumpur over a gin and tonic, the gin containing juniper as a medicinal and the tonic containing quinine as an antidote to the scourge of malaria. Gertrude would have been dressed in the most modern haute couture, freshly supplied to her detailed specifications from London, and Sir Frank would be resplendent in his tropical uniform and bedecked in medals. Conversation could have switched to any number of languages designed to bamboozle the curious, not to mention half-brother Hugo, tasked by his parents with the impossibility of keeping an eye on his unruly half-sister.

The two developed a passionate affection for each other and after Gertrude's return to England corresponded regularly.

Eventually on Sir Frank's return to England they were reputed to have consummated the affair, although all is pervaded by doubt and surmise; in any event, Sir Frank was still a married man, and in turn-of-the-century Britain this relationship could only end like her disastrous liaison with Henry Cadogan.

⁓

It was the summer of 1907. A lovely summer week of sunshine hovered over the north of England, just right for a wedding. Elsa, Gertrude's half-sister, was marrying none other than Herbert Richmond, Jacky Fisher's most trusted confidante, destined to become an admiral. It was an outlandish coincidence that would cause the worlds of two exceptional people having absolutely no apparent overlap of interests to collide. Both Gertrude and Jacky were in attendance.

The groom wore his naval uniform and the bride white broderie anglaise. Gertrude, conscious of not wishing to make too much of a statement, wore a midnight-blue creation by Worth, obtained by her mother Florence from Worth's store on Rue de la Paix in Paris.

The wedding took place in the grounds of the family home, Rounton Grange, Northallerton, in North Yorkshire. The house was designed by Philip Webb. Building had begun back in 1872 at the height of the family fortune. It was three-storeys high, gothic, with a peaked slate roof and a myriad of high chimneys plus a bell tower. Inside, a broad staircase spiralled up from a majestic hall with a huge fireplace. The drawing room had two grand pianos and an Adam fireplace. The dining room featured a huge tapestry frieze illustrating Chaucer's *Romaunt of the Rose*. Hugh had inherited the house together with the baronetcy in 1904 when his father died. The estate had sweeping lawns, a daffodil garden and two lakes – one suitable for messing about in boats, which Gertrude of course did. That year the garden was particularly beautiful, and a profusion of flowers abounded on the hot summer day. The whole property spread over almost 3000 acres. Proceedings were shaded by an ancient oak tree, most appropriately naval oak, and a profusion of acorns had been raked into a tidy pile. Half the population of Northallerton were employed there.

The guests, including Gertrude, enjoyed the generous hospitality of Hugh and Florence. Standing back from the proceedings as if he were an observer was the powerful figure of the First Sea Lord, Jacky Fisher. It was late in the day as the sun was slipping towards the distant hills that Gertrude found herself being escorted by her new brother-in-law to meet his superior officer. Gertrude, having looked through the guest list, of course knew well who he was. Fisher's complexion – but more the intensity of his expression and the odd combination of both good humour but innate command – meant almost all the guests were well aware of his presence. Gertrude was amused to see that Fisher had picked up a couple of acorns and was absent-mindedly spinning them around in the palm of his hand. Jacky bowed, shifted the acorns to his pocket, and lifted Gertrude's hand to his lips. Herbert, having performed a graceful introduction, turned away and a short silence ensued until broken by Jacky. 'Since time is short, will you forgive me if I come to an important point?'

Gertrude simply nodded.

'Herbert has told me of your most adventurous career to date. I must say, quite remarkable.'

'Would that be because I am a woman?'

'Not at all; it would be remarkable for anyone, man or woman, British or not. However, it does mean that I am asking your permission to approach you, at a more appropriate time and venue, to ask for your assistance in an important decision that is under current consideration by the navy. It would result in the navy having a commitment to the East and, specifically, Persia. Before we make such a decision which could involve high risk to Britain, I need to know much more than I currently do. We are still in the early stage of our consideration, but your opinion would be much valued.'

Gertrude considered him in silence. She already knew that Fisher himself had had a remarkable career and also that, unlike some of his fellow officers, he was extremely bright. Furthermore, she saw no signs of condescension so common in many men she had met, but rather a genuine desire to explore her knowledge. 'I would be happy to help, sir,' she said. 'I can see you have a serious purpose, but I must leave it to you to make contact and tell me where and when. Perhaps, however, you can tell me the central purpose before we meet?'

'Of course, of course,' said Jacky. 'But perhaps for now I might just say that firstly, it is about oil, and secondly, can I ask you to keep that entirely to yourself?'

'Does Herbert know?'

'Naturally he does, and after he returns from his honeymoon he will provide you with the background. Now I rather think this is time for champagne. By the way do you like to dance?'

'I do indeed.'

'Well, perhaps I could have the pleasure of a dance later?'

Gertrude had been told by Herbert that Fisher had a reputation for being an excellent ballroom dancer and was inexhaustible on the dance floor. *A strange man*, she thought; but, then again, she rather preferred strange men.

Gertrude had to admit that Fisher was indeed a very good dancer, and not at all handicapped by being rather shorter than her. They had several dances and then Gertrude judged it was time to leave the floor. She had a feeling they were becoming the centre of attention which she emphatically did not want.

'Thank you,' she smiled. 'You are certainly a fine dancer, but I really must have a rest.'

'Well, I thank you for partnering me. It has been quite exhilarating. We will sadly have a more serious purpose when we meet next. A good dancer and an expert on Persia; I was not expecting that!'

Gertrude gave a small curtsey and walked away. Richmond had been watching and came over to her with a glass of water.

'You two were excellent!' he said. 'Jacky will not forget you. He's an extraordinary man, you know. Not an old naval salt, but he might just save our navy and maybe even England. This meeting's important, Gertrude, but I'll tell you everything when we meet.'

On Richmond's return to London he arranged to meet Gertrude for afternoon tea, something of a ritual in the new Hyde Park Hotel, well-sited in the strip of land between Knightsbridge and Hyde Park. The hotel was lavishly appointed, and service provided by liveried waiters and maids in discreet uniforms. Its entrance originally was from the park, but since the Queen objected to anything as vulgar as advertising appearing in her park, the entrance was moved to Knightsbridge. Richmond and Gertrude seated themselves in a corner table beneath a window, the velvet drapes drawn back and a pale sunshine illuminating the heavy décor of the tea room. They carefully perused the comprehensive list of teas. Gertrude, with a little smile, ordered cardamom tea, a favourite in Persia, and Richmond thought it might be wise to follow suit. The traditional tea was served over a samovar. The cardamom would aid digestion, as Gertrude explained. 'Recommended by Hippocrates; although perhaps we should avoid the traditional Persian custom of holding a cube of sugar in your teeth whilst drinking it?'

Richmond took a cautious sip and grimaced. Carefully putting his cup down, he came straight to the point. Fisher's plan, which the majority of the navy endorsed, was to switch propulsion in his ships to oil from coal, but the rub was that the only significant source of oil in anything like the quantities required might come from some new wells in Persia, which rumour had it were very significant in quantity. The area was a quasi-British zone, but what Fisher wanted to know was how much they could rely on the Persians to keep to the very attractive agreement they had made with a rumbustious Australian Englishman called D'Arcy.

'Admiral Fisher would like to explore your opinion about this as soon as is convenient,' he stressed.

Gertrude took a sip of tea. 'As it happens, a young friend of mine who has a wonderful knowledge of the Middle East is briefly back in England, doing some work in the Bodleian Library in Oxford. His name is Lawrence, T. E. Lawrence, and I will be down in Oxford and will catch him up for a chat. Bright chap; first class honours from Jesus.'

That all sounded satisfactory to Richmond, and swallowing the remains of his tea, they parted until Gertrude's research could be completed.

～◦

May was an inordinately wet month in southern England, so when the end of the month neared the racecourse for the Epsom Derby was described as 'heavy'. The derby, started in 1780, was named after the 12th Earl of Derby and was the original 'Blue Riband' of the turf. It became so popular that Parliament was adjourned so members could attend, and a fair was set up to cater for families and children so that it became a marquee day out for the English.

On Derby Day on 26 May 1909, a Wednesday, William Knox D'Arcy was present in his box alongside the King and Queen in their own adjoining box. King Edward even tipped his hat to D'Arcy. The race this year was over one mile, four furlongs and six yards. The King's horse Minoru was something of a favourite. It had won the 2000 Guineas in April and was reckoned to be good on a wet track. The odds were 7/2 in a field of fifteen. The favourite was US-bred Sir Martin, with Bayardo the second favourite.

There was a little gasp as Minoru broke slowly from the start on the inside, but she quickly recovered and was fourth at the turn behind Louviers, then Brooklands, with Sir Martin just ahead and William the Fourth just behind. Then Sir Martin stumbled and lost his rider, badly impeding William the Fourth. In the straight, the race turned into a battle between Louviers and Minoru. Over the last two furlongs the lead swapped, as the jockeys applied the whip, and the horses went stride for stride. The two colts crossed the line together just ahead of William the Fourth, finishing strongly considering the interference. The result was in the hands of the judges; after a considerable delay Minoru was pronounced the winner by a short head. The supporters of Louviers believing their horse had won were outraged, but the enthusiasm from the rest of the crowd for the King's horse was ecstatic. Hats were tossed in the air, three cheers for the King rang out and the words of the national anthem resounded with cries of 'Good for you, old sport' and 'Well done, Teddy'. The victory was the first by a reigning monarch and the King received bundles of telegrams, his favourite being from Argentina: 'Minoru, England. Congratulations from your father – Cyllene.'

Cyllene was a mountain in Greek mythology, but also the name of a British thoroughbred with an outstanding career in the 1890s. Cyllene sired four Epsom winners, including Minoru.

D'Arcy was delighted to have been in attendance and provided Cristal, the champagne developed for the King's cousin Tsar Alexander II, for all his equally delighted guests. Of course, it helped that he had had an inordinately large bet on Minoru.

Out at sea when the news finally reached him, the King's firm friend Admiral Jacky Fisher was equally satisfied, although horse racing was for him a sport for idiots.

CHAPTER 22
Mesopotamia

⌒

GERTRUDE'S PASSION for Mesopotamia, now called by many westerners the Middle East (so named by the American naval strategist Alfred Mahan in 1902), had seen her continuing to journey to the area. Over six or seven voyages she visited archaeological sites and remote mountain or desert settlements, all the time carefully avoiding the Ottoman Turks who nominally ruled the area. She had learned both Persian and Arabic, despite the latter proving most difficult. How to deal with a language that has five words for a wall and thirty-six ways of forming a plural? Then there was the pronunciation – the aspirated 'h' which seemed almost impossible without contorting the tongue – but she would not give up a battle which would see her eventually speaking as if born into an Arab tribe. She was capable enough to choose either common patois or the purer dialect which would encompass the sheiks and tribal leaders she would need to impress. Her fluency allowed her to travel where most Europeans had never ventured, and probably saved her life.

Gertrude was an accomplished rider and preferred a horse to a camel, the latter being only for relaxation and a comfortable ride.

She had originally ridden her horse side-saddle but then decided to switch to a normal saddle and ride like a man. This was much better; for decorum she now had a split skirt made so it would fall both sides of the saddle. She quickly took to the Arabic style of dress, wearing the traditional white cloth, the keffiyeh, tied over her hat and wound over her lower face, with a blue veil with slits cut for her to see out. Over it all she wore a khaki cotton coat, made for a man. To any observer she would be mistaken as a man, which would often be desirable.

One of her early journeys took her into the country of the Druze, a closed Muslim sect, dangerous, and answering only to themselves. She set off with two cooks, two muleteers and five mules carrying everything. She also had adopted the habit of finding a rafiq, or friend, who under the unwritten rules of desert travel, if he was properly credentialled, could guide a caravan. More importantly he would ensure attack from hostile tribes would be unlikely. She later discovered, to her discomfort, that the rafiq's other function was as a member of the Order of Assassins. The rafiq was tasked by the society to prepare the way into the area of interest, and helped sanction the large number of assassinations carried out over centuries by this sinister and secret organisation.

To her surprise, when Gertrude eventually made it to a Druze village near Mount Kuleib she was warmly welcomed. With her excellent Arabic she could join complex discussions and found herself taking turns with the narghile or the bubble pipe in which tobacco or more likely marijuana or opium was smoked. She might have been ten or twelve hours in the saddle, and it was a relief to sit and be accepted in such company. Over the years she was to cover some 20,000 miles of desert and mountains; Jerusalem and Damascus, Petra and Palmyra, Mosul and Mardin, Al Quaim and Aleppo; dozens of towns and archaeological sites and places like the mountain town of Hayyil, where only a handful of Europeans had ventured before. Somehow, she managed to avoid the murderous tribal conflicts between the Druze and the Sakhr, the Sakhr and the Sherarat and the Howeitat and the Daja, and back to their allies the Druze.

Islam and sharia law was everywhere. In Damascus she entered the Great Mosque, leaving her shoes outside. The comments in her diary are revealing. 'Islam is the greatest Republic in the world, there is neither class nor race inside the creed ... I begin to see dimly what the civilisation of a great Eastern city means – how they live, what they think; and I have got on to terms with them.' She found that, although Islam ruled, their society allowed the Greeks, Armenians, Persians, Egyptians and Assyrians to thrive. Among them all dwelled prosperous Jewish traders. The Turkish overlords were moving from Islamic law to the Napoleonic Code and using Turkish not Arabic as their language of governance, removing them further from their connection with the local people.

Gertrude's life was about to take a turn for the better. While in Adana, which sits on the bank of the longest river in Turkey, the Sehan River, full of snow melt and flowing down to the Mediterranean opposite Cyprus, she was introduced to Fattuh. Fattuh was an Armenian Catholic with a wife in Aleppo. He became Gertrude's most faithful guide and servant.

Gertrude had a great advantage: as well as being brilliant she was very rich, thanks to her grandfather's extraordinary endeavours. She could travel with an entourage including an extensive wardrobe, numerous tents and even a bath, which turned out to be a great comfort as Fattuh heated the water and she lay back to recover from her day's exertions. Fattuh also knew 'every inch of ground from Aleppo to Van and Baghdad'. She began to develop a reputation, became a 'Person'. One sheik was heard to ask, 'Have you seen a queen travelling our land?' She packed couture evening dresses, blouses and riding skirts, cotton shirts and fur coats, sweaters and scarves, canvas and leather boots. Hidden beneath the clothes was an assortment of guns, cameras, pairs of binoculars and pistols. She carried hats, parasols, soap, and especially Egyptian cigarettes in a silver case; insect powder, maps, books, a Wedgwood dinner service, silver candlesticks and hairbrushes, crystal glass, linen and blankets, folding tables and chairs, and of course the canvas bath and bed.

She learned the ways of the local tribes little by little and especially the rituals by which they lived. One evening she was invited to dine with a local sheik. She listened to the music of the *rababa*, a single-stringed instrument which accompanied long and mournful songs of the desert.

When the music was over, she rose, leaving the other guests enjoying the dinner. But back at her camp her soldiers told her she had perpetrated a great insult by leaving the dinner so early. A sheep had been killed in her honour and was being prepared. Not only that; she should have taken the sheik a suitable offering. She quickly chose a pistol and wrapping it in a handkerchief sent it to the sheik, where fortunately it was well received. She returned for the feast and participated in the men's talk around the table.

In 1905, in appalling cold wind and rain, Gertrude camped near Madaba, east of the Dead Sea. She was joined by Bedouins of the Beni Sakhr tribe. She had some trepidation, as always, that they might be hostile to the arrival of this strange foreign woman, but the tribe acknowledged her. '*Mashallah! Bint Arab*. As God willed! A daughter of the desert.'

Evelyn Baring, 1st Earl of Cromer, consul-general of Egypt, wrote of Gertrude: 'Gertrude Bell knows more about the Arab and Arabic than almost any other living English man or woman.' This was a remarkable admission from a pillar of the establishment, who believed in the innate superiority of the English aristocracy. He opposed broader education for the lower classes and the 'indigenous' races, and especially opportunities for women. He talked down the skills of women trained as doctors, and in general discredited their expertise. To say the least, Gertrude would have been something of a conundrum.

Gertrude decided to expand her list of destinations to ones that had been barely visited by any Europeans, let alone women. She settled on Hayyil (Ha'il) in Saudi Arabia. The city's most important function was to serve as a resting place for the Hajj, as people moved by camels from Damascus to Mecca. It was also the homeland for the Rashid royal family, bitter rivals to the Saudi royal family. Her visit would take place during the rule of Talal Al Rashid. Gertrude had been inspired to visit by the tales of Charles 'Dick' Doughty's visit in 1888. Perhaps for her it was something of a pilgrimage.

Hayyil is situated close to the two mountain ranges of Aja and Salma and is overlooked by As Samra mountain, where the poet Hatim al-Tai, well before Muhammad's preaching of Islam, had lit a fire to welcome all visitors, part of a continuing welcoming attitude to strangers. The local tribe was Shammar, headed for generations by the Rashid. Fortunately for Gertrude, the current amir, Tala, was quite welcoming to foreigners, in contrast to his attitude to his hated opponents the Sunnites and particularly the Wahhabis. Gertrude's affection for the Hashemites, another tribe, would develop into a close, long-term friendship and put her clearly on their side in the battle with the Saudis, a battle which would continue for decades and out of which would eventually emerge the nations of Saudi Arabia, Iraq and Jordan.

Gertrude came across Hayyil after a particularly hard journey over the harsh terrain of the Nefud, an inhospitable desert with great sand dunes heaped by violent storms. At last she found herself gazing up at the mud walls of the fortress crowned with dogs'-tooth battlements and with tall towers sitting high above the walls. The forbidding austerity was softened by surrounding gardens, growing robustly under the shade of a forest of gently waving palm trees.

Gertrude was assigned to her own special quarters. After she had been attended to by slave girls she was taken to meet Turkiyyeh; exotically clothed, this talkative Circassian was a powerful-looking woman who had been a gift from the sultan in Constantinople to the late king, Muhammad ibn Rashid. Gertrude quickly discerned from Turkiyyeh that the real power in Hayyil was the amir's formidable grandmother, who ruled with an iron fist while the young amir was away raiding the Ruwallah camps.

The fact that Gertrude was a woman, and so fluent in Arabic, allowed her to discover the truth of how the women of the royal harem in Hayyil lived. They were overseen by foreign eunuchs. They could leave their household only three times in their entire lives. At least ordinary women could venture out after dark, veiled, though they were only allowed to see female members of their family. The women of the harem each had a male guardian who would organise her contract in marriage. A husband could have four wives, and as many concubines as he wished. He could rid himself of a wife by the recital of a few simple words. She would later write that Turkiyyeh had said, 'The people here think of women as dogs, and so treat them.'

Gertrude had no money. She had arranged for an agent of the Rashids to provide a letter of credit for £200 to be cashed in Hayyil, but no one professed to know anything about it. She started to sell her camels, and then dismissed her retinue one by one; but even if she could get permission to leave, how would she recross the Nefud? Worse, she was confined mostly to her quarters and surrounded only by slave girls. She became alarmed as she realised that she was not free to go; she was effectively imprisoned. She managed to ascertain from Turkiyyeh that she was within a city beset by the murderous internal family civil wars of the Rashids. Brother murdered brother, cousins murdered cousins, sons murdered fathers. As she was to later write, 'Not one grown man of their (Rashid's) house remains alive. The Amir is only sixteen and all the others are little more than babes, so deadly has been the family strife. Their history is one long tale of treachery and murder. I should say the future lies with Ibn Saud. He is a formidable adversary. If he combines with Ibn Sha'lan of the Ruwalla tribe, they will have Ibn Rashid between a hammer and an anvil.' She could hardly have known how accurate this projection would be.

Gertrude became part bored and part alarmed by her inability to move freely within the city or to discover how she would be allowed to leave. It was then that Turkiyyeh took her to meet Mudi, the mother of Amir Talal, wife of Muhammad-ibn Rashid and the head of the royal harem. They walked through the city after dark. There were a few lanterns lighting the way, but mostly the alleys were shrouded in shadows, almost deserted, but with a belt of stars visible above the high walls of the houses lining the way. Windows were mostly shuttered. Those that were out went about their business with their heads down. The few women were covered from head to toe in their black robes. Mudi, though still quite young, had been married to three amirs. Gertrude described her as 'beautiful and charming, plus both intelligent and receptive.' They chattered incessantly as the women of the harem looked on bewildered. Here was a woman, uncovered, white as alabaster with hair the colour of an orange, who behaved exactly as a sheik and a warrior.

It was a fresh insight into the life of Hayyil. As she would write, 'I passed two hours, straight from the *Arabian Nights*, with the women of the palace. I imagine that there are few places left wherein you can see the unadulterated East in its habit as it has lived for centuries and centuries; of these few, Hayyil is one. There they were, those women – wrapped in Indian brocades, hung with jewels, served by slaves. They pass from hand to hand; the victor takes them ... And think of it! His hands are red with the blood of their husbands and children. Truly, I still feel bewildered by it.'

Finally, and with no explanation, after almost two weeks Gertrude was free to go. The amir had still not returned, but she felt certain it was Mudi who had managed to engineer her departure.

⁓

Gertrude and T.E. Lawrence met on the steps of the Bodleian Library in Oxford, underneath the giant wooden doors decorated with the coats of arms of several Oxford colleges. Lawrence had been busy studying, apropos of nothing at all, a collection of Sanskrit literature just donated by the prime minister of Nepal. He emerged into the sunshine rubbing his eyes. Gertrude suspected he might have dozed off over this challenging exercise. They greeted each other as old friends and colleagues.

'Hello, Gerty,' as he liked to call her. 'Fancy seeing you here.'

Gertrude had never seen Lawrence wearing anything other than clothes suitable for the desert, mostly Arab garb which was more comfortable in the heat but infuriated the British officers. Here he was, looking very uncomfortable, in a suit and tie. She looked him up and down. 'You look like some absentminded don out for a wander. You're much better in your keffiyeh.'

Lawrence was even more uncomfortable. He reflected that Gerty always looked smart, even in a dust storm.

Gertrude had met Lawrence at the archaeological site at Carchemish, the ancient capital of the Hittites. Two difficult personalities, the meeting could have ended badly but they found that in fact they were kindred spirits, united in a determination to try to preserve the ancient artefacts that were literally priceless and in need of protection from the crusader armies that were sweeping across the Arab lands. Lawrence described her as 'not beautiful', which was rather harsh, but went on to add, 'She is a success and a brave one.'

Lawrence was only five feet five inches tall and Gertrude rather looked down on him physically, if not intellectually. She wondered to herself what it was about these small men: Lawrence, but also Churchill and Fisher. How strange.

Gertrude knew that Lawrence had received his first-class degree for his paper, ponderously titled, 'The Influence of the Crusades on European Military Architecture – to the End of the XIIth Century'. Lawrence had written his thesis based on first-hand experience. Against all advice he had set out in the height of summer with temperatures of 120 degrees and walked across tracks and old Roman roads with nothing more than a rucksack. He had been warned he would be treated with hostility, but he found the opposite was the case. The impoverished tribesmen treated him with such generous hospitality that he formed a fondness for the people of the lands that he never forgot. His facility with language, like Gertrude's, gave him an insight into the tribes that very few foreigners could hope to gain, and more, he saw the world of the Middle East through the eyes of the traditional owners, not those of the foreign interlopers. His strange upbringing and the harsh treatment he'd received from his mother had given him a tolerance for pain that was almost masochistic. It was if he was punishing himself.

'Are you hungry?' he asked.

'Not at all,' Gertrude answered.

'Then let's take a stroll. Such a nice afternoon for wandering about Oxford, don't you think?'

Gertrude thought Lawrence looked like he needed a good English roast, but she agreed, and after a few pleasantries Gertrude explained her mission.

Lawrence laughed. 'Huh, so now they need us; but should we help? Oil is messy and dirty. The wells and refineries are a blight on the desert landscape.'

Gertrude agreed, but was a firm believer that 'your country needs you,' as she put it. 'We must help,' she argued. 'If not, Germany and the Ottomans will just run the place and they will treat our Arab friends as slaves. We could have some influence over what the British do. I am hopeful that I can at least persuade the Admiralty to keep us involved.'

She explained the close connection to Admiral Fisher. Lawrence smiled at her. 'Well, you've always moved in exalted circles. But you're right; we need to be involved. The army will be much closer to the action than the navy and we're aware most of them don't know one Arab or Turk from another. They treat them as minions, making them fetch the water and build the fire. Whatever they agree to, they won't stick to it where it matters: on the ground. It will end in tears when some bone-headed officer insults one of the sheiks.'

Gertrude agreed. 'Of course, I have thought the same. But if we cooperate we should be able to exert some control over the way they behave. I made a few enquiries of my own. The risk is that if the British don't do it, the Russians will. If it's the Russians, there will be carnage in the area. They are even greater vandals than our army colleagues. Furthermore, we do know some good people in government and even in the forces. We have a chance to influence how this turns out. Anyway, with some luck they might find nothing worth the effort and go away.'

As that seemed to be agreed they discussed, back and forth, whether the Persians, the Shah and the tribal sheiks could be trusted to keep to any agreement. It was a long afternoon strolling through the back streets of Oxford and eventually stopping at one of Lawrence's favourite tea rooms, which just happened to serve excellent coffee. Lawrence seemed to relax. Gertrude thought him usually quite tense, but he sat back as he thoughtfully stirred a few teaspoons of sugar into his coffee. They chatted a little of affairs in the East. Lawrence ventured the opinion that it would be hard to keep all the warring factions apart. At the lowest levels roamed hundreds of tribes, the mixture of unforgiving religions and, behind the local conflicts, the great powers circling around, always looking for an opportunity to extend their zones of control or influence.

'I'm really heartily tired of it,' said Lawrence. 'Tell me, why is it that men seem to be only happy if they have some confected cause they are outraged about enough to take up arms? Of course, that's why I prefer the remote corners of the desert.'

Gertrude laughed. 'Do you know the old Persian fable of the scorpion and the turtle?'

'Go ahead, tell me.'

'The scorpion is stranded on a rock in a rising river. He asks a turtle to carry him to safety, but the turtle is reluctant, fearing he will be stung. Eventually he agrees but halfway across the river the scorpion stings him. Luckily, the turtle's shell saves him. On the other side the turtle indignantly asks the scorpion why he did such a thing, something which could have killed them both. The scorpion could only reply, "It is my nature."'

CHAPTER 23
London

⌒

I T H A D B E E N a delightful dinner at the Army & Navy
Club in the Mall, with a convivial group of military officers
and Conservative peers and MPs. Rear Admiral Lord Charles
William de la Poer Beresford had particularly enjoyed the roast beef
and Yorkshire pudding, a club staple, and always reliable. The food
belied the club's popular nickname, 'The Rag', which had been coined
after some chap years ago had complained about the poor quality
of the food. 'The Rag and Famish,' he had christened the club, after
a squalid gaming house in the East End. The name 'The Rag' had
stuck, but the food was now 'top hole'. Beresford was the third son
of the Marquis of Waterford. His family home was at Curraghmore,
in Ireland's County Waterford. The palace at its heart is surrounded
by ten miles of stone walls. The stables housed 100 horses, the
estate employed 600 people, and its patron saint, St Hubert, is the
patron saint of hunters. The marquis thought it amusing to have
his buttocks tattooed with a hunting scene. The family were classic
Anglo-Irish; vehemently opposed to Irish independence and deeply
conservative. It was Beresford's intervention that postponed the
abolition of flogging in the navy for eight long years.

By some remarkable acknowledgement of Fisher's extraordinary gifts, which did not include birth, Fisher was Beresford's senior officer.

Beresford had repaired to the smoking room for a cigar and port with his friend, Admiral Sir Frederick Charles Doveton Sturdee, Bt. They found themselves a table by the fire and watched as the butler filled their port glasses. There was a short silence. Beresford finally spoke. 'He has to go, you know. We can't have it.'

Sturdee nodded agreement. 'Indeed.'

'Fisher will wreck the damn navy if we're not careful. Torpedoes and now these damn submarines. Damn rubbish.'

'And this obsession about oil. Where does he think we'll get that from? You know the trial the other day? You heard it failed.' There was a silence as they each knocked the ash off the cigars.

'He's a dreadful fellow, you know,' puffed Beresford. 'All that damn dancing. I ask you. Apparently, he was running around the wardroom on *Invincible* doing the bloody hornpipe. The men had to join in. I ask you. What sort of example is that?'

Sturdee stood up and stirred the fire with the poker. Sparks shot everywhere and he hastily brushed them off his dress trousers. 'Not sure how we're going to do it. He's close to Winston, and he and the king appear to be great palls. He knows which side his bread's buttered. I'm never sure; is he part punkah wallah or not?'

'They say not, but it damn well looks like it.'

The butler refilled the port glasses. 'Perhaps I'll have a chat with Asquith. Might as well go to the top.'

On the steps outside the club they waited for their coach. Sturdee turned to Beresford. 'By the way, how did your Irish problems turn out?'

'Damn good. Half of them are on a ship to Australia. Gone to join their relations. A bunch of bloody convicts. Serves them damn well right.'

⁓

Kitty came home from visiting a friend in Ladbroke Grove. She had been held up and it was rather late when she arrived to find Jacky seated in his study, the light fading behind the buildings across the street. Unusually, he didn't leap up to greet her and only managed a rather mournful 'Hello, Kitty' as she moved to switch on the lights. He was in his uniform but his tie was undone, as was the top button of his shirt.

'Jacky, are you all right?' she asked. 'Has something happened?'

'No, no … Well, actually yes, I suppose.'

'What on earth is it?'

Jacky sighed. 'I suppose it is that I am determined to force through a momentous decision, and I have just wondered what the consequences are if I'm wrong. It is possible, Kitty, it could go horribly wrong.'

Kitty took off her coat and seated herself in the armchair by the window. 'What do you mean, Jacky?'

'I know with absolute certainty that we should switch the navy to oil. But yesterday there was a trial, and it all went wrong; nothing to do with using oil but its opponents see it as a great victory. I am sure oil is right, but I will have to burn all my bridges if I am to win.'

'But who supports you? Surely they will stay firm.'

'Many do. The engineers and scientists, and many in the navy like dear Richmond and Winston, of course. But if it's wrong Kitty … The consequences don't bear consideration.'

Kitty put an arm around Jacky's shoulders. 'One thing I have learned from you, dear husband, is that hesitation and self-doubt are not in your vocabulary. You are at your best when you have a conviction, as in your religion. You have weighed it all up, listened carefully to advice and reached your conclusion. Be who you are and fight every inch of the way. Do not blink. That is the Jacky way.'

Jacky squeezed her hand.

She smiled. 'Three-H's-Jacky, that's the Jacky way: "Hit first, hit hard, keep on hitting". Now, let's have a drink and I want no more of this.'

'Yes, my dear,' said Fisher. 'As you say.'

Kitty rang the bell to summon the maid.

~

Fisher strode into the officers' mess at Portsmouth looking for Herbert Richmond. Richmond was seated with a group of other officers, most of them admirals. At the start of the twentieth century there were dozens of admirals in the Royal Navy. Admirals were everywhere. At least half a dozen would be appointed each year and those appointed in the nineteenth century were mostly still around, the more sclerotic ones being the more determined to play a role.

Fisher was waving a sheaf of papers. He strode over to Richmond. 'Have you seen this, Herbert? It's a paper on submarines. Fascinating, fascinating and bloody frightening.'

Richmond knew all about submarines. He had been quietly promoting them with Jacky against some stiff opposition; but Jacky loved them. 'We need to raise our game, don't you think?' he said.

Richmond was sitting with Fisher's old friend and admiral, A.K. Wilson, known to all as 'Old 'Ard 'Art', who was about to reply in agreement when the elderly admiral Sir Robert Penruddock Harris wandered up and overheard the discussion. He went red in the face. 'Damn disgusting,' he sputtered. 'Hide yourself under the waves, fire a torpedo and slink away. Bloody things should be banned. No decent man would ever have anything to do with them. They're not proper ships at all.'

Old 'Ard 'Art was the wrong man to say that to. Clever, outspoken and a devotee of submarines and torpedoes, he needed to be listened to; he had a Victoria Cross to his name and more importantly was an Old Etonian. He was about to explode when Richmond leapt up and dragged Sir Robert out of the firing line.

Fisher, Richmond and Old 'Ard 'Art loved submarines. They had no time for the nostalgia for wooden boats and canvas sails: all nothing but toys, as far as Fisher was concerned.

'Well, I can tell you we will have submarines, and lots of 'em,' said Old 'Ard 'Art. 'You agree, Richmond?'

Richmond did agree. He sighed to himself. 'We must face facts. One submarine can sink a battleship with one torpedo. They may not look nice, but they are a very serious weapon.'

Sir Robert had wandered back and overheard the conversation. 'Look nice! They look like a row of coffins. Underhand, unfair and damned un-English.'

Fisher turned to Richmond and Old 'Ard 'Art. 'Come on,' he said. 'We need to go and have a sensible discussion.'

No one was ever going to persuade Sir Robert and his cohort to change their minds, but Old 'Ard 'Art, Richmond and Fisher quietly sat down and went through the new briefing paper. They agreed; if submarines were here to stay, they'd better have the best. In 1901 they imported one from America and in 1903 they had a fleet of five based in Portsmouth. They were disdained by the blue-water types, but they were there to stay.

CHAPTER 24
London

GERTRUDE WAS FINALLY ready to speak to Fisher. She called her brother-in-law Herbert Richmond to arrange a time and a place. They agreed they would go to Fisher's office in the Admiralty. Gertrude arrived and met Herbert in the entrance to the foyer. Two street urchins were sheltering under the lintel, one with bare feet. They wore wretched rags for clothes and their thin jackets were far too small, the sleeves stopping at their elbows. Cloth caps were pulled down hard over their heads. It was pouring, the rain blowing in horizontal gusts down the street.

Herbert waved his umbrella at them, muttering 'Be off.' The urchins ran away, one of them shouting something indecipherable. As Gertrude watched the larger of the two turned and gave a two-fingered gesture before disappearing up an alley.

Herbert and Gertrude shook the rain from their umbrellas. Drips slid off their raincoats and small puddles formed on the tiled floor. 'Delightful,' muttered Gertrude. 'Do take me back to the desert!' Then: 'Will I be wasting my breath, do you think?'

Herbert laughed. 'Not at all. Believe me, the admiral is the last person to let old-world prejudices stand in his way of modernising the navy, as a lot of naval officers have found to their cost.'

Fisher greeted them warmly. 'I must say you are an excellent dancer, Gertrude. Excellent!' Gertrude was slightly taken aback but well recalled a pleasant turn around the floor with Fisher at the family wedding.

They seated themselves opposite Fisher. Gazing down at them from the wall was the Spy cartoon of Fisher in naval uniform, one of Fisher's favourites.

Fisher got straight to the point. 'So Gertrude, what do you have for me? How do we handle these people?'

Gertrude sat back, took a long draw on her cigarette, exhaled a cloud of smoke, and slowly stubbed it out in an ashtray. 'First,' she said, 'I have to say that D'Arcy has negotiated a very favourable deal for himself which, in itself, creates a problem. It is quite clear the parliament in Tehran, the Majlis, don't like it one bit and the Russians are stirring the pot. I think you know this.'

Gertrude was hardly exaggerating. There was in fact considerable unrest in Tehran, with the Shah at odds with the Majlis, particularly over the exceptional leniency of the agreement. The Majlis had ordered the First Exploration Company to provide copies of the 1905 agreement and Burmah Oil's articles of association.

Gertrude continued. 'But to go back a little, you should start by treating these people as your equals and not some inferior race to be condescended to and cheated. They are as sensitive to insults as the rest of us. You must stick strictly to your agreement, and you must take seriously any complaints – and there will be many – which are thrown at you. They are exactly as trustworthy as the people you deal with here, but they have a sense of pride and honour which you must not offend. I would strongly recommend that you have a Persian-speaking intermediary who understands their culture. This should save you from creating unintentional offence and avoid the misunderstandings that come with translation. One thing I assume you already appreciate is that you are dealing with Persians and not Arabs. Their culture and language are quite different. They speak an Indo-European language, and more importantly they are Shiite Muslims, based on the Prophet's cousin and son-in-law. The Arabs speak Arabic, an Afroasiatic language, influenced by Semitic tongues, and they are Sunni Muslims. To repeat what I have already said, you need someone full time in Tehran to monitor the mood and keep an eye on the Russians, not to mention Standard Oil.'

Fisher stood up and walked over to the window. After a long silence he returned to his seat. Gertrude took the time to light another cigarette.

'Please continue,' said Fisher.

'The tricky part,' resumed Gertrude, 'is that the drilling is now taking place, I believe, at Masjid-i-Sulaiman. As I think you know, this is close to the Gulf and beyond the writ of the Shah. The area is a tribal land of the Bakhtiari. Bakhtiari can be taken to mean "companion of fortune", by the way. They are a powerful nomadic tribe in considerable conflict with Tehran. They move their livestock around the country to the best grazing lands near the Zagros ranges, but much of the time they will be in the area in which you'll be drilling. They are of course proud; they believe they are descended from Fereydun, a legendary hero from the Iranian national epic, *Shahnameh*. You will need to pay them if you don't want serious trouble, but really not very much. You may guard your rigs, but they can destroy them overnight if they wish. Again, you must have someone available who speaks their language and is in constant contact when they are in the area. You must also understand their internal tribal conflicts. For example, there are two tribal divisions, Chahar Lang, meaning "four shares", and Haft Lang, "seven shares". I am certainly not going to go into the subtleties of this particular dispute, since I assume you don't want to be here all morning. However, there is constant movement between them.'

This warning turned out to be prescient. The Bakhtari turned out to be a constant thorn in the side of the engineer in charge, George Reynolds, and the drillers on site. They were well aware of what was taking place on their land and rode into the camp from time to time demanding compensation or damaging the drilling equipment and threatening the drilling gang. Constant small 'contributions' would have to be made to ensure a few more weeks of relative peace.

Fisher clasped his hands in front of his mouth. 'Essentially it sounds as if there is just too much risk to bet the navy on. Is that what you're trying to tell me?'

'No, that's not what I'm telling you,' said Gertrude. 'You can rely on these people. They have no reason to interfere in your endeavours; they need the money. But what I'm trying to say is that you must deal with them from a position of knowledge and understanding, and sadly that has rarely been the position of the British military in the East. However, there are a surprising number of our citizens who know a lot about the subjects we've been discussing and can protect your interests, not militarily but by remaining very close to the tribes and shifting groups that matter. I would be happy to make some suggestions.'

Richmond intervened. 'What about your young friend from Oxford. Could he help?'

Gertrude laughed. 'Oh yes. But somehow, I think not. He's really only interested in digging holes in the middle of the desert. Besides, the Arab world is his territory and you need someone who knows Persia.'

Fisher grunted, then thanked Gertrude for her contribution. 'We have some work to do and then we will get back to you, but please do have a think about who might assist us. I think we understand quite well that we will need to handle these relationships with care. This seems a significant difference from our vertical line of command structure. The navy likes giving orders!'

There was silence for a minute. Gertrude looked at Fisher. 'Do you think there will be war with Germany?"

Fisher lifted his chin and stared straight back at her. 'It is more likely than not.'

'I think you know them, their admirals. Can it not be stopped?'

'"The kingdom of heaven suffereth violence, and the violent take it by force": Matthew 11. War is part of nature. It's God's will.'

Gertrude gave a wan smile. 'Do you know what you are dealing with?' She quoted: '"I will destroy whom I have created from the face of the earth; both man and beast, and the creeping things, and the fowls of the air; for it repenteth me that I have made them." Genesis, I believe. All complete nonsense, of course.'

Fisher smiled at her. 'Genesis indeed. Excellent, my dear.'

Gertrude stood and frowned at Fisher. 'Do not call me "my dear".' She turned to leave, and Richmond jumped up to follow her. At the door she turned back to Fisher. 'I do hope and pray that peace will be your goal. I'm not optimistic about the prayer bit, though.'

They stepped outside to find Herbert's car and driver waiting. The rain and brisk wind had eased but a heavy fog was cutting visibility. Gertrude shivered and pulled her coat tight around her as Herbert busily buttoned up his overcoat. Suddenly the two urchins they had seen when they arrived appeared at her elbow from nowhere. They were both soaked through. She could hardly follow their cockney twang, but it was obvious what they wanted. As he climbed into the carriage, Herbert turned to the kids. 'Get away with you. Go on, go home.'

'What home, mister?' one child yelped.

Gertrude thought of her stepmother and her dear father and how they tried so hard to give some justice to the impoverished people up north that they employed. She reached into her purse and gave each child a shilling. They stood stock still in amazement. A whole shilling!

~⊙

A long-running dispute with France in North Africa continued until brought to a head at Fashoda on the Nile. War nearly erupted during the Fashoda Crisis. France sent a column of troops overland to protect their African interests by trying to seize control of the upper reaches of the White Nile.

Britain, with overwhelming force available, including a flotilla of gunboats based on the Nile, intervened, and forced France out. A face-saving compromise was reached by acknowledging France as the new 'dominant power' in Morocco. This precipitated a debate in France which caused them to recognise that the predominant threat was in fact Germany, leading in turn to the Entente Cordiale between Britain and France in 1905.

Events came to a head when France, responding to the apparent agreement of the British government, deployed a substantial force in Morocco in April 1911, and took effective control. Germany responded by sending first a gunboat, SMS *Panther*, and then the Bremen-class cruiser SMS *Berlin*. The British were initially slow to react, but then it dawned on Sir Edward Grey, the foreign secretary, that this would give Germany a naval port on the Atlantic. Agadir faced westward over the Atlantic. From Agadir, ships could range north towards the south coast of England, west to America and south around the Cape of Good Hope into the Pacific. Worse, Tangiers was an alternative, and it was situated only a few miles across the Strait from Gibraltar. You could sit on the wharf in Tangier and watch every ship that entered or exited the harbour at Gibraltar.

The response was an immediate threat of war. Germany backed down. In 1912 the Treaty of Fez was signed, giving France complete control of Morocco. Britain backed France thus fuelling significant resentment in Germany, particularly from the Kaiser.

Home Secretary Churchill observed the events and watched the performance of the German cruisers and then the British battleships sent in response to Morocco. All the while, Fisher continued to prompt Churchill on the subject of oil. Prime Minister Asquith appointed Churchill First Lord of the Admiralty, which prompted Churchill to restate his public support of the switch to oil – but now with real authority. With the Persian oil strike proving to have huge reserves, objections about sourcing supply had now been overcome.

The fact that not long after the French were confronted with a German threat to their authority in Tangiers only confirmed the Entente with Britain.

CHAPTER 25
Turkey

⌐

CHARLES Hotham Montagu Doughty-Wylie VC, CB, CMG was born in Thebarton Hall, Suffolk, and educated at Winchester College and the Royal Military College, Sandhurst. His military career was colourful from the start. After the Chitral Expedition in 1895 and in 1898 the occupation of Crete, he had postings in Sudan and served with Lord Kitchener in the Mahdist Wars. In 1899 he took part in the final defeat of the Khalifa as a brigade major, then the second Boer War, the Boxer Rebellion and the Somaliland expedition, commanding the Camel Corps.

Doughty-Wylie, for some reason called 'Dick' by everyone, was a handsome, educated, decorated hero: enough to turn any young woman's head. In 1904 he married Lilian Oimara Adams, daughter of John Wylie, a no-nonsense nurse and the widow of Lieutenant Henry Adams. As with her deceased first husband she insisted on incorporating her maiden name in their surname. Lilian, for some unknown reason called 'Judith' by friends and family, was not to be trifled with.

Gertrude had met Dick at the door of the consular office in

Konya, in the Anatolian highlands, where Dick had been appointed British military consul. She had been poised to ring the bell when the door opened and out stepped a dashingly good-looking officer, immaculately dressed in his military uniform. He doffed his cap and asked how he could assist. Gertrude was very seldom taken aback but at that moment she found herself lost for words; she quite forgot what she wanted to say when, just in time, he stepped aside for her to enter. Recovering, she explained she had come to let the consular office know of her whereabouts in the area.

Unfailingly polite, he invited her to join him and Judith and some local dignitaries for tea in the consular gardens, it being early afternoon. Dick had adopted the new pastime of drinking tea rather than coffee. It was served in the Turkish style: two stacked kettles, one above the other, water boiled in the lower kettle and infused into the top kettle with a spoonful of loose tea leaves. The maid carefully managed the process and then the tea, very strong, was served in small tulip-shaped glasses, with cubes of beet sugar added as required. Gertrude added a cube and then carefully picked up her glass which she knew to be called *ince belli*, holding it carefully by the rim to avoid burning her fingers. Dick watched and could see that she was clearly familiar with the protocol. Small, sweet biscuits, *kurabiye*, were served with the tea. Gertrude preferred coffee but understood that the tea-serving was becoming an established afternoon ritual.

Judith went inside to attend to some domestic matters and Gertrude and Dick were left to talk. She found that he had an excellent knowledge of the East and especially some areas that she had not in fact experienced. She was also gratified to find he was as enthusiastic as she was about the people of the East, their history and customs. Judith had not returned by the time Gertrude left so she passed on her thanks and agreed with Dick that they should meet again before she left Turkey.

Gertrude was to visit Konya and the consulate several times before she left for England.

Judith stood by her husband during the outbreak of the revolution by the Young Turks. The revolution began by systematically massacring the local Armenians, but Doughty-Wylie was not going to stand by. He persuaded the Turkish governor to provide an escort of Turkish troops plus a bugler and, despite being shot in the arm, he managed to restore order. His wife turned part of the dragoman's house into a hospital for the wounded Armenians. Dick was awarded a CMG in the Birthday Honours and the Order of the Medjidie by the Ottomans. Gertrude wrote him a letter of congratulations which started an increasing exchange of letters, but then Dick found himself in London alone, while Judith visited his mother in Wales. Suddenly Gertrude found she had to be in London. Gertrude introduced Dick to her circle of the aristocratic, the sophisticated, the bohemian. It was becoming clear that Dick's marriage was floundering, and Judith was nowhere to be seen.

The relationship blossomed over the years, and Dick and Gertrude could be found in a variety of London destinations talking and laughing, seemingly oblivious to those around them. When Gertrude was with Dick, other people could not mistake the light that would come into her life. Even the densest observer could see that Gertrude had found a soulmate; but this was the dawning of the twentieth century and old rules of behaviour died hard. Edward VII could have as many mistresses as he liked but he was the king; different rules applied. Many of the royal circle followed his example (admittedly, mostly with less flamboyance) but it became slowly clear to Gertrude that however much Dick loved her he could not and would not leave his wife. In addition, true to the rules Hugh and Florence had applied over her abortive love affair with Cadogan, they would not countenance Gertrude having a public affair with a married man.

Eventually Gertrude invited Dick to a house party at Rounton, without telling Hugh or Florence. She was deliriously happy when he accepted. He somehow ended up in her room long after midnight, but it seems that Gertrude, a virgin still, remained a virgin when the party was over. Dick wrote her a warm and affectionate letter of thanks but at the bottom he ended it by saying, 'All the good luck in the world, Yours ever, R.' Gertrude read it and reread it, but the final words were a knife in her heart. 'Yours ever, R.'

The stream of letters backwards and forwards continued, but as much as Gertrude could persuade herself otherwise, they had begun to take the tone of a friend. She had written to him in Albania and when she tore open his reply her face fell as she read: 'Of course call me Dick in letters, and I shall call you Gertrude. There is nothing in that – many people do – my wife doesn't see my letters as a rule, but as she often writes to you herself we have always passed them across – but oh, how I shall miss them! There is another thing that has to be done. Tonight I shall destroy your letters. I hate it but it is right. One might die or something, and they are not for any soul but me.' Then in a later letter: 'and you'll go on being the wise and splendid women that you are, not afraid of any amazement and finding work and life and the fullness of it always to your hand. And I shall always be your friend.' Gertrude was in her forties. 'I shall always be your friend': this was goodbye, she thought, and there was not going to be another Dick Doughty-Wylie in her life.

CHAPTER 26
France

ACROSS THE CHANNEL in London, a different battle had been taking place over the proper role of the navy. The two protagonists were the two great friends, Winston Spencer Churchill, First Lord of the Admiralty, and John (Jacky) Arbuthnot Fisher, the First Sea Lord.

The two had first met a decade earlier in Biarritz. Fisher claimed he fell 'desperately in love with Churchill' and later claimed that Churchill had told him that 'you are the only man in the world I truly love'. The residents of Biarritz were somewhat intrigued by these two boisterous figures strolling along laughing and arguing, waving their arms about and gesticulating violently in support of a point of view or a joke. What was more intriguing still was that both men stood five feet seven inches tall, reinforcing the impression of two dynamic sources of energy in two very small packages. Whatever the truth, they had the tumultuous relationship of an old married couple; but they shared an enthusiasm for life and a poetic, even romantic view of the world that stood them apart from the grizzled old-style men of the navy. They loved to be together even though Churchill was half Fisher's age. Edward VII christened them 'the chatterers'. Worse still for the British establishment, they were both radicals and liberals in political attitudes. More scandalously (as far as the establishment was concerned) was the fact that Winston's mother, the American-born Jennie (Jennie Jerome from Brooklyn, NYC) and married to Lord Randolph Churchill, had been Edward's mistress. Edward had introduced her to Randolph at a regatta on the Isle of Wight. Randolph and Jennie were engaged three days later.

Of course, everyone who was anyone knew about it. Fisher tried to avoid the subject fearing that Winston might be upset, but as it turned out Winston raised it himself. They were chatting in the hotel reception when he was handed a letter. He looked at the handwriting and announced to Fisher, 'It's a note from Mother.' Opening it, he glanced at the content. 'She's heading to Paris and wondering if Paris is on my agenda. Sadly not. A pity we couldn't go together. She's such fun. One of the most entertaining women I've ever met. Not really the motherly kind, though. Never mind. We must find another occasion. You two would get on famously. She's a pretty damn good dancer, you know.'

When Fisher retired in 1911 after being appointed a baron, he moved to the country. In an extraordinary stroke of luck for Fisher, who had no means outside the navy, his son Cecil had been adopted as family by the arms maker Josiah Vavasseur. Upon Vavasseur's death in 1908 Cecil had inherited the country mansion, Kilverstone Hall, plus 3000 acres of its estate, subject only to changing his name to Vavasseur. Located beside the Little Ouse River, near Thetford in Norfolk, the huge mansion had room for both families, and Cecil's wealthy American bride could well afford the upkeep. Fisher became a country gent. It was claimed that on one occasion the Fisher shooting party had bagged 1100 pheasants in a day. Fisher had the mailed fist and trident that formed his baronial crest fixed to the gatepost, where it remains.

But Churchill was not going to let Fisher spend his time shooting pheasants for long.

It was a summer night in 1912 at around 2 am when two figures wandered to the quay at Naples. Dressed in stylish white suits, Churchill was to head up the gangplank of the Admiralty yacht *Enchantress* and Fisher would return to his hotel, the Excelsior, from where he could survey the Bay of Naples and the *Enchantress* at rest in the Porto Grande. Both Churchill and Fisher believed the Royal Navy must switch to oil at the soonest opportunity, notwithstanding that Britain actually had no oil. Fisher would come home to head up the Royal Commission on Fuel and Engines. The first report, classified secret, would be presented in November 1912. He was seventy-one, but had more than enough vigour to handle this task. The commission's purpose, as far as Churchill and Fisher were concerned, was to put the navy en route to Persia.

CHAPTER 27
London

ERTRUDE had received a message from Lawrence, who was briefly back in London. He proposed they meet at the bridge over the Serpentine in Hyde Park. They would take a stroll through the park. It was a mild day, sunny with a light breeze. A few fluffy clouds drifted across the sky. The park abounded with couples or nannies pushing prams. Children ran about playing games, some flying kites. Gertrude arrived to find Lawrence, dressed in a rather worn pair of army trousers and a blue silk shirt with a paisley cravat, feeding the ducks from a small bag full of breadcrumbs. He had created a riot amongst the ducks.

He greeted her as usual with a 'Hello, Gerty,' but added a peck on the cheek. They strolled for a while before he turned to her. 'You know I am very fond of you, so I am going to stretch our friendship, I fear.'

She looked at him hard. 'Go on.'

'Gerty, you have a terrible taste in men. First that poverty-stricken poet in Persia, an addicted gambler, then the roving aristocrat from Singapore and now the glamorous Lieutenant Colonel Doughty-Wylie. I admit even I find him attractive. But Gerty, he's married.

Do you think you can run away with him to Arabia? He will never leave his wife. He is English establishment.'

Gertrude stopped. 'Why are you of all people lecturing me on relationships? Your relationships are an absolute mystery to all of us. You have no relationships, as you call them.'

Lawrence laughed. 'My private life is a mystery even to me. Is it because I don't have one? Never mind – I'm not heartbroken about anything. But I know full well that you are. Am I wrong?'

Gertrude took his arm. 'No, you're right.'

'Gerty, you are one of the smartest people I have ever met, male or female. You must know that you need to forget him, or you will go on suffering nothing but pain. You know I care deeply about you, which is why I am daring to say such things. Find some dreary middle-class solicitor who will worship the ground you walk on.' He paused. 'Actually, forget that last bit.'

Gertrude gave what he thought was a laugh then turned on her heels and walked away without a backward glance.

⟿

Florence walked into the sunroom at her home in Rounton to find Gertrude sitting on a sofa, gazing out the window at the garden and trees beyond. She had a book open, but it was by her side, upside down on a cushion. Born in 1851, Florence was only seventeen years older than Gertrude. She was young enough to understand her. Florence was making coffee and poured a cup for Gertrude, then sat beside her.

'Gertrude, tell me. What is the matter?'

'There is nothing at all the matter.' Her hands were trembling.

Florence hesitated. 'Gertrude, that's not true. I know you too well, usually with all that bonhomie and energy … But I know something is not right. Are you not well? You don't seem to be in your usual rude health; you appear a little subdued.'

Gertrude suddenly burst into a flood of tears. She sobbed uncontrollably. Florence wrapped her arms around her. She had never once seen Gertrude cry before. Finally, she asked again.

'What is it, Gertrude?'

Gertrude sighed. 'I think you're aware that I had, I have, this great love for Dick Doughty-Wylie. You know him. But he is married, and now I know he will never leave his wife and family. That's as it should be. I didn't want children anyway. Never. Never.' She put her head in her hands. 'I should have known. I deluded myself; but I know we can never be together. It will never happen. I must accept that. I am a sensible person – you appreciate that. So I should be able to get over him and go forward but try as I might, I cannot. I just cannot.'

There was little Florence could say that would be any more than platitudes. She rocked Gertrude in her arms.

Suddenly Gertrude pulled away, stood up, announced, 'I must get on,' and marched from the room.

That evening Hugh and Florence had guests for dinner. Gertrude arrived, dressed beautifully, her hair carefully done, her makeup carefully applied. During dinner she was witty and excellent company. Florence watched carefully. Who would ever have known?

CHAPTER 28
Germany

❧

KAISER WILHELM II, or William in the anglicised form, was a conundrum: on the one hand he was gifted, quick to pick up new ideas with a strong desire to be modern; on the other superficial, far too hasty, unable to give serious thought to serious problems, thin-skinned when disagreed with, and compulsive with decision-making. He could not countenance the presence of Bismarck, who was the opposite to all these things in every way. So Otto von Bismarck – who wanted detail, planning and objectives measuring risk against reward, who had checkmated the French over Alsace–Lorraine – eventually lost patience, and in 1890 walked away from his pivotal role as chancellor just when he was most needed.

Wilhelm's sensitivity was greatly increased by being born with Erb's palsy, a condition in which his right arm was six inches shorter than his left, a condition he constantly, and unsuccessfully, tried to obscure.

More difficult still, Wilhelm was insanely jealous of the British and especially of his Uncle Bertie, the Prince of Wales, later King Edward VII. Wilhelm usually visited England for Cowes Week and competed in his magnificent yacht *Meteor*, the old America's Cup yacht *Thistle*, a truly awe-inspiring sight when in full sail. She had won the Queen's Cup in 1893, but over the years his main competitor was his uncle, then Prince Edward, in *Britannia*, and Edward, being the more experienced yachtsman won nearly all the races. No matter what Wilhelm did, somehow he believed the British and his uncle would never see him as their equal.

Edward became king after the death of Queen Victoria. He was in Cowes in early August for Cowes Week, but not sailing; however he returned to his suite at the Royal Yacht Squadron on the evening of the last races of the week.

The Royal Yacht Squadron was founded on 1 June 1815 in the Thatched House Tavern in St James's, London, by forty-two gentlemen interested in yachting. Membership was restricted to those owning vessels not under ten tons. They were undeterred by the Battle of Waterloo breaking out two weeks later.

Organised yacht racing began in 1826. From the Cowes Roads yachtsmen can see the Yacht Squadron Castle as battlements, a round tower and a flagstaff. The building was originally built by Henry VIII in 1539 as a deterrent to the French. An uninformed spectator might have originally mistaken it for a prison with an excellent view. Its cannon and brass one-pounders, which once belonged to the ship *Royal Adelaide*, were donated to the squadron by Edward VII. They are now fired at five-minute intervals to start yachtsmen in their races.

Edward's mission was a critical meeting with his friend Jacky Fisher. The issue was urgent. When Jacky arrived at the squadron the doorman directed him immediately upstairs to the King's suite. Edward was delighted to see him, but he had business he needed to attend to. The King walked around the room, his hands behind his back.

'This is the situation, Jacky,' he said. 'As you know, the Kaiser is here and of course he raced today. During the race there was an incident seen well by most of the competitors. His yacht was on port tack when it attempted to cross a British yacht on starboard tack.'

This violated a core rule of yacht racing, introduced in 1828.

'The yacht was called *Derwent*,' Edward continued. 'A much smaller yacht but sailed by a Captain Jamieson; you will know he is a serving officer in the Royal Navy. Jamieson hailed him to give him right of way. Clearly the Kaiser was in the wrong, but he refused to give way. There was very nearly a catastrophic collision. There was a lot of shouting and some ungentlemanly language. Jamieson has lodged a formal protest and it is due to be heard by a protest committee appointed by the squadron, headed by a retired admiral. Of course, the outcome is certain, and the Kaiser will be disqualified. You're no doubt aware of how proud and unduly sensitive Wilhelm is. If he is disqualified for all the world to see, we are concerned there will be a major diplomatic incident. At the very least it will be another nail in the coffin of his jealousy and resentment of the British. Jacky, we don't need this. Can you get your man Jamieson to withdraw? I don't know how, but I do know you can be very persuasive.'

Jacky had listened in silence. 'Jamieson's stubborn and will be no fan of Wilhelm and his bully-boy tactics. All I can do is my best. When is the protest hearing?'

'Tomorrow, eleven am, here at the squadron. He can withdraw up to then.'

'Shall I see you here at nine am tomorrow? I'd best be on my way.'

The next morning Jacky met the King in his suite having breakfast. Edward's first question as Jacky opened the door was, 'Well?'

'He will withdraw. Reluctant, in a rage at the Kaiser's failure to stick to the rules of sailing, but more at his behaviour as someone who is supposed to be a gentleman. Notwithstanding, I managed to persuade him that there is much, much more at stake.'

Edward grasped Jacky by the hand. 'I can't thank you enough. But this is just another warning to us all. The Kaiser is no friend of ours. I am afraid he is jealous of me and of Britain's achievements. You know all about the German naval building program. It is, I understand, extremely impressive. Thank god you are here to force us to modernise. Thank god for the dreadnoughts. There is another thing you should consider. Whatever Wilhelm thinks of me as his uncle and the King, I have some influence over him. I might be able to make some accommodation with him if necessary. But if I am gone I very much doubt George will have the same influence. You will be on your own.'

CHAPTER 29
London

⌒

JAMES HAMILTON was the director of Burmah most closely involved with D'Arcy and George Reynolds and the frustrations of the drilling programme. On 14 May 1908 he dispatched a letter to Reynolds. Part of it read: 'We would like if possible to put two wells at Masjid-i-Sulaiman down to 1500/1600 feet, and if no oil is found at this depth, to abandon operations, close down, and bring as much of the plant as is possible to Mohammerah ... With regard to packing of the plant, you will arrange same to stand a voyage to Burma. Is it possible to charter a small vessel to carry it direct there?'

Notwithstanding, argument continued. On 19 May the Burmah board was meeting, with the drilling program high on the agenda. On the day before, Hamilton called D'Arcy to meet him in his office next to the Burmah boardroom in the City. It was an old-fashioned oak-panelled room with the usual portraits of stern directors staring loftily down from their oil paintings. D'Arcy was startled to be confronted by two miniature dachshunds, one black and tan and the other just tan. Both barked furiously until a secretary removed them. 'My constant companions. Such good company,' Hamilton explained.

'Bloody German spies,' D'Arcy thought, but contented himself with remarking that he had a very favoured pair of cocker spaniels on his estate. This intervention over, they seated themselves in two armchairs whereupon an ancient butler shuffled in precariously carrying a silver tray with silver teapot, silver sugar bowl and silver milk jug. He very carefully and slowly poured two cups and removed himself.

Hamilton didn't waste any time. 'The fact is, D'Arcy, we have used all of the allowance we made for this venture. None of the drilling has come to anything, and my personal opinion is that enough is enough! However, I have to say there are a variety of opinions around the Board.'

D'Arcy replied with his usual enthusiasm. 'There is oil in Persia. There is evidence everywhere. We started in the wrong place, but I am convinced we are now in the right spot. There are shows, there are signs on the surface and the topography is most conducive to its presence in the area. We are close. We must not retreat now, so close to success.'

The door opened and the butler shuffled back in like Banquo's ghost, collected the tea set and, after enquiring if anything was required and receiving an answer in the negative, reversed out.

Hamilton sat silent for a minute. 'I will convey your views, but I advise you to consider other strategies.'

At the board meeting, Hamilton as promised conveyed the discussion with D'Arcy. The chairman then reported that he had had a long discussion with the First Sea Lord who had made it clear he regarded the exploration as in the vital interests of the navy and therefore, as they would all understand, the nation. Not only that, his friend in the Foreign Office had made it clear that they thought the Russians were sniffing about again and their presence would be 'most unwelcome'.

After a long debate a reluctant board consented to loan a further £40,000 to the venture, bringing the total to £140,000. D'Arcy escaped scot-free.

⌒

On the ground conditions were near intolerable. The temperature in Masjid-i-Sulaiman was 110 degrees Fahrenheit in the shade. Workers were being paid off. Everyone knew that the end of the exploration program would be sometime soon.

About midday George Reynolds gloomily tidied up some papers and left his office. He walked over to the drill rig, for no particularly good reason. When he got there, he sniffed, and sniffed again.

'My god.' He called one of the riggers, then demanded, 'What do you smell?'

'That's gas,' gasped the rigger. 'Phew, it's strong! Like rotten eggs.' He backed away.

Number 1 well was at a depth of about 1000 feet and moving quite quickly. The tension rose when the hardest stratum of rock was encountered. The drill bits might fracture. The men stood around, anxiously listening to the drill motor grinding away at intervals and reaching a crescendo when a particularly hard stratum was struck. If it broke, they would probably all be fired. They could tell from Reynolds' grim demeanour that he was worried. As he strode up and down no one could talk to him; but everyone by now could smell gas.

The drill finally burst through the rocky stratum. On 26 May at 1180 feet the gas pressure surged and shot oil 300 feet above the derrick. The oil was pure, undiluted by water, and flowed at fifty barrels a day. All those standing around, including Reynolds, were covered in it, but to a man they all cheered.

The men on the ground were ecstatic; at last, some reward for all the pain and doubt. But they had no idea what they had found. One way or another it took several more days before bits and pieces of the news flowed to Burmah directors in Britain and eventually to D'Arcy.

D'Arcy was at home when he received the news. For once he was shocked into silence. His wife, Nina, walked in to find him propping himself with one hand on the dining-room table. In the other was the telegram. He simply passed it to her. He was still the driving force at the centre of the ocean of oil that lay beneath Persia's soil.

~⌒

Having driven back from London, Fisher was walking through his front door when the maid called him to the telephone. It was Winston.

'Jacky, glad to have found you. Have you heard the news?'

'I just walked in. What news?'

'Wonderful, wonderful news from Persia! They have struck oil. Not a trickle but a huge stream! A lake of oil – no, an ocean of oil, I understand. Of course, not exactly proven but they are very confident. Can you believe it?'

Fisher felt a huge wave of relief. His hand shook as he held the telephone. 'Hurrah! That is splendid. Our whole plan depends on it. Now we can go ahead. Could it be a false signal?'

'Apparently not. It shot 300 feet in the air and covered them all. They were dancing about, covered in oil. It's still going like a huge fountain. Reynolds has never seen anything like it before. "Unprecedented," was what he said. Now we spring into action. I must tell the King. He has been asking, you know. They asked me to tell you, but we need to keep it to ourselves for now. Ha! Those thieves at Standard Oil and Shell will be furious.'

When Jacky told Kitty, she was thrilled to see how happy he was. As he said, 'All my plans, my wishes to create the modern navy – they all depended on this. Truly, God has been on my shoulder.'

A little later she was passing the bathroom when she heard the muffled sound of singing. She went closer and stopped to listen.

And did those feet in ancient times, walk upon England's mountains green,
And was the Holy Lamb of God on England's pleasant pastures seen?

She really thought Jacky had rather a good voice. He was singing in tune.

～

It took more drilling and two more successful wells, more testing and some third-party confirmation, but eventually the truth was out. A handful of men led by the determination of George Reynolds had just encountered the most extensive oil field thus far known to man. In the space of a few hours, the economics and logistics of oil had been turned on their head.

On 14 April 1909, Burmah Oil created a new subsidiary company. The new company would be called the Anglo-Persian Oil Company, or APOC. Its tasks would be to raise the oil, and build a pipeline to Abadan where a new refinery would be constructed. The navy would have its oil. As Winston Churchill was to say, 'Fortune brought us a prize from fairyland beyond our wildest dreams. Mastery itself was the prize of the venture.'

APOC went public on 19 April 1909 and the public offering of the stock on the day resulted in the Glasgow branch of the Bank of Scotland being mobbed by customers eager to invest in the shares. Burmah held the majority and D'Arcy received shares to the value of £895,000 - a very considerable sum in 1909.

Over in the United States John D. Rockefeller, sole owner of Standard Oil, the largest oil refinery in the world, was busy fighting a lawsuit with the US government over the Sherman Antitrust laws that was to break his company into thirty-four separate companies. Finally, someone caught his attention for long enough to inform him that there might be some serious competition from some wretched godforsaken place, thousands of miles away in the middle of a desert. Up until then he would have had the greatest difficulty locating Persia on a map. It had been of no interest. Now they were very late in the game.

In his office in Amsterdam, Henri Deterding, the chairman of the Royal Dutch Petroleum Company/Shell (and who was known in the more excitable sections of the press as 'the Napoleon of Oil'), was marching up and down cursing this highly inconvenient development. He had always suspected there was significant oil in Mesopotamia, but could never work out where. He was not at all accustomed to losing. It took him some time to fight back but, after a series of abortive tilts at Burmah Oil, in 1911 he purchased the oil field in Azerbaijan from the Rothschild family.

D'Arcy's enterprise had proceeded on the basis that eventually oil would be found and on this proposition a refinery would be needed. Reynolds had chosen Abadan, a long narrow island of mudflats and palm groves on the Shatt-al-Arab delta of the Tigris and Euphrates rivers, and a mere thirty miles from the Persian Gulf from whence the world could be reached. It would take until 1912 before the refinery could be opened, by which time the flow from the oilfields was significant. Tankers began to arrive from both the Indian Ocean and the Mediterranean, making their way up the Gulf to take the oil back through the Strait of Hormuz to wherever it was needed. It hardly mattered that, being at sea level, it was even hotter than the surrounding areas, temperatures reaching fifty degrees Centigrade quite frequently. Still, as Reynolds reflected, that was hardly his problem.

~o

Gertrude met Lawrence at a tiny Persian restaurant in the East End. It was one of Lawrence's favourite hideaways, removed from the noisy babble of London society. The young Persian waitress knew him well. She asked him if he wanted his favourite and he nodded. A secret Druze sauce comprising roasted red peppers with onion shards accompanied by cauliflower harissa soon appeared.

Lawrence hadn't indicated what he wanted to talk about. 'Good chance for a catch up, Gerty,' was about all he'd volunteered.

But at the restaurant he went straight to the point. 'I've been thinking about your advice to Fisher, Gerty. I can't get past the fact that if there is oil there will be an oil pipeline and an oil refinery and then tankers and probably trains. It's likely to make a huge mess about which the operators will not care a jot. The archaeological sites will just be forgotten. Babylon is only one hundred-odd miles away on the Euphrates. It is a jewel that must be protected. We can't let anything happen.' He took a sip of wine. 'How do we stop the buggers?'

Gertrude stared into her glass as she swirled the content around. 'I can speak to my brother-in-law, and of course Fisher himself. I genuinely believe they get it. But still, how much control can they exert?'

Lawrence thought about that. 'Trouble is, although they're the so-called "Senior Service" it appears the army and navy see little point in combining forces so it's unlikely the army will pay attention to anything the navy have to say. The navy won't be in Mesopotamia, but the army will. You probably didn't hear but there was a significant row. One of the admirals called the army officer corps a bunch of boneheaded Sandhurst bores, and somehow it made *The Times*. Not very well received. Nevertheless, maybe you should speak to Fisher and Richmond.'

'I've got a better idea. I'll go and see Winston. He's a serious power in the Commons, he's ex-Sandhurst and he and Fisher are the best of pals. But apart from all that, I think he will really understand the priceless nature of the sites.'

Gertrude eventually pinned Churchill down to a meeting in his office in the Commons. He gave her a cordial welcome, but she well understood that, like the military, he was principally engaged in shoring up British power and he and Fisher were determined to secure the oil the navy would need. He waved her to a chair in front of his desk. Gertrude knew he was busy, and she too had limited time.

'Winston,' she said immediately, 'I have undertaken to help the navy secure its oil but – not to put too strong a point on it – I will not do so if it will lead to the destruction of some of the world's great archaeological treasures. They must be protected. I have had the good fortune to work with Professor Reinach in Paris and listen to his theory that the whole basis of European civilisation descends from Mesopotamia. I think he is right. We cannot allow our own heritage to be destroyed before it is even discovered.'

Churchill leaned forward. 'Go on.'

'As you may know, the site of the major find at Masjid-i-Sulaiman is close to the ancient site of Babylon on the Tigris and Euphrates rivers. Babylon itself goes back to nearly 3000 BC. It was first either Akkadian or Sumerian; either way, they seem to have spoken Aramaic. Much confusion exists, but it is central to both the Christian and Jewish bibles. In the Christian, Babylon is referred to in Genesis. It is the site of the Tower of Babel whose construction is halted by God, when he scatters the people around the world turning them from a common language and culture to many, so now no one can understand another. It's also in the Book of Revelations. I'm sure you know the "Whore of Babylon", riding on a scarlet beast with seven hearts and ten horns and drunk on the blood of the righteous.'

Churchill smiled. '"Mystery, Babylon the Great, Mother of Harlots and Abomination of the Earth", is it not?'

'Exactly. Babylon has been trampled over time and again through the ages. It was part of the Assyrian Empire until destroyed in 689 BC, then Nebuchadnezzar rebuilt it; it was then conquered by Cyrus the Great in 539 and then Alexander in 321. Finally, of course, it was overpowered by the Sword of Islam in the seventh century AD.'

Churchill nodded. He was about to speak but Gertrude continued. 'In 1855, not so long ago, came the Al Qurnah Disaster. Two hundred cases of priceless antiquities from Fresnet's mission were being shipped out of Babylon down the river when they were attacked by river pirates. A transport ship and four rafts were sunk. Hardly anything could be recovered.' Gertrude had stood up to deliver this missive. Now she slumped back into her chair. 'So, I need some help. Please?'

Churchill had a chess set on the corner of his desk. While she was talking, he had picked up the black queen and was revolving it back and forward between the index finger and thumb of his right hand. He stopped and replaced it on the board. 'Gertrude, I must go to the House now. But let me state that I have heard what you say, and I do absolutely understand your concern. Our history is essential to the world seeing us for who we are. You must leave it to me for now while I work out how best to go forward. But I will go forward.' He stood up and walked down the corridor to escort her out. 'By the way, I think you know Jacky Fisher is a great devotee of the Bible, but he especially loves the Old Testament. He will take no convincing.'

Gertrude thanked him. 'But please also remember there are wonderful fragile sites all over Mesopotamia. All over. We must also protect them.'

It was a warm, sunny day and she decided to stroll part of the way home. As she observed the bustle of a busy London morning, she vowed to herself: 'I'm not going to be bullied into this by forked tongues and seductive language. They must act or I will turn into their sworn enemy.' But in the back of her mind was the certain knowledge that if she walked away, they would go ahead anyway. The oil was too important to them, and if she and Lawrence were not there, they would have no restraint. She must stay strong, but she must stay engaged.

CHAPTER 30
London

To coincide with the Epsom Derby week, the ball of the year was held in the ballroom of the Savoy Hotel. The Savoy was the first luxury hotel in London. It was built in the Strand overlooking the Thames and opened in 1889. It had electric lights, an electric lift, bathrooms, hot and cold running water. The hotel boasted the services of Escoffier and César Ritz, enticed out of Paris, as chef de cuisine and manager. No wonder the rich and famous flocked to the Savoy. Presided over by the developer and owner, Richard D'Oyly Carte (or Oily Carte as some of his detractors named him), it was a very grand affair. D'Oyly Carte, ably assisted by his wife Helen, had done what no one else in London was prepared to do. He had built a hotel to match or exceed the other great hotels of the world. Before then, English hotels had been rather dreary establishments, run without panache or flair, mean-spirited. D'Oyly Carte had spent without restraint and in the period of Edwardian decadence, presided over by 'Tum Tum', the fun-loving King Edward VII, England was ready to party; it was indeed the Belle Époque.

D'Oyly Carte died in April 1901 but his twenty-five-year-old son,

Rupert, was on hand to inherit the empire Richard had assembled. By twenty-seven he was chairman of the Savoy, Claridge's, the Berkeley, Simpson's in the Strand, Marivaux and the Grand Hotel in Rome. He also had the theatrical business that his father had so successfully begun by backing the irrepressible Sullivan and the dour Gilbert. If all else failed, a revival of *The Mikado*, which had run at the Savoy Theatre for 671 consecutive performances, would always do the trick. Luckily, he had his father's great manager of everything, Helen, quietly and efficiently doing the hard and boring jobs that kept the show on the road. Helen had had a major role in exposing the outrageous thefts that Ritz and Escoffier, notwithstanding being extremely well paid, had perpetrated on his father, which had resulted in them both being marched off the premises. Ritz had then set up his own hotel, the Ritz, in direct competition. Rupert had his father's flair. The game continued.

D'Arcy had booked a large table for the ball at the Savoy. The ballroom was exquisitely decorated with huge bowls of flowers and a row of potted palm trees at the entrance. His guests included a variety of London's glitterati, although he included one or two pals closely connected with the racing industry. D'Arcy's wife, Nina Boucicault, daughter of the Rockhampton newspaper proprietor Arthur Boucicault, accompanied him. Across the table sat her famous cousin, also Nina Boucicault, the celebrated Irish film and stage actress. D'Arcy's wife had arrived dressed in the latest creation of the House of Worth from Paris, with a quadruple string of pearls. As Lady de Grey whispered to her partner, 'One string too many, don't you think, darling?' Nina's cousin was no less immaculately attired in something black from Chanel.

Rupert D'Oyly Carte was of course there in person, immaculate in his dinner jacket, and circulating the floor ensuring a little more champagne here, perhaps some caviar there. The sixteen-piece band was playing away watched by an enthusiastic crowd.

A table in the front row stood empty when in stalked a short trim figure dressed in evening dress. He was deferentially escorted to the table with his retinue by D'Oyly Carte. D'Arcy looked over and saw it was the unmistakable figure of the First Sea Lord, none other than Jacky Fisher. D'Oyly Carte naturally knew very well who Fisher was. Fisher had attended a performance of the light opera, *HMS Pinafore*, performed to excellent reviews at the Opéra Comique and written by Carte's friends and business partners in the theatre, William Gilbert and Arthur Sullivan. The plot daringly involves the captain of HMS *Pinafore*'s daughter falling in love with a lower-class sailor, although her father intends her to marry the First Lord of the Admiralty. Naturally, Fisher was delighted.

Jacky eventually looked up and, seeing D'Arcy, gave him a cheerful wave. Jacky was soon on the dance floor with an assortment of ladies, showing the great flair for the art of dancing for which he was renowned. Finally, he walked over to D'Arcy's Nina. Bending low, he took her hand and requested permission for the next dance. She gracefully assented and soon they were the centre of attention with D'Oyly Carte rapturously applauding, followed by the other guests. It was not long before the whole floor was filled with couples, inspired by Fisher and Nina. She was indeed an exceptionally graceful dancer, and so was Fisher. However, as Fisher was quite short and the ladies in the main wore extremely high heels, Fisher's face was normally aligned with a generous decolletage, a fact that seemed not to trouble him at all. Fisher's long-suffering wife Katherine bore it all with her usual good humour. This was her Jacky. Nothing would change him and, in truth, she never really minded. Only D'Arcy was left alone as a spectator. Dancing was not a skill he had ever mastered and nor did he wish to.

Later in the evening, D'Arcy was about to enter the gentlemen's toilet when Jacky walked out. They both stopped and Jacky enquired how things were progressing in Persia. D'Arcy smiled and clapped him on the back. 'Excellent. I shall soon be buying myself the best stallion they have at Newmarket. I have my eye on him.'

Jacky stepped back, his eyebrows raised. 'It is easier for a camel to pass through the eye of a needle than it is for a rich man to enter the kingdom of heaven. Just remember that.' He turned and walked away. D'Arcy for once was totally lost for a reply.

It was close to midnight when there was a sudden flurry of activity. Some guests were rapidly cleared from the front row, mollified with a free bottle of champagne. A clean table was set up. Then in strolled King Edward VII, or 'Tum Tum' to his friends, to a round of rousing applause and trumpet blast from the band. He was accompanied by a few friends and Alice Keppel, his aristocratic and beautiful mistress of some years. He waved merrily to the crowd, glanced around and waved his cigar in acknowledgment of D'Arcy before strolling over for a brief chat with Fisher. A Strasbourg pie and some truffles appeared from nowhere, and the King returned to his table to share this modest snack with his guests. To follow was pêche Melba, prepared by Escoffier and named after another of the hotel's favourite guests, Dame Nellie Melba. Champagne was of course in attendance.

D'Oyly Carte was in ecstasy.

While the Savoy was at the peak of the social ladder in London society, by no means was everyone impressed. Prime Minister William Gladstone on one occasion had visited the Savoy. He ordered a piece of toast and a boiled egg, glared at the plate, nodded to the doorman, and departed.

~๏

D'Arcy's birthday was coming up, and where else could you have it but at the Savoy? At first, he was thinking of something modest, at least by his standard, but he had some good fortune. One of his horses had an unexpected win at Ascot and D'Arcy, of course, had placed a large bet on it at excellent odds. He was very much in pocket. 'Let's have a bit of a fling,' he remarked to Nina.

He called Rupert D'Oyly Carte and gave his instructions: 'No expenses spared,' as he put it. Rupert hardly needed encouragement. It was winter and a floor of artificial snow was created in the restaurant. Guests in winter finery arrived to walk past icebergs of silver tissues to tables decorated in snow drifts. Waiters dressed as Eskimos. The pièce de résistance happened when it was time for the cake. With a roll of the drums from the orchestra the curtains parted, and in walked a baby elephant, borrowed from London Zoo for the night. It was escorted by its keeper dressed as a mahout. The elephant was draped in a pink cover with 'Happy Birthday D'Arcy' stitched on each side; hitched behind it was a five-foot-high birthday cake. The candles were lit, and D'Arcy with Nina's help blew them out to rousing cheers. Finally, members of the chorus from *HMS Pinafore* appeared to sing 'Happy Birthday'.

The Savoy continued as *the* place for Edwardian London to party, and each event was more outrageous than the one preceding it. Extravagance was the word. Any publicity was definitely better than none.

Over a decade later there was an unfortunate incident which, of course, did nothing to dent its popularity with the inhabitants of La Belle Époque. Courtesan Marguerite Fahmy was staying at the Savoy as a resident with her husband, Prince Ali Kamel Fahmy, in the fourth-floor furnished apartments. It's safe to say her relationship with her ten-years-younger husband was characterised by continuing and often public rows and physical abuse.

On that particular night they had attended the perspicaciously named *Merry Widow*. Marguerite was strikingly dressed in a platinum-coloured lace cocktail dress, purchased in her recent Paris shopping expedition from the Place Vendôme couturier of

Madeleine Chéruit. The prince wore full evening dress. Back in the restaurant at the Savoy there was a series of explosive rows, culminating with Marguerite threatening to hit the prince with a wine bottle. Marguerite stormed upstairs and, when the prince returned to their room, she pulled out the Browning semi-automatic she kept under the pillow, took aim, and shot him three times in the chest.

At her trial for murder at the Old Bailey she was swiftly acquitted. Her defence barrister described the prince as 'a monster of Eastern depravity and decadence, whose sexual tastes were indicative of an amoral sadism' and his weeping wife as a 'helpless European wife; a woman of the West married to an Oriental.' Particularly powerful words from an outraged barrister.

It turned out some time later that one reason for the rapid termination of the case was that Marguerite had previously been the mistress of the then-seventeen-year-old Prince of Wales, the future King Edward VIII. The echoes of Bertie's exploits with the Curragh Wrens ricocheted around the cognoscenti. The young prince had been unwise enough to commit his affection for Marguerite to paper, including all too much detail. Marguerite had carefully retained these amorous epistles, just in case. 'His name is to be kept out,' as Foreign Secretary Lord Curzon made crystal-clear to the judge, fortunately a fellow ex-Etonian, a sentiment with which the English establishment, and no doubt the judiciary, would have been in violent agreement.

Curzon, along with most of the most significant holders of high office in England, knew well the extravagance of Edward VII's bohemian lifestyle when he could escape the middle-class mores of England. They were much more concerned with the current king than the next one. Edward VII had developed the habit of removing himself to Paris whenever (which was frequently) he felt the urge for some fun. He was a repeat customer of Le Chabanais, a high-class

Parisian brothel, and even had his coat of arms above his bed there. However, his love of the best things in life had led to him becoming extraordinarily obese and this was restricting his sexual exploits, which included some jolly pranks with more than one young lady at a time. The solution was to construct a 'love chair', *a siège d'amour*, which resided at the brothel. The King could entertain a number of courtesans at the same time but no one, except the participants, knew exactly how. The chair was described as a 'mindboggling contraption', as pictures of it attest. The one certainty was that the English establishment in the person of Lord Curzon could not on any account have the King's activities in Paris becoming common knowledge in what remained, outside a very exclusive 'set', a highly conservative and respectable Britain.

CHAPTER 31

KING EDWARD, sometimes 'Bertie' and sometimes 'Tum Tum', died on 6 May 1910. He had been on holiday in Biarritz with his mistress Alice Keppel, but had caught a chill and returned to England where the condition worsened into bronchitis. His health was always precarious. Edward loved his food and drink and was an inveterate smoker: up to twenty cigarettes and a dozen cigars a day. In hospital it was clear he would not recover, although he managed a wan smile when told his horse had won at Kempton Park. Both Queen Alexandra and Alice Keppel were there at the end.

It was the final chapter in an era of flamboyant self-indulgence by the rich; of glamour and entertainment, when women wore extravagant gowns and even more extravagant hats, and men wore impeccable evening dress and expansive whiskers, and it was great to be British and control an empire that covered more than half the known world.

The funeral of Edward VII took place on an exceptionally warm day and London came out on mass to farewell their king. D'Arcy was invited to attend at his friend Henry West-Watson's club in Piccadilly. Their group had pride of place on the club's expansive balcony overlooking the route the funeral would take. The procession was to move along Whitehall, the Mall, Piccadilly and Hyde Park to Paddington station where the train would carry the body to Windsor for burial.

D'Arcy heard the procession before he saw it. Above the murmur of the crowd came the muffled chimes of Big Ben signalling 9 am and the procession's start. The tolling of Big Ben was followed by the strains of the 'Dead March' from Handel's *Saul*, played by the band of the Royal Horse Guards. Then the most impressive collection of the royal heads of Europe ever assembled in one place came into view. Nine kings rode behind the coffin, accompanied by five heirs apparent, forty more imperial or royal highnesses, seven queens and an assembly of special ambassadors. The coffin appeared covered by the Royal Standard and carried on a gun carriage draped in red, white and purple. Alongside the gun carriage, which was drawn by the Royal Horse Artillery, walked the late king's eighty-three aides-de-camp, all colonels or naval captains and all peers. England's three field marshalls, Lord Kitchener, Lord Roberts and Sir Evelyn Woods, rode together, followed by six admirals of the fleet. One of the admirals, striding purposefully along with his head held high, was Edward's great friend, Jacky Fisher.

In the centre of the front rode the new king, George V, flanked on his left by the Duke of Connaught, the late king's only surviving brother. On his right rode Wilhelm II, Emperor of Germany, soon to be known to all Englishmen as Kaiser Bill, resplendent in the scarlet uniform of a British field marshall. It was the Kaiser's fierce stare from behind his huge, upturned moustache that drew D'Arcy's attention. Somehow, mounted rigidly upon a grey stallion, the Kaiser managed to convey an impression that he was now the most important person present at the gathering. *The Times* seemed to endorse this primacy by acknowledging that to him 'belongs the first place among all the foreign mourners who, even when relations are most strained, has never lost his popularity amongst us.'

All of England's famous regiments were represented. The Household Cavalry, The Coldstream Guards, the Gordon Highlanders, the Royal Fusiliers. Behind them marched the hussars and dragoons of the German, Austrian and Russian armies, together with other foreign cavalry units plus, provocatively, Grand Admiral von Tirpitz, representing the German navy. The passing parade was truly magnificent. Crimson sashes and jewelled orders contrasted with plumed helmets and gold braid.

The dead king's horse, with an empty saddle and his boots reversed in the stirrups, was led by two grooms. Trotting behind came his wire-haired terrier, Caesar.

Adding to the pageantry were representatives of the dearly held traditions of England. Pursuivants of arms in emblazoned medieval tabards, Silver Stick-in-Waiting, white staves, equerries, archers of Scotland, judges in their wigs and black robes and the Lord Chief Justice in scarlet, bishops in ecclesiastical purple, Yeomen of the Guard in black velvet hats and frilled Victorian collars, an escort of trumpeters, followed by a glass coach bearing the widowed Queen Alexandra and her sister, the Dowager Empress of Russia, and twelve other coaches of queens, ladies and oriental potentates. The mourners filled the road and stretched as far as the eye could see and the spectators stood quietly, hats in hand, to farewell their king.

D'Arcy thanked West-Watson and headed back to his club for lunch. At the Albemarle Club the question was quietly raised whether the Kaiser could have portrayed a less militaristic air.

One of the members turned to D'Arcy. 'I wonder what Fisher was thinking. I hear the Kaiser wants to turn Agadir into the base for the German Mediterranean fleet.'

D'Arcy was proud to say he knew Fisher. He had some credibility when he pronounced, 'He won't stand for it.'

D'Arcy had only recently managed to join the Albemarle Club. It had been formed in 1874 and remarkably had an almost equal number of male and female members. In the 1880s things had unravelled when the Marquis of Queensbury had stormed into the club to confront Oscar Wilde. Blocked from entry he had left a card: 'For Oscar Wilde: posing somdomite (sic)'. Wilde sued for libel and then found himself facing a very public criminal prosecution for homosexuality. The club's membership had collapsed, and D'Arcy was therefore welcome.

D'Arcy was just about to leave the club when, to his dismay, he saw 'Boofy' Dacres-Fitzmaurice sidling up to him. Boofy was dressed in an ill-fitting dark brown tweed suit with an accompanying club tie, whose colours clashed horribly with the suit. He looked like a bookie.

'Good morning, D'Arcy,' grinned Boofy. 'Well, what an event! Exceptional, exceptional.'

D'Arcy grunted assent.

'Must say you look a bit peaky. Late night?'

D'Arcy acknowledged reluctantly it had been rather a late night; actually, he did feel pretty grim. A little too much champagne.

Boofy giggled. 'Haven't been chasing the fillies around down at the Pink Panther have you, you naughty boy?'

Boofy had three claims to fame: his attendance, briefly, at Eton; a distant duke in the family; and, most importantly, membership of Boodle's Club in St James's Street, where he normally resided.

D'Arcy particularly hated Boofy, mainly because he knew that Boofy knew that D'Arcy had been blackballed from Boodle's. Boodle's was established in 1762 and is, after White's, the second oldest gentleman's club in the world. It was the Boodle's Club tie Boofy was proudly wearing. D'Arcy didn't exactly know why he had been blackballed; reasons are never given. Probably, he gloomily surmised, the disgrace of his father's bankruptcy or, more likely, the fact he was considered an Australian and therefore, logic dictated, he must have been a convict. D'Arcy turned on his heel and stormed out.

~⌒

D'Arcy continued to attend the Epsom Derby each year after Edward's death. He maintained his box, but somehow it was not as much fun without his friend Tum Tum. The new king, Edward's second son, George V, was rather a dull cove and no friend of D'Arcy. Still, one must attend. D'Arcy donned his tails and Nina found something très chic by Coco Chanel. It was the derby of 1913, held on 4 June. The King and Queen Mary were in attendance and an enormous crowd, reckoned to be 500,000, had turned up.

The race began in a fever of expectations and the King's horse, Anmer, was well in the running when a slight figure in a dress, waving two small flags, climbed under the rail and ran out on the course. She was immediately bowled over by Anmer. Horse, jockey and the young lady, Emily Davison, all went down. It took some time before it was clear that Emily Davison was a suffragette and had darted out to protest in front of the largest audience she could imagine reaching. She had devoted her life to the movement and been to gaol several times, including the brutal Holloway Prison, where she had gone on a hunger strike. They had force-fed her with a tube rammed down her throat. None of this had deterred her from the cause.

The race was won by Aboyeur, after a steward's protest was upheld in an eerie replay of the win by Edward's horse, Minoru, in 1909. D'Arcy was well satisfied with his day at the races. He was gratified to learn that Anmer and his jockey had survived. In addition, D'Arcy had had a not immodest wager on Aboyeur, at the staggering odds of 100-1.

Emily died four days later. A huge crowd attended her funeral. On her gravestone was written the suffragette motto: 'Deeds not Words'.

Gertrude was in Yorkshire with her mother when she read the sad story of Emily Davison's death, amply covered in *The Times*. Passing the newspaper to Florence, she said, 'Read this.'

Florence took up her glasses, carefully read the article and returned the paper to Gertrude.

Gertrude took Florence's hands. 'We should join the movement. We need to stand up for women. It's well past time we had the vote. You and I know that a good half of the men we've ever met are pompous idiots.'

Florence hesitated. 'Of course, I have thought about it often and like you am constantly being invited to join the cause. I've decided, though, that I'm not going to, and this will not change my mind.'

Gertrude was taken aback. 'Why are you opposed? It has to be a good thing.'

'I believe it is a distraction for women up here.' Florence sighed. 'The vote for women is a push from the well-educated and wealthy. They have the money, influence and time to campaign, and I wish them well. But you know very well, Gertrude, that our women in the factories could not care less about the vote. They would hardly know, much less care about, the prime minister's name. Their whole life revolves around getting through the day with enough pennies to buy some food and stopping their husbands drinking it all, then punching them when they object. You've seen them. Mothers and children dressed in rags and half-starved. I know they would swap one good meal on the table for getting the vote anytime. You do it if you wish, but I will not.'

Gertrude for once had nothing to say. She had rarely seen Florence so forthright. She would decide when she returned from her forthcoming trip to the Middle East.

The telephone rang. It was her brother-in-law, Herbert Richmond. 'When are you heading back to London?' he asked. 'Fisher and I would like to see you if you have some time.'

Gertrude was returning in two days, and they agreed to meet at a smart coffee and tea room, newly opened in Knightsbridge. 'Central for all of us,' as Richmond put it.

Both Richmond and Fisher were in civilian clothes for a change and Richmond had arranged a table in an annex. Fisher did not want company. He was dressed in a plain charcoal suit, the inconspicuous look rather spoiled by a blue velvet bow tie. After some brief preliminaries, Fisher got straight to the point.

'Here's the thing, Gertrude. We look like we have all the oil we need from this remarkable discovery by that rascal D'Arcy. But if we put all our eggs in one basket, as we are going to have to, what happens if the Persians renege and we can't change their mind? It could be disaster. No oil. It would mean defeat for Britain if we were at war. It's a huge risk.'

Gertrude sat back in silence. There was not a sound. She picked up her coffee cup. 'They will not renege,' she said. 'Pay what you owe, be meticulous, pay the Bakhtiari too. In the scheme of things, be generous; it is nothing.'

'Yes, yes,' huffed Fisher. 'But still something could go wrong. What if the Russians or the Ottomans intervened or bribed the Shah, more than we do?'

'You have significant armed forces in Egypt and further away in India. Military is not my thing, but if the refinery is planned for Abadan and you have a proper contingency plan you could put troops there very quickly. Across the desert from Cairo, very close, or around the Gulf. If the Shah wants to send troops, it's not his country and he would have to cross the Zagros Mountains. Very unappealing.' Gertrude sighed. 'You should maintain some troops there anyway, but for god's sake make sure they are not led by an idiot who provokes the local tribes.'

'The tribes will do what they're told.'

'They will *not* do what they're told. We must disabuse ourselves of this absurd idea that anyone who is not English will "do what they're told". Do you do what you are told?'

'No. The opposite.' There was a pause. 'What do you think, Richmond?'

Richmond tapped his chin slowly. 'I've studied the map closely and Gertrude is right. But as a precaution, I also suggest we make sure we at all times have one largeish naval ship in port at Abadan. A cruiser equipped with batteries of 8-inch guns is usually a compelling reminder to behave yourself. In any event, it is actually a good strategic location if we need to go down the Gulf or even to India.'

Fisher sat back while Gertrude lit a cigarette. 'Hm, well, all right. I agree,' he said. 'A quiet voice but a big stick then. Thank you, my dear.'

~⊙

Gertrude headed back to Yorkshire. On the train she was reading *The Times* when she saw a report that there was to be a mass rally in Manchester in support of women's suffrage and that it would be addressed by several prominent suffragettes, including Emmeline Pankhurst. On a whim, Gertrude decided to attend. She descended the train at the next station and arranged a change of trains to Manchester. She booked herself in at the newly opened Midland Hotel in central Manchester.

The next day she was a little late arriving at the rally. As her taxi, on a supposed short cut, passed through some back streets she stared out the window. A grey morn with a grey sky, grey clouds, grey houses and grey, sad people walking with their heads down. It was a tough, unforgiving life working in the cotton mills, processing the raw cotton from the southern states of America.

She had not allowed for the huge size of the crowd. There were thousands of people there, young women and old, well dressed and in rags, some with children attached. She was surprised to see quite a few men. She did feel a little self-conscious, a little over-dressed for the occasion with her mink stole. When Emmeline Pankhurst mounted the stage there was an uproar of cheering as everyone pushed closer to get a view. The police were out in force, several them mounted. The cool, fine drops of rain and the relentless easterly wind were hardly noticed by the crowd, intent on catching every word.

The noise reached a crescendo. Gertrude could see several scuffles had broken out. Placards were being waved, then poked at the police, then broken. Paving stones and bits and pieces of paraphernalia were being hurled. She looked around to see women being beaten with truncheons. One woman close to her was pulled away by two policemen, another was in a head lock, a third was kicking and wrestling as three policemen had hold of her. The woman bit one on the hand and he kicked her in the stomach as another one smashed her head. Blood spurted from the wound. Gertrude thought she looked pregnant. Then three horses trotted into them, the riders flailing about them with their batons. The women fled and Gertrude found herself trying to scramble away.

In the melee she tripped and felt her ankle give way as a large, red-faced woman screaming indecipherable abuse fell on her. She lay still until a hand touched her arm; looking up, she saw a young gentleman, well dressed and apparently unperturbed, was helping her to her feet. She stumbled as her ankle gave way again, but he caught her. 'Here, hold my arm. Let's get you out of here.' She limped painfully alongside him until they found a clear patch with a raised garden bed, and he sat her down on the wall.

'Thank you, young man,' she murmured, then tried to tidy her hair and rearrange her dress and the precious stole.

'William Loveless, ma'am,' the man said. 'Happy to be of assistance. If you will allow me, can I escort you out of here? I know a spot where you can sit down and then we can see about getting you home.'

Gertrude quietly acquiesced and they hobbled down a side street around the corner into a small alley. At the end was a charming little tavern with window boxes and gabled windows. Suddenly the crowd had vanished. Gertrude's acquaintance helped her inside and appeared to know the landlord, who fussed around until he found them a small table and commandeered two chairs. William ordered himself a pint of lager and insisted she have brandy along with the water, which is all she had ordered. Gertrude wanted to know what such a well-presented young man was doing at such a rally.

He put down his pint. 'It's a little complicated, but Emmeline and I are friends, and I do believe completely in the cause. Perhaps I can explain. My grandfather, James Loveless, was one of the six Tolpuddle Martyrs. Do you know the story?' Gertrude did know the outline but told him to go on anyway. 'They formed a secret society to protest against agricultural wages in Dorset. Ten shillings a week they'd been getting, but the landlords tried to reduce it to six. That meant they were starving. Their society was a friendly society and supposed to be allowed but they were quickly arrested, and the judge sentenced them to transportation to Australia; Sydney, it was. Horrible. But there was uproar in England and marches and petitions, including one with 800,000 signatures. Can you believe it? The Home Secretary, Lord John Russell, supported them and eventually they returned to England in 1839. I was brought up at my grandfather's feet and I will never forget what happened to him. I suppose I am a revolutionary.' He took a sip of his pint. 'Now we need to organise to get you home.'

Gertrude explained that she had only come here for the rally and was staying at the Midland Hotel in central Manchester. William was talking to his friend, the landlord, about transport when the front door swung open, and in swept Emmeline Pankhurst herself, escorted by a retinue of men and women.

She surveyed the room and spotted William. 'Well, well!' she said. 'And what on earth are you doing here, Will?'

Will explained what had happened. He realised he did not actually know the name of the lady he had rescued. Gertrude introduced herself first to her rescuer and then to Emmeline. Emmeline's eyes widened. 'My God, I know who you are. You're the secretary of the Anti-Suffrage League. You're against everything we stand for. You're spying on us.'

Gertrude laughed. 'Spying! Who would need to spy?'

'What on earth are you thinking, you and the thirty peeresses sipping afternoon tea and doing what their husbands tell them? You're a traitor to us all!'

William looked horrified but Gertrude was not the least perturbed. 'I might support your ambition, but certainly not your encouragement of violence and law-breaking. That was a rabble and the women caused it.'

'We will succeed, you will see.'

'And then what? My friend Lord Fisher, the First Sea Lord, says there will be war with Germany. What will you do then "Admiral" Pankhurst? We have seven principal objections and allow me to quote you the second. "The modern state depends for its very existence on naval and military power, diplomacy, finance and the great mining, construction, shipping and transport industries, in none of which can women take any practical part." If you are honest, you know that is true.'

Emmeline stared at her and turned to leave. As one of her flunkies opened the door, she looked back. 'And if you were honest, you would know that women would never allow such a war. It's the disgusting ego of the male. Unsurpassed and murderous. Go to your friend Fisher and stop the war.'

CHAPTER 32
London

Y EARS HAD PASSED until a thoroughly frustrated
ex-First Sea Lord Fisher found himself with Winston
Churchill, now the First Lord of the Admiralty, essentially
the civilian boss of the Royal Navy. Fortunately for Fisher, he
and Churchill were cut from the same cloth. In early 1911 Fisher
went to see Churchill at home in London. His wife Clementine
had heard Fisher was coming and decided to absent herself. She
found Fisher's friendship with Winston disturbing; she felt it
excluded her. They were frequently either arguing noisily or in gales
of laughter, in either case about what she could not imagine. She
walked into Winston's study. 'I shall take myself to Claridge's whilst
your over-exuberant court jester friend is present. I shall be home
this afternoon; late this afternoon.'

When Fisher arrived the talk quickly moved to oil. Fisher
strolled around the room while Churchill sat listening, wearing his
silk dressing gown over his day clothes, the stub of a cigar on the
ashtray. The study reeked of stale cigar smoke. Fisher had resigned
as First Sea Lord on his seventieth birthday in 1911. Without
Fisher having other responsibilities, Churchill saw him as ideal

to be appointed chairman of the Royal Commission on Fuel and Engines, reporting to parliament. The new chairman made his views crystal clear. 'What you require is super-swiftness, all oil. And don't fiddle about with armour – it really is so very silly. There is really only one defence; that is speed.' He meant twenty-five knots. Twenty-five knots was, indeed, twenty per cent faster than anything the admiralty believed Germany could throw up.

One way or another, enough parliamentarians were finally convinced. In 1912 the first Queen Elizabeth-class battleship, a super-dreadnought, was laid down. It was 33,000 long tons, had a complement of nearly 1000, had four twin 15-inch guns and fourteen 6-inch guns. Its boilers were to be fully fired by oil. It was fast. The battleship's speed was twenty-four knots, one knot less than intended but two knots faster than the fastest German ship. D'Arcy was invited by Fisher to see the first outing. He stood on the aft deck of the navy launch with other dignitaries as the *Queen Elizabeth* charged down the viewing course, ensigns streaming. A huge bow wave was set up which washed all the way across to their launch, which had to be powered up and turned to head into the wave to avoid being thrown about uncontrollably. D'Arcy was busy watching when the wave hit. He pitched to his side and landed on his shoulder on the cockpit floor. A seaman helped him to his knees, but he was writhing in pain, his shoulder feeling like it was broken.

HMS *Queen Elizabeth* sailed on. It looked what it was: a fearsome machine for making war.

The medical staff on shore bound D'Arcy's shoulder in a sling, gave him a pill, a good tot of rum and sent him back to London. After a disturbed night trying in vain to find some comfortable way to sleep, Nina took him to the hospital the next day. Sure enough, the shoulder was dislocated. Fisher sent him some flowers and a card, noting that D'Arcy was the first casualty of HMS *Queen Elizabeth*.

After the successful trials there was no turning back. In 1913 Winston Churchill, as First Lord of the Admiralty, had presented the cabinet with his memorandum on 'Oil Fuel Supply for His Majesty's Navy'. The cabinet agreed and in June 1914 he presented it to the House of Commons. The motion was passed that the government would invest £2.2 million in APOC, acquiring a 51% interest and placing two directors on the board. They would have special powers relating to naval matters. Unrevealed was the twenty-year contract to supply oil to the navy.

The lead had been given. From 1912 to the outbreak of war in August 1914 the British navy turned to oil.

TIMELINE TO WAR

28 JUNE 1914   Archduke Franz Ferdinand assassinated.

20 JULY 1914   Austria-Hungary declares war on Serbia. WWI begins.

29 JULY 1914   Russia mobilises.

1 AUGUST 1914   Germany declares war on Russia.

3 AUGUST 1914   Germany declares war on France and invades Belgium and Luxembourg. France invades Alsace. British forces arrive in France.

4 AUGUST 1914   Britain declares war on Germany.

10 AUGUST 1914   Austria-Hungary invades Russia.

9 SEPTEMBER 1914   First Battle of the Marne. Allied forces halt German advance into France.

CHAPTER 33

T HE FIRST SHOTS of the war had barely been fired. Far from Europe, down on the toe of South America, a British squadron was making its way up the Pacific coast of Chile. Since the outbreak of the war, a number of the Kaiser's new German fast cruisers, accompanied by single armed raiders disguised as merchant ships, had been cruising the Pacific wreaking havoc with Allied shipping.

Vice Admiral Sir Christopher Cradock was tasked with finding them. It was an unenviable task. His fleet was not large and to cover more ground he had to split it in two. He had stayed with the Pacific squadron, comprised of the armoured cruisers *Good Hope* and *Monmouth*, the light cruiser *Glasgow*, and the armed merchant cruiser *Otranto*. He had been forced to leave behind his only battleship, HMS *Canopus* with its 12-inch guns. She was old and slow, managing only twelve knots; modern German cruisers would simply steam out of range. Worse, his intelligence was inadequate. He did not know how many ships the Germans had in the area nor exactly what size. Prudence suggested caution, but the British navy was not into caution, and in the back of his mind he thought of the fate of his old friend, Admiral Troubridge. Troubridge was now under court martial for allowing the German cruisers, *Goeben* and *Breslau*, to escape to Constantinople from his Mediterranean fleet. The British admiralty, particularly Lord Fisher, were not amused.

Cradock's ships steamed up the Chilean coast towards Coronel when his lookouts spied smoke, but it was the smoke of three ships, a German cruiser squadron commanded by Admiral von Spee, and including the *Scharnhorst* and *Gneisenau*, with sixteen 8-inch guns between them. He had been hoping for one or, at most, two opponents. Cradock was steeped in British naval tradition – the modern navy had learned the lessons of Nelson, and had not lost a naval battle since 1812. He must turn and fight.

The Germans had the favourable inshore position, the battle grey of their ships hard to distinguish against the grey green of the Andes rising behind them. The British ships were starkly outlined by the rising sun. Firing began at a range of six miles with salvos every fifteen seconds. *Good Hope* was soon ablaze; her forward section exploded then she broke apart and sank, with no one witnessing the end and no survivors. *Monmouth*, severely damaged, was caught by the late arriving *Nürnberg* and, declining an invitation to surrender, was also sunk. *Glasgow* finally managed to separate herself in the darkness and *Otranto*, a less compelling target, slipped away to the south. Cradock and 1600 of his men had been lost. The Germans suffered three casualties.

Fisher's phone rang on his desk at the Admiralty. It was the First Lord of the Admiralty, Winston Spencer Churchill. It was hard to know who was more outraged by this humiliating defeat in the first naval battle of the war. Britain had been humiliated in front of the world. The headlines in *The Times* read, 'Disaster in the Pacific'.

Fisher had only a few weeks earlier taken over from First Sea Lord Prince Louis of Battenberg, a great patriot, but German-born and therefore quite unacceptable to the British public. Fisher's reappointment was broadly welcomed across England. There could hardly have been a time when a commander of experience and competence was more needed, and who did England have that more accurately fulfilled that description?

The Times reported that Fisher 'was now entering the close of his 74th year but he was never younger or more vigorous'.

Churchill, as First Lord of the Admiralty, had been delighted to bring his old friend back. But now this. Fisher strode around his desk and then called for an immediate briefing. Where were the nearest British ships capable of striking back? Incredibly, it now appeared that the nearest suitable and available ships were the two battlecruisers HMS *Invincible* and HMS *Inflexible*, with 12-inch guns and twenty-five knots of speed. They had been built in 1907 before the switch to oil, but they had Parsons' turbines powered by water tube boilers and carried 3000 long tons of coal and 750 tons of fuel oil sprayed on the coal to increase burn rate. There was only one problem: they were currently refitting in Plymouth.

Fisher picked up the phone. 'When will they be ready to sail?' he asked the Plymouth dockyard.

'Two weeks,' was the response.

'They will leave port in two days. Have I made myself clear?'

In two days the two battlecruisers cleared Plymouth for the South Atlantic.

Flush from such a comprehensive victory, von Spee headed south around Tierra del Fuego heading for the South Atlantic. He had in mind a second decisive blow against Britain. He would land a force at Port Stanley and destroy the facilities at the Falkland Islands. He stopped for three days at Picton Island at the eastern end of the Beagle Channel. The commanders of the *Dresden*, *Leipzig* and *Gneisenau* were not so sure about the Falklands; the intelligence was not altogether clear. Von Spee was determined to press on.

HMS *Canopus*, detached from Cradock's squadron, had wallowed her way slowly towards the Falkland Islands, where it was finally determined she was not fit for service. In Port Stanley she was beached on the mudflats in a position where her guns could cover the harbour. To ensure she could not be seen from offshore, her top masts were removed. On 7 December 1914 the two British battlecruisers arrived in dire need of coaling after their high-speed passage from Portsmouth. Worse still for von Spee, the harbour contained the armed cruisers *Carnarvon*, *Kent* and *Cornwall* plus the light cruisers *Bristol* and *Glasgow* and AMC *Macedonia*.

An unlikely source of intelligence on the movement of the German ships was from Mrs Muriel Felton, wife of the manager of a sheep station at Fitzroy, and her maids Christina Goss and Marian Macleod. Their property was situated high above the Fitzroy River in the East Falkland island. They were alone when Mrs Felton received a telephone call from Port Stanley advising that the German ships were approaching the islands and asking if she could maintain a lookout. The maids took turns running to the top of a nearby hill overlooking the ocean and quickly spotted the German ships steaming along the coast. They recorded the movements of the ships, ran down to Mrs Felton who then relayed the information to Port Stanley by telephone. Her reports allowed *Bristol* and *Macedonia* to take up the best positions for interception. The Admiralty later presented the women with silver plates and Muriel Felton received the OBE.

At first light, von Spee's fleet cautiously approached the port, unaware they were being watched from a station high on the headland.

The first they knew about any opposition was when a shot from *Canopus* skidded across the water, the shell splinters splattering *Gneisenau*. Not sure if he should press on with the attack, von Spee finally decided to turn away. Sturdee, the commander of the British squadron, coolly finished his breakfast while his battlecruisers finished coaling. He then set off in pursuit. A bright, sunny day lit up the Southern Ocean, ideal for gunnery. A few small fishing boats had been enjoying the summery conditions enough to lay some nets. Sturdee well understood his superiority. Aping Nelson at the Battle of the Nile, he ordered, 'General chase'. Travelling at twenty-five knots, *Invincible* and *Inflexible* ran down *Gneisenau* and *Scharnhorst* and opened up with their 12-inch guns. The two German ships were soon on fire and the British ships could only watch as each settled in the water, and finally capsized and sank. There were no survivors, including von Spee and his two sons. The *Nürnberg* and *Leipzig*, also outgunned, were also sunk; only the *Dresden* escaped.

Back in London a nasty grey fog was seeping through the streets and keeping visibility to a few yards. Fisher was visiting the Foreign Office, discussing a number of locations of concern including the South Atlantic. He had been given pride of place in the meeting, underneath the painting of Lord Canning, first Viceroy of India, in a huge boardroom lit by a large crystal chandelier. Fisher's task was to bring some sense of reality to the assembled group of executives. Coronel had made them extremely nervous. He was about to begin when an aide poked his head around the door and nervously asked if he could speak to the admiral on an urgent matter.

'Urgent?' demanded Fisher.

'Yes sir, very urgent.'

Fisher muttered to himself but agreed. Outside the door the aide explained. 'Excuse me, sir, but we have an urgent message from the radio station in Port Stanley. It is marked "for your eyes only" and is given our highest priority.'

Fisher nodded, his stomach tightening. This could be either very good news or, quite possibly, very bad. 'All right, give it here, man.'

The aide handed over one sheet of paper, typed on both sides.

Fisher read it carefully and turned back to re-enter the Foreign Office. The executives looked up expectantly.

'Gentlemen,' Fisher announced. 'It appears the British Navy has just won a comprehensive victory in the Falkland Islands. I have here a message from Vice Admiral Doveton Sturdee. Apparently our ships have engaged a large German naval force just offshore from the Falklands. As a result, our ships have sunk the two German armoured cruisers, the *Scharnhorst* and the *Gneisenau*, plus two light cruisers *Nürnberg* and *Leipzig*, plus some supporting merchant ships carrying coal. This is a truly momentous victory. As you will appreciate only one ship, the *Dresden*, has escaped but we will hunt her down. The Germans have suffered nearly two thousand casualties, including von Spee and his two sons. Our casualties, at the moment, are about nine. We have revenged Coronel and by god we needed to.' Without a word the Foreign Office directors stood up and gave three hearty cheers.

There was only one tiny downside. Fisher and Sir Doveton Sturdee were engaged in a long-running feud. Fisher and Sturdee were never going to be friends. Sturdee was a pompous establishment naval officer who was opposed to every one of Fisher's changes. One of Fisher's first actions when Churchill recalled him was to remove Sturdee from his post as Chief of War Staff.

When Fisher got back to his office, he of course sent a message of congratulations, but he demanded to know how it was that *Dresden* had escaped and gave orders that at all costs she was to be found.

In fact, *Dresden* was not to be found for over three months.

She was eventually cornered off the Juan Fernández Islands and after a short battle she was scuttled, and her crew interned. Victory was complete.

In the aftermath, discussion revealed that when the German flotilla approached the Falklands they were unaware that the two

British battlecruisers were at the end of two days' coaling in the harbour and could not immediately leave port. Admiral von Spee turned away after the salvo from *Canopus*. Had he, in the tradition of Nelson, pressed on, the outcome would have been much different. As Fisher remarked later to Churchill, 'If they had attacked, then taking two days to coal could have sunk us; another case for oil, I think.'

The British press responded in force at this famous naval victory. The story was wonderful news for *The Times*, the *Express*, the *Daily Mail* and the *Evening News* and, after Coronel, much needed. The Public Orator of Oxford University expressed the public gratitude: '*Hoc Tibi Piscator Patria Debet Opus.*' Fisher had no more knowledge of Latin than the ordinary man in the street but, when translated, he could not but enjoy the sentiment: 'The nation is in your debt.'

Britain had a new hero: First Sea Lord Admiral Jacky Fisher, the man who sent the battlecruisers to the Falklands.

Messages of approbation flooded in. Winston rang and he and Jacky had a good chat. As Winston said, 'Thank god you forced the hand of the dockyard in Plymouth. If it had taken two weeks for the cruisers to make it, the Falklands would have been lost. On such small decisions are battles won and lost.' They chatted for some time on other naval matters and arranged to meet in Westminster in a few days for a full briefing on all the many issues which were vital to naval development.

When Fisher hung up Kitty came in to say that William Knox D'Arcy had been on the phone and wished to pass his heartiest congratulations to Jacky. 'He was very jolly, I must say,' she said.

Fisher laughed. 'Oh, yes, he would be. He knows how much oil we're buying from him. "Black gold" he calls it, and he's right.'

'He does have a rather odd accent.'

'Westminster School overlaid by Australian. Yes, very odd. I like him. "Takes no prisoners," as he says, but you know exactly where you are with him. Which is a refreshing change from the hypocrites I am saddled with.'

CHAPTER 34

ALLIED GROUND TROOPS were bogged down in France, and it was apparent that breaking the German forces in a European ground war was going to be a long and bloody war of attrition. On top of that Russia had been severely handicapped by the inept British handling of relations with Turkey, leading to the Ottomans joining the war as allies of Germany. The Ottoman intervention left 350,000 tons of shipping bound for Russia bottled up in the Mediterranean. Grain from Russia could not exit the Black Sea and military support could not be supplied to Russia.

Winston had an idea about how the problem could be solved. He went to see Fisher and explained. 'The Turkish forces at the end of the Dardanelles are weak, their guns are old-fashioned, and morale is poor. If we move fast, we could send in a naval force, smash their forces, and land army units to take the Gallipoli peninsula. From there Istanbul would be at our mercy. Greece would see the writing on the wall and join us and I have no doubt the Ottomans would soon sue for peace. That's it, in a very short nutshell.'

Fisher rose from his desk and began walking around the room

but saying nothing. Winston sat puffing on his cigar. Finally, he could stand it no longer. 'Well?'

Fisher stopped. 'It could work. As you know, we have frantically been modernising the fleet. As a result we have quite a few redundant battleships. No good in the high seas or against the modern German fleet but they are in effect floating siege guns. But, whatever happens, the attack must be simultaneous; none of this army stuff of waiting to see how we go before committing. You know my motto. "Hit first, hit hard. Keep on hitting."'

Churchill had no problem with that; it was now up to him to persuade the government and Field Marshal Haig, who would need to persuade Kitchener that this second front was essential. Churchill received the backing he needed, and the Admiralty came up with a plan involving a mixture of old battleships both British and French. The fire power to be deployed would be formidable. Fisher by now was becoming more enthusiastic and finally allowed Churchill to persuade him that the fleet should be led by his brand-new dreadnought, HMS *Queen Elizabeth*, sporting 15-inch guns. It was then of course that the army started to push back. They had a variety of excuses. They could not release any troops, they had none with experience, the navy should be able to do it on their own. Finally they agreed, but only if the ground landings took place after the bombardment so the troops would face limited if any resistance. The navy would 'force the Gallipoli straits' and then the army would go in.

Fisher stormed into Churchill's office. 'I do not agree. What did I say? "Hit first, hit hard." This is dispersing our forces!'

Churchill tried to calm him down, but Fisher would have none of it. The next day a war cabinet was called. All parties voted in favour of the plan and Fisher, seeing he was the sole dissenter, eventually agreed.

The task force was formed. Fourteen allied battleships, four from France, with mine sweepers, cruisers and other smaller craft. The new aircraft carrier HMS *Ark Royal* was also deployed. So was the *Queen Elizabeth*.

Fisher was quietly beside himself. As he said to Herbert Richmond, 'What happens if she hits a mine and is sunk? It's not like the bloody army. You can't call up more troops. It will be a global disaster; a giant propaganda coup for Germany and they will know it. She will be the target and those blithering idiots have forgotten about submarines. The Dardanelles is only thirty miles long and a mile wide. It's no place for the *Queen Elizabeth*.'

Over the course of the campaign Fisher raved, threatened to resign, and threatened to go to the Dardanelles and take command. Nine times Churchill talked him out of it.

Fisher scribbled notes in the middle of the night. 'YOU ARE BENT ON FORCING THE DARDANELLES AND NOTHING WILL TURN YOU FROM IT. NOTHING. I know you so well. You will remain … I shall go.' It was as if he was having a breakdown. He scrawled a letter to Andrew Bonar Law, the leader of the opposition: 'A very great national disaster is very near us in the Dardanelles.'

Finally, Fisher disappeared. He saw Lloyd George, the Minister of Munitions, and told him he was leaving but after that no one could find him. Prime Minister Asquith ordered him to return but it was to no avail. If Fisher had been a seagoing commander, he would have been blindfolded and shot on the quarterdeck.

The naval attack was a disaster. The essential precursor to the attack, the clearing of mines, failed. The minesweepers were shelled and machine-gunned and rapidly withdrew. The battleships went in anyway. The *Bouvet*, the *Irresistible* and the *Ocean* were sunk by the mines. The *Suffren* and the *Gaulois* were damaged; as were the *Agamemnon*, the *Lord Nelson* and the *Charlemagne*. The *Inflexible*, returned from her heroic exploits in the Falklands, hit a mine and had to be beached.

Now General Sir Ian Hamilton decided to send in the troops, but in the delay German General Liman von Sanders took control of the Ottoman Turkish troops, and Kemal Ataturk had arrived with him. The fatal delay.

⁓

Fisher was in his study at Kilverstone Hall, hunched over his desk, scribbling furiously. Kitty came in with a cup of tea. She knew Jacky was in a state of high tension.

Waving his glasses he looked up. 'Kitty, read this. It's to Asquith. I'm sending it today. What do you think?'

Kitty read it as quickly as she could.

'If the following conditions are agreed to,' it began, 'I can guarantee the successful conclusion of the war:

'That Mr Winston Churchill is not in the cabinet to be always circumventing me;

'That there shall be an entire new Board of Admiralty, as regards the Sea Lord and the Financial Secretary (who is utterly useless). New measures demand new men;

'That I shall have complete professional charge of the war at sea, together with the absolute sole disposition of the fleet and the appointment of all officers of all ranks whatsoever, and absolutely untrammelled sole command of all the sea forces whatsoever;

'That the First Lord of the Admiralty should be absolutely restricted to policy and parliamentary procedure;

'That I should have the sole absolute authority for all new construction and all dockyard work of whatever sort whatsoever, and complete control of the whole of the civil establishments of the Navy.

'These conditions must be published verbatim so that the fleet may know my position.'

Kitty stared at him. 'Jacky, are you mad? You can't send this to the Prime Minister.'

'I can and I will.' He snatched it back, laid it on the desk and with a flourish signed it. Then he rose and marched out clutching his magnum opus. He was off to post it.

When Asquith received it, he took one look and, noting that he had not previously responded to Fisher's letter of resignation, promptly sent a telegram accepting it.

The other major casualty to lose his job was Churchill.

Fisher's juvenile behaviour incited all his numerous enemies. Queen Alexandra declared he should be hung from the yardarm, Violet Asquith proclaimed that he 'had behaved in a lower, meaner and more unworthy way than any Englishman since the war began'. *John Bull* magazine advised: 'Stick to your post like Nelson!'

Admiral Beresford and Sturdee met up at the club. Sturdee swirled his port around his glass. 'Lack of breeding, that's what it is. No class and no ticker either.'

Beresford agreed. 'Punkah wallah, he is,' he blustered. 'Shames what it is to be an Englishman.'

It was a week later that a smart young lad, dressed in a striking uniform of black with red edges and a cap arrived at the front door at Kilverstone. The maid answered the knock to be presented with a telegram for Sir John Fisher. The maid took it to the study.

Kitty heard a bellow from the study. She opened the door to find Jacky brandishing the telegram. 'The swine! Asquith's accepted my resignation.'

He crumpled into his armchair, head down. Kitty put an arm around his shoulders.

'It's better, Jacky, it really is. You are exhausted. A return would be a herculean demand on you. Why don't you go to see Richmond? He is a friend, almost family and wise when wisdom is needed.'

'Yes, yes, I will.' He clutched his head in his hands.

Kitty tried to think of something appropriate from the Old Testament, but nothing came to her. For once she wished she had spent less time daydreaming in chapel.

She was in the kitchen when Fisher shuffled in. He perched on a stool.

'I fear I may have made a terrible error,' he said sadly. 'I have put my heart into the navy, the biggest, fastest and best-armed battleships on the water. The *Queen Elizabeth* was the apogee. But in my heart, I've realised that it's now the opposite. The waters are becoming the realm of the small. Submarines, torpedoes and mines. They cost nothing, you can have hundreds of them, and they can sink the largest ship in the ocean. Now there are aeroplanes. Can fly wherever they want, spy on you, drop bombs or torpedoes. I have looked the wrong way.'

Kitty hardly knew how to respond. 'But you *have* known, Jacky. I've heard you talk about all those things.'

'I know. I have talked about them, but we've moved too slowly. We've hardly looked at aeroplanes, but when you think about what you could do with an aeroplane properly armed, it's the stuff of nightmares. We must react, and I could make that happen.'

Kitty could only repeat her words. 'Talk to Richmond, and Old 'Ard 'Art. We have those weapons too, do we not?'

'Yes, we do. You are correct. But still.' And he lapsed into silence.

CHAPTER 35
England and France

⌒

SOMEHOW DOUGHTY-WYLIE'S letters kept coming to Gertrude.

'Tonight, I should not want to talk. I should make love to you. Would you like it, welcome it, or would a hundred hedges rise and bristle and divide? But we would tear them down. What is a hedge that it should divide us? You are in my arms, alight, afire. Tonight, I do not want dreams and fancies. But it will never be … The first time, should I not be nearly afraid to be your lover?

'So much a thing of the mind is the insistent passion of the body. Women sometimes give themselves to men for the man's pleasure. I'd hate a woman to be like that with me. I'd want her to feel to the last sigh the same surge and stir that carried me away. She should miss nothing that I could give her.'

Gertrude replied: 'Dearest, dearest, I give this year of mine to you, and all the years that shall come after it. Dearest, when you tell me you love me and want me still, my heart sings – and then weeps with longing to be with you.'

What could have been any clearer? And yet …

Gertrude received a letter, written as he left for yet another continent, containing the following: 'Africa draws me; I know I shall have things to try for … But of them I scarcely think. It is only that I love you, Gertrude, and shall not see you …'

Was this indeed a declaration of commitment?

Gertrude wrote to her stepmother Florence, offering to leave France immediately and come to help her in the north of England.

'Boulogne, Saturday 28th November 1914.

'Dearest Mother, I hear that you have your convalescents, and even twenty of them. (Where have you put them all?) Now would you not like me to come back? I am quite ready to come … If you send me a telegram, I will come at once and no more said. They can get someone else here. You understand I should not be happy here if I thought you needed me. I reckon you would be able to manage eleven without difficulty, but twenty is a different matter. Your ever affectionate daughter, Gertrude.'

Still the three-cornered relationship went on. Dick's wife was well aware that she was in a ménage à trois. Judith wrote a letter to Gertrude, but the content is lost. She would not be giving up her husband for anyone. Her misery was as great as Gertrude's, and it became clear that she was contemplating suicide. Christmas arrived and Gertrude stayed in France. She went with friends to inspect the nearby hospital they were running. The state of the wounded and dying alarmed her but the staff were doing their best. She wrote to her father Hugh, 'I hope we shall never spend another Christmas like this one.'

She was back in her room when a letter was delivered, this time from her mother. She opened it, read it carefully and then flopped into her bedroom chair. Her mother wanted her to know that among all the major news that was constantly before her she imagined no one had told her that two German battlecruisers, from out in the North Sea, had shelled the ruins of one of the favourite places they shared, Whitby Abbey. The firing had continued for some time. The damage was substantial. Just another body blow, Gertrude supposed. She wondered to herself what on earth the point of shelling the ruin had been.

Gertrude continued in France, working impossible hours with the Red Cross running the Missing and Wounded Enquiry Department. She was trying to manage the grizzly task of identifying the dead and wounded. She was up before the first French cockerel crowed and filled her day trying to arrange notification of the families (often unrecorded), names missing or addresses not known. It was then she received a letter from Dick. She was amused to find her hand trembled as she opened it.

It was good news and bad. He would be heading to the Allied forces in Gallipoli, but he was briefly about to return to London for a furlough. If it was not too difficult, was there a chance they could meet? Gertrude dropped everything, took a train then a ferry then a train, and was back in London when Dick arrived.

They met at his old bachelor flat in Half Moon Street in Mayfair, just across Piccadilly from Green Park, and were alone together for four nights and three days. They talked non-stop, laughed at nothing, held hands, and wandered about the streets of London. In the evenings they paid visits to the gilded watering holes of Mayfair; enjoyed a French delicacy, a glass or two of wine or perhaps a cocktail, the speciality of the house. In the mornings a stroll to Green Park, or across Park Lane to Hyde Park. Anyone who observed them would have smiled to themselves and thought how good it was in such troubled times, times when death was a constant, always slyly squeezing your shoulder, to see some happiness. But again, both his letters and hers confirm that this passion was never consummated.

Judith was soon away in Greece running yet another field hospital. She was dealing with hands-on triage and treatment of the wounded, many not much more than scared children. She was probably like Gertrude, not unhappy to have such an unrelenting twenty-four-hour demand on her resources.

Gertrude never returned to France.

⤚

Herbert Richmond drove up the semicircular gravel drive to Kilverstone Hall and parked his car in one of the numerous spaces provided. He had driven from Cambridge where he was much sought after for his contribution to the history department. He looked up at the substantial front of the house, which had only just been remodelled in Jacobean style, buttoned his blazer, and rang the doorbell.

There was a lengthy wait until eventually the door was opened by Kitty. She looked rather nonplussed. 'Admiral Richmond, what a surprise! But it is good to see you. Do come in. What brings you all the way down here?'

Richmond was taken aback. 'Did you not get my letter then? I had to be in these parts and wrote to say I would drop in to see you and Jacky. I do apologise. War time. The post is so unreliable.'

Kitty recovered, and smiled. 'Do come in. I'm afraid Jacky's not here at the moment but it is good to see you. Let's have some tea.'

She rang the bell for the maid as they made their way down the delicately detailed panelled passage through to the drawing room. Richmond had not appreciated what a huge house this was. He shook his head in wonder that the property had been bequeathed to Jacky and Kitty's son Cecil, who had so curiously been adopted by the childless owner Josiah Vavasseur and his wealthy American wife. Well, Jacky certainly had earned his luck. The tea came and Kitty asked after Elsa, and then Gertrude.

'Such an astonishing woman,' Kitty said. 'I so admire her; an example of what women can do when given a chance, yes?'

Richmond was happy to agree. He then enquired where Jacky might be and if he would be back that day.

Kitty hesitated. 'I don't know when he'll be back. He disappeared over a week ago. He's gone to see his friend the Duchess of Hamilton. They seem to be great chums.'

Richmond knew very well who that was. She was married to the gnome-like 13th Duke of Hamilton. An irascible recluse with a foul tongue and an endless supply of money. Richmond expressed surprise that Fisher should find the Duchess much company.

'Oh yes,' said Kitty. 'They are great friends. Both very religious; quoting the Bible endlessly to each other like some sort of contest. Always on their knees in church. You know Augustus John is painting Jacky? The Duchess goes to the sittings and offers encouragement.'

'Well. I didn't know. How extraordinary.'

Kitty put her hand to her neck and adjusted her necklace. 'I think it's something else. I think Jacky, like half the other admirals, feels in the shadow of Nelson. He is so superstitious. You know very well that Nelson's long-term mistress was Lady Hamilton. I sometimes wonder if Jacky thinks that providence has provided him with the Duchess of Hamilton as some sort of second coming of Nelson. Ridiculous, I know.'

Richmond was endowed with natural charm and a keen intelligence, but he found himself searching frantically for something intelligent in response, finally excusing himself to visit the bathroom. On his return, Kitty had ordered a fresh pot of tea. Richmond could see she wanted to continue the conversation. He felt sorry for her. Kilverstone Hall was in Norfolk, but quite remote. The property was on 3000 acres of parkland and the village itself had less than twenty houses. Kitty must have been quite lonely when Jacky was not there. She was hardly the fox-hunting type.

Kitty poured him another cup of tea and continued just as the maid arrived with a plate of sandwiches. Richmond was pleased to see them, not having eaten since breakfast. Kitty continued. 'Of course, everyone knows Jacky's history, and in the face of the circumstances of his upbringing what a tribute it is to his capacity that he should have reached First Sea Lord. The trouble is, he is well aware of the disdain he receives from some of the establishment. He has been snubbed many times, especially by such people as Beresford and Sturdee who are always trying to destroy him. He bitterly resents it. I think being seen with the duchess is a way of poking a finger in their eyes. Silly I know, but there you have it.'

Richmond shook his head. 'That is England, I'm afraid, Kitty. Nothing has changed for a century, and who knows if it ever will.'

Kitty took Richmond for a short tour of the main part of the house and garden. As they walked to the car, Kitty turned to Richmond. 'You know, Jacky has been a wonderful man to be married to. A whirlwind; like a boisterous child, unpredictable, a little bit a genius but a little bit mad. But I like to believe he still loves me as much as ever.'

As they said goodbye, Richmond promised to do more to involve Jacky, but he admitted to Kitty that he himself had more than enough trouble with the old English naval establishment. 'They are battle-hardened in their resistance to change. It may well sink England.'

It was April 1915. The navy having tried and failed to run the straits at Gallipoli, it was the turn of the army.

The British forces were heading to the beach at Gallipoli. On board the transport *River Clyde* were 2000 men led by Dick Doughty-Wylie and Lieutenant Colonel Weir de Lancey Williams. The boat was run aground on the beach and a bridge of lighters made to bring the men ashore. The plan was to break the group into three. One part would try for the castle and village, one would join the troops already on 'W' beach, and the third would head for Hill 141.

Dick had watched the men from the ship as the carnage took place in front of him. Then, without warning he came ashore, and unarmed, he picked up his cane and marched towards the village. A bullet knocked his cap off. The village was taken but Dick marched steadily on, now alone, towards Hill 141. Carrying his cane and maintaining an eerie calm, he led a cheering crowd from the Dubliner, Munster and Hampshire regiments. They made it all the way to the top, the Turks retiring but turning to fire back. At the very moment when the men knew they had managed a rare victory, Doughty-Wylie was shot through the head.

He was buried where he lay, with the chaplain of the Munsters reading the burial service. Doughty-Wylie was the most senior officer to win the Victoria Cross during the Gallipoli campaign. His grave is still there, surrounded by the wild lavender and two cypress trees, the only Allied cemetery on Gallipoli with just one grave. It was Sir Ian Hamilton, Commander of the Gallipoli forces, who wrote, 'A braver soldier never drew sword. He had no hatred of the enemy ... Tenderness and pity filled his heart ... He was a steadfast hero ... Now, as he would have wished to die, so he has died.'

It was here in the Dardanelles, overlooked by the ancient ruins of Troy, where the legend of Hero and Leander was created. Hero was a young priestess serving the goddess Aphrodite. Even though Aphrodite was the goddess of love, beauty and eternal youth, Hero was forbidden to marry. Leander was a youth who lived at Abydos, across the waters of the Hellespont, the Greek name for the Dardanelles. Somehow, they met and fell in love. Hero lived in the tower of a castle at Sestos, on the Asian shore. She would leave a light burning in the tower; each night Leander would follow its flame to swim to his lover.

One night, Hero succumbed, and broke her vow of chastity. When the winter came the lovers agreed to part until the warm spring weather arrived. But driven by so strong a desire, they could not stay apart until winter ended. It was too much. Hero climbed to the top of the tower and lit the flame. Even though the weather was poor, and the water cold, Leander set out to swim across. The strong wind blew out the flame. Leander lost his bearings and was caught in the strong current of the strait. The strait is nearly a mile and a half wide opposite Çanakkale. Though a powerful swimmer, Leander could not prevail. In darkness, with waves breaking all around him, he drowned. Wracked by grief Hero threw herself from the tower. Their bodies, caught in an embrace, washed up on the shore together. They were buried in a lovers' tomb above the beach.

So powerful a myth could only attract the poets of the world. The story appeared in Virgil and Ovid, Shakespeare, Keats, Marlowe and of course Byron. Lord Byron, to honour the legend, began a tradition carried on to this day by, in 1810, swimming across from the Asian shore to Europe. As Byron wrote to commemorate the myth:

> *The winds are high on Helle's wave,*
> *As on that night of stormy water*
> *When Love, who sent, forgot to save*
> *The young, the beautiful, the brave,*
> *The lonely hope of Sestos' daughter.*

The whole area surrounding the Dardanelles is steeped in mythology, in legends of heroes, of great loves and of greater tragedies. Few of the soldiers fighting for their lives on the Gallipoli shores would have known anything of Byron's swim or the myths and legends surrounding the area, but Dick Doughty-Wylie and Gertrude Bell certainly would.

Gertrude was at a luncheon party in Chelsea, organised to raise funds for the Red Cross. The guests were mainly women. Gertrude noticed they were modestly dressed. No one wanted to look too gay in a London preoccupied with a brutal war. They were gathered in a spacious music room, the grand piano pushed into a corner. The room was an elegant example of early Victoriana with a large Persian rug on a parquet floor, but it was showing signs of neglect with its fading wallpaper and the need for a lick of paint. The hostess's husband was in the navy, at sea; she had no idea exactly where.

A huge oil painting in an elaborate gilt frame hung on the chimney. It depicted an eight-point stag staring superciliously from what Gertrude presumed was the banks of a Scottish tarn. A decrepit waiter was serving drinks while a young waitress walked about with a tray of cucumber sandwiches, the crusts carefully removed. Gertrude was chatting rather aimlessly with an acquaintance of her stepmother when an army officer in uniform walked into the room. He looked about him and then strode over to the hostess, more elegantly dressed than the rest, who was busy talking to a younger male guest; by his uniform, also an army officer. The new arrival, ignoring the hostess, immediately addressed the latter.

Gertrude and her friend were standing close by.

'I presume you already heard, but such a shame,' said the army officer. 'Doughty-Wylie was a damn fine soldier, and a damn decent chap to boot.'

'What are you talking about, Adrian?' asked the younger man. 'What am I supposed to have heard?'

Gertrude would have picked up the name even had she been across the room. She paused her conversation in mid-sentence.

'You didn't know then?' said the officer. 'KIA under extraordinary circumstances on the slopes at Gallipoli. Marching in front of his men; setting an example. Deserves the VC from what I hear. Just heard the news at the barracks.'

There was no reason why anyone would have told the news to Gertrude. She was not family, and few even knew of the relationship.

Gertrude used every nerve in her body to stay calm. But turning white, she dug her fingernails into her palms trying to avoid betraying even a trace of emotion. She had grown her nails and painted them auburn to match her hair. She looked down to see a thin line of blood across her palm. With the thinnest of excuses she made her departure, muttering a few words on her way out to her bemused hostess. She rushed into the park opposite, found a deserted bench and sat head in hand, tears pouring down her cheeks. She could hardly think but somehow she managed to find her way to Hampstead to her half-sister Elsa. Married to the admiral and now Lady Richmond, Elsa took one look and assumed it was their brother Maurice who had been killed.

Gertrude stammered out the truth. 'No, it's not Maurice. It's Dick.'

Every adult in Britain lived each day fearful that the messenger could arrive at their front door and some father, brother, uncle or son would be reported a casualty in this hideous and never-ending conflagration. People lived, tossing and turning in bed at night, clinging to the hope that tomorrow would not be their day. Then would come the sound, the 'soft footfall of the Black Angel'. A knock on the door. The door would open and there would be the postman, cap on head, face expressionless. 'A telegram for you, sir (or madam)'. Sometimes it was no more than a roneoed letter, with only the name and date written in by hand. 'Captured, wounded or dead' would be the choice.

Elsa for once was at a loss for words. Instead, she lay Gertrude on the sofa, plumped the cushions around her, took off her shoes and gently stroked her head. What use would words be anyway?

~⃝

It was a two blankets morning at Gallipoli, the grey sky accompanied by icy gusts of wind, when a small launch putted to a stop alongside the hull of the SS *River Clyde*. The date was 17 November 1915 and winter was coming. The *River Clyde* was a collier and had been run ashore on 'V' beach to provide access to the French base, situated on the southern tip of the Gallipoli peninsular. Under intermittent shelling she was still being used as a landing wharf, breakwater and field station. The launch ran alongside, and a figure dressed in an ankle-length coat, scarf and wide-brimmed hat scrambled up the ladder, looked about her and set off for what little was left of the nearby Seddülbahir castle. Those French soldiers close enough looked and then looked again, astonished to see that the unexpected visitor was a woman.

The visitor strode past the ruins and headed up the rough track, pulling her coat around her as the chill wind rustled the few leaves that remained on the scrub and bushes that still grew along the way. The guns had fallen silent as she climbed up what was the road from Seddülbahir across to 'W' beach. On the way the road would pass her destination, Hill 141, one of the highest points on the peninsula. At the top of Hill 141 was the only grave to be allowed on this part of the peninsula, a stone construction barely bigger than the coffin it held, topped by a wooden cross and surrounded by one sagging strand of barbed wire. Two Cypress trees were the only vegetation. The woman was carrying a wreath. She placed it carefully on the cross, bowed her head for a few seconds, then turned and made her way back down the hill to the *River Clyde* and her waiting launch. Without her speaking a word the launch departed.

The grave is the most isolated on the Gallipoli peninsula and belongs to Lieutenant Colonel Dick Doughty-Wylie VC of the Royal Welsh Regiment.

The French officers, splendid in their uniforms, gathered that evening in the officers' mess. They discussed the mysterious intruder over a round or two of absinthe. All agreed it must be his wife, Lillian, apparently a matron on the Greek Island of Thassos. However, among the wider community who knew the story of Doughty-Wylie the conviction grew that the visitor was actually Gertrude Bell, compelled by her inconsolable grief to pay the final tribute available to her, to the only man she truly loved.

CHAPTER 36
London

⌒

THE HEADMASTER of Westminster School was busy at his desk when his secretary put her head cautiously around his door.

'Excuse me, Headmaster, but there is a gentleman on the phone. His name is Knox D'Arcy, and he says he is an old boy, and he would like to come to see you about making a bequest. What shall I tell him?'

'A bequest, eh? How much?'

'He didn't say, sir.'

'Well, one can't look a gift horse in the mouth, can one? I trust it's not some piffling sum and he wants a schoolhouse named after him. Better make an appointment, half an hour at most, and in the meantime see if you can find his record at the school.'

A week later Knox D'Arcy seated himself comfortably in a spacious leather armchair in the headmaster's study. Nothing much seemed to have changed, he hazily recalled.

The headmaster said a few words of welcome and then got straight to the point. 'So, what is you had in mind, sir?'

'I enjoyed my rowing at the school,' said D'Arcy, 'and I have understood that, to say the least, your rowing equipment is rather decrepit. I wondered if you would like two brand-new eight-oar racing shells. Must give good young chaps good equipment is my view! And I am aware that rowing is still a most prestigious event. You will want to perform rather better than at the last Head of the River, I suspect.'

The headmaster nodded. Second from last: that had been embarrassing. He understood that the school's rowing equipment needed money spent on it and especially the shells. 'Well, that's a most generous offer, I must say. I need to clear it with my Board, but I am sure they will welcome new equipment. By the way, I took the liberty of looking up your time here and I see you didn't stay to the end of senior school, and in fact left in mid-year. That is, in my experience, unusual, and I wondered how that had come about, if you don't mind my asking?'

D'Arcy coughed. 'No, no, that is quite all right. Nothing particularly remarkable, but my father had been offered a senior post in the government of the new State of Queensland in Australia. By appointment to the Queen, you understand. It was quite an opportunity. He was rather adventurous, but we had a limited time to reach Australia, so we had to leave immediately. It worked out extremely well. He was up for a knighthood but sadly died before it could be awarded.'

The headmaster nodded. 'Such a pity.'

'It was indeed. We trace our family back to the fourteenth century. Lord D'Arcy de Knayth, you understand. It would have been most appropriate.'

'Ah, Anglo-Irish. I see. Well, Australia must have treated you well. Let me check as I said but I feel sure the answer will be yes. Are there any conditions you might require?'

'Only one. I would like to name the boats.'

'I quite understand and I'm sure we would have no objection.

Do you have a name in mind? Two names?'

'Indeed. "William Knox D'Arcy 1" and "William Knox D'Arcy 2" I think would look well.' D'Arcy leaned back, took out a cigar and contemplated the headmaster while he lit up.

The headmaster hesitated for just a few seconds. 'Well, I'm sure that would be quite acceptable. The Board will confirm, of course.'

CHAPTER 37
England

WINSTON picked up the phone and called Kitty
Fisher. 'How are you faring down in the country?' he
asked. They chatted briefly and then Winston got to
the point.

'Kitty, I haven't seen or even heard from Jacky for a while. I'm just
checking that he's all right. I would hate it if something happened,
and I didn't know.'

Kitty reassured Winston that Jacky was quite all right, although
feeling his age a bit.

'Look,' said Winston. 'I know we didn't part well but I would
like to just catch up with him. Face to face. Just a drink and a chat.
Do you think he would do that? After all, we are such good old
friends.' Kitty promised Winston she would talk to Jacky .

A few days later she called Winston to say Jacky had agreed;
perhaps they could meet in the smoking room at the Army & Navy
Club. It had a quiet alcove where they would be private.

It was two weeks later when Fisher entered the club, the 'Rag' as
it was called, a little anxious that they would not know him. After
all, it had been over a year since he had visited. He need not have

worried. The doorman snapped to attention. 'Welcome back, sir. We have missed you.' Inside the welcome was equally warm. Who could possibly forget this small man with a huge presence, and who could ever forget the compelling magnetism of Fisher's face?

He was early and Winston was late. While he waited, he stood admiring one of his favourite paintings. *Elephants in a Sandstorm*, otherwise known as The Heffalumps, had been painted and donated by a member, Henry Pilleau. Fisher particularly liked it; after all, it was the only painting in the club not containing an admiral, a battleship or endless vistas of water.

Winston eventually bustled in the door, hastily tucking his fob watch back in his waistcoat. Jacky stood up to greet him. 'Late as usual,' Jacky pointed out. Not a trait admired in the navy. Winston apologised then clasped the older man around the shoulders and stood back to look closer at him. Yes, he did look older.

'Jacky, I've missed you. We've all missed you. I just had to see you, and of course as always I want to see what you're thinking. Things are still tough as you know. Very tough.'

They sat down and ordered a couple of Scotches. Winston passed Jacky a parcel he had been carrying. 'Here, a small present. I do hope you like it.'

Jacky cautiously unwrapped it. Inside was a glass case enclosing a tiny scale model in steel and brass of a piston. Jacky knew immediately what it was: a miniscule, intricate model of the pistons in the engine of a dreadnought. He read the inscription. 'To a great naval officer from a grateful navy.' Jacky seemed to relax. He shook Winston's hand warmly, sat back in his chair and lit his cigar.

'Well, that is a lovely surprise.' He turned it around, admiring the intricacy of the work. 'Thank you indeed. I am sure Kitty will allow me to award it a pride of place.' He placed it carefully down beside his chair. 'I hope you've been getting my letters?'

'Indeed, indeed. Always entertaining and enlightening.'

'My successor, that Jackson fellow. Nice chap but completely out of his depth. You did well to remove him. Jellicoe is very sound, very sound. A little cautious, if you don't mind me saying so. I hope you received my letter.'

'I did, thank you. Yes, there is certainly a lively debate about the "fleet in being" issue.' Winston sat back and tapped the ash off his cigar. 'Jacky, I wanted to reassure you on two things. The first is that we all acknowledge without reservation that you may well have saved Britain. I was talking about it the other day with Richmond and one or two others. We listed your accomplishments. Engineering pre-eminence, water tube boilers, the turbine, the submarine, the dreadnought, promotion on merit and most of all, oil. The last a masterstroke. Not to mention getting rid of that accumulation of floating rubbish we called a navy; "a miser's hoard of useless junk" you famously phrased it.'

The butler entered to draw the curtains against the fading light, tip some more coal on the fire and replenish their glasses. Jacky smiled. He was most comfortable in the club's frayed elegance and appreciated the presence of servicemen from all the forces, each trying to forget the struggle that otherwise wholly engaged their lives.

Winston stood up and leaned on the mantelpiece. 'The second,' he continued, 'is more difficult, but you should know I fought hard against the campaign that Lord Charles Beresford waged on you. Dreadful, dreadful. British aristocracy at its absolute worst. He went on for so long, everywhere, to Parliament, the press, to anyone who would listen. Tried to destroy you. At least the King was on your side. Thank goodness for that.'

The two friends continued chatting for a while about old allies, hated enemies, how much they missed the King, what a great companion Bertie had been, and how George was rather dull, it had to be said. They strayed back to the war: the worrying rate of sinkings by German submarines of British merchant ships, 600,000 long tons in one month. 'Unsustainable,' was Winston's observation.

Jacky waved his arms about, spilling his whiskey. 'Winston, I wrote to you. Convoys, convoys are the solution. Surround the merchant ships with destroyers and, where you can, put up some aircraft. You must keep the submarines below the surface.'

Winston nodded his agreement. 'Jacky, I have to say I agree and luckily so does Jellicoe. We have rounded up every destroyer we can. First signs are hopeful. Much smaller losses on the last Atlantic convoy. It must succeed.'

After that the evening progressed enjoyably for a while until Jacky expressed himself as 'rather weary', and excused himself. Winston sat back and reflected. As he said to Kitty when she rang to thank him, 'Jacky tired? I never heard of such a thing. He is the least tired man I have ever met.'

~⌒

It was spring 1918 when Kitty fell seriously ill. Jacky rushed to her side but in July she died. Jacky was devastated, but he kept Nina informed with a stream of letters. He wrote that Kitty had had 'a most perfect, peaceful, blissful end'. She was buried at Kilverstone and on her gravestone was written, 'Her children rise up and call her blessed, and her husband also, and he praises her.' There seemed to be no sense of irony with Jacky's added words: 'For fifty-two years the wife of Admiral of the Fleet Lord Fisher of Kilverstone, having married him as a young lieutenant without friends or money or prospects, and denied herself all her life for the sake of her husband and her children: to them she was ever faithful and steadfast, and to such as condemned them she was a dragon.'

It is hard not to imagine that, on reflecting, he might have felt a pang of regret that he had so neglected her in favour of his strange and almost certainly platonic infatuation with Nina.

CHAPTER 38
Scotland

BETWEEN THE 25th and 27th of November 1918 the capital ships of the German fleet made their way slowly to Scapa Flow on the Scottish coast to surrender. Scapa Flow has been the fleet base for the British navy for hundreds of years. It is in the north of Scotland, protected by a ring of islands and giving immediate access to the North Sea and the Baltics. The flowers of the Reichsmarine steamed slowly between the assembled might of the British fleet, anchored in two parallel lines on either side of them. Germany, starving and in turmoil, had collapsed, and on board the German ships there were already clear signs of rebellion. The communists had made good progress with the ordinary sailors of the German navy; the 'Red Guard' was growing fast. Seventy-four ships were interned at anchor there.

Among the 370 ships of the British fleet assembled, the 90,000 smartly dressed sailors and the white ensigns displayed on every top mast, twenty admirals of the British fleet enjoyed their moment. There was no sign of Jacky Fisher. He had not been invited.

The precursor to the surrender had been the Battle of Jutland out in the North Sea, back on 1 June 1916. Sir John Jellicoe commanded the British fleet and Vice Admiral Reinhard Scheer the German. The purpose was for the Germans to break the vice-like blockade Britain had placed on Germany, which was slowly starving them to death. Two hundred and fifty ships were involved, including twenty-eight British and sixteen German battleships. 175,000 tons of shipping went to the bottom. Three British battlecruisers plus three armoured cruisers and eight destroyers were sunk. For the Germans, one battlecruiser, one pre-dreadnought, four light cruisers and five torpedo boats were lost. There were 9823 casualties, almost all killed. In terms of total ships displaced it is still the biggest surface naval battle in history. The Germans had won numerically in both tonnage and casualties, but the British still had the largest fleet and denied Germany access to the North Sea and Atlantic. The Germans continued to starve.

From Kilverstone, Fisher raved to the duchess and anyone else who would listen about Jellicoe's commitment to the 'fleet in being'. 'They've failed me, they've failed me!' he cried. 'I have spent thirty years of my life preparing for this day and they've failed me.' Fisher was still committed to all-out attack; he had himself failed to remember Gallipoli.

At the surrender of the German fleet the ships were moored until an armistice was signed on 11 November 1918. Signed on the eleventh hour of the eleventh day of the eleventh month, it led to joyous celebrations around the world. People danced in the street, hugged total strangers, laughed and cried. Church bells rang out and people gave thanks to God, although perhaps some wondered if he could not have stopped the fighting a little sooner.

Casualties, including dead, wounded, those who died from disease and vanished were reckoned at about 40 million, but could never be accurately calculated.

Just one week earlier the poet and company commander Wilfred Owen MC had died, killed in action in France. A random German bullet went cleanly through his head.

His poems lived on, particularly 'Dulce et Decorum Est'. The last verse reads:

> *If in some smothering dreams, you too could pace*
> *Behind the wagon that we flung him in,*
> *And watch the white eyes writhing in his face,*
> *His hanging face, like a devil's sick of sin;*
> *If you could hear, at every jolt, the blood*
> *Come gargling from the froth-corrupted lungs,*
> *Obscene as cancer, bitter as the cud*
> *Of vile, incurable sores on innocent tongues –*
> *My friend, you would not tell with such high zest*
> *To children ardent for some desperate glory,*
> *The old Lie:* Dulce et decorum est
> Pro patria mori.

None could foresee that before a year was out the Spanish flu pandemic would seep into the weakened limbs of the survivors. Give or take a few, 50 million more would die.

Post Armistice, the victorious Allies could now set about agreeing how to share the vast spoils among themselves, including the ships. Germany awaited instructions. Months dragged by and finally the German sailors settled the matter themselves. On 21 June 1919, fifty-two of the seventy-four interned ships, their skeleton German crews evading their guards, were scuttled. As the seacocks were opened, carefully prepared for this moment, one by one the ships settled in calm seas and sank to the bottom of Scapa Flow. The few Royal Navy sailors on guard managed to prevent around twenty sinkings, including the sole battleship to survive, the *Baden*. A few rusting remains still lie in the shallow waters, visited by divers from time to time.

Fisher was staying in the Hamilton summer residence, a shooting lodge on moorland close to Strathaven in southern Scotland. It was a bright sunny morning, just a few low clouds drifting across the horizon. Outside a gardener was clipping the rose bushes. On the far side of the lawn in the home paddock a herd of Highland cattle were browsing quietly on some scattered hay bales. Fisher loved to escape here whenever Nina invited him, away from people and away from the noise of politics and warfare. He was enjoying a leisurely morning coffee when the butler delivered him *The Times*. The headline was the scuttling of the German fleet at Scarpa Flow. Fisher threw the paper down and struggled out of his chair. Nina came in to see what the fuss was about.

Fisher picked up the paper and pointed to the headline. 'How did this happen? What were those nincompoops doing that they allowed it?' Fisher's health had deteriorated recently under the depravations of cancer. He was stooped and his face now was deeply imbedded with the damage wrought by age and a life upon the ocean. He shuffled back to his armchair while Nina tried to calm him. 'They have made damn fools of us,' he cried. 'That's what happened. They have made the British Navy a laughing stock.'

Nina nodded, made him sit up and plumped his pillow. As she remarked, 'The Lord giveth and the Lord taketh away.'

Fisher smiled. 'Ah, indeed. The Book of Job.'

EPILOGUE

WILLIAM KNOX D'ARCY died on 1 May 1917 aged sixty-seven at Stanmore Hall of bronchopneumonia. His death attracted a surprising amount of attention but, after all, he was really the founder of the Persian, later Iranian, oil industry. Without D'Arcy there would have been a whole series of potential outcomes involving Russia, Shell Oil or Standard Oil, or any number of players who could have ended up in control of these vast supplies of oil. Most of the alternatives would not have been good for Britain.

D'Arcy died with his wealth intact; in today's terms around £50 million worth. An array of the rich and powerful attended his funeral in Stanmore. D'Arcy's largesse had much benefitted the residents and farmers. The procession was watched by hundreds of local spectators, as the hearse, drawn by horses with black plumes, slowly carried the coffin through the village to the church of St John the Evangelist for the service.

The black granite gravestone read:

WILLIAM KNOX D'ARCY. Aged 67.

*Erected in most loving memory by his wife Nina and his children.
'I have fought the good fight, I have finished my course, I have kept
my faith.' (Timothy IV.7.)*

The eulogy was read by D'Arcy's stable master. He finished by saying, 'William has ended his life by being responsible for two extraordinary achievements: Mount Morgan mine, one of the largest silver and copper mines ever discovered, and at one stage the world's largest gold mine; and the oil find in Persia – when it was found, described as "the biggest oil field ever discovered in the world". For the son of a bankrupt solicitor, truly, truly remarkable.'

Perhaps something to the effect that 'when you roll the dice and lose, double up' might have been more the essence of D'Arcy, than Timothy 4:7. D'Arcy's was a philosophy for which at least the British navy should be grateful.

In 1935 D'Arcy's company APOC was renamed the Anglo-Iranian Oil Company (AIOC) (being the name of the country in Persian). A series of vituperative arguments between the Iranian government and the company then took place until a complex new agreement was finally reached. APOC later expanded its business elsewhere and in 1954 APOC became the British Petroleum Company, later BP.

D'Arcy's old partner in Mount Morgan, Walter Hall and his wife Eliza, continued their philanthropic activities in Australia. After Walter died in 1911 Eliza set up the Walter and Eliza Hall Trust. It was to be used to relieve poverty, advance education and for the general benefit of the community. The trust still exists today and is renowned for its funding of medical research, having supported some of Australia's most successful programs.

~

John (Jacky) Arbuthnot Fisher died of cancer at St James's Square on 10 July 1920, aged seventy-nine. He was given a national funeral at Westminster Abbey. The coffin was drawn on a gun carriage through the streets of London by blue jackets, with six admirals as pall bearers and an escort of Royal Marines, their arms reversed, to the slow beat of muffled drums. The body was cremated at Golders Green Crematorium and the following day the ashes were moved to Kilverstone, escorted by the Royal Navy. They were placed in the grave of his wife, underneath a chestnut tree, overlooking the figurehead of his first seagoing ship, HMS *Calcutta*. The obituaries were lavish, including those by his old friends at *The Times*. An unctuous poem was published by Sir William Watson. 'His ageless eyes burned with unsquandered power ...' etc, etc.

It is strange to reflect though that this man – who had had a dynamic effect on the development of the British navy – never commanded a fleet in battle.

There were various moves to try to have busts erected in Trafalgar Square alongside Nelson and later Jellicoe and Beatty, but it was to no avail. His old friend the Duchess of Hamilton had a memorial slab erected on the wall of a church at Berwick St John. There it remains above a large photograph of Jacky and, for some reason, an empty metal deed box with his name on it. Fisher had provoked strong emotions and criticism over Gallipoli and the failure of his battlecruisers at Jutland. In England he was no darling of the establishment. His background and his delightful eccentricities, including his failure to give precedence to birth, were too strong a provocation to many in power – with the honourable exceptions of Winston Churchill and King Edward VII.

~

The annual Trafalgar Day celebrations were coming up. This would be a universal celebration of England's greatest naval victory against Spain and France on 21 October 1805. Admiral Lord Nelson in particular would be remembered in towns and cities all over England and in every wardroom and on every British ship. Nelson had died on the deck of his ship, HMS *Victory*, at just the moment when it seemed the battle was won. He had been shot by a sniper in the rigging of the French ship *Redoubtable*.

Fisher's great friend and ally, Sir Herbert Richmond, was expected to be in Portsmouth for the event, but he was now established in the hierarchy of Cambridge University. He felt a great reluctance to leave the university for what he was certain would be a repeat of the endless speeches by almost every admiral in the fleet, none of which would contain anything new.

It struck him that it was not long – a mere three months – since First Sea Lord Jacky Fisher had died, and though his funeral had indeed been a very grand affair perhaps it would be timely to arrange a small gathering of the families that had been involved in the seminal decision to switch every ship in the fleet from coal to oil. The Master of Trinity Hall, a great friend, was prepared to lend him the college hall for the evening. The issue remained who to invite. After some thought, he decided it would be most appropriate to ask some of Fisher's family, but also whoever he could locate from the family of William Knox D'Arcy and, of course, his own wife Elsa and her sister Mary, both half-sisters to Gertrude Bell. Gertrude was now living in Baghdad but had been a significant if reluctant contributor to Britain's search for oil. In any event his family would like to see her.

From Fisher's family he asked his son Cecil, now Cecil Vavasseur and the owner of Kilverstone Hall, together with his three sisters Beatrix, Dorothy and Pamela.

He then invited D'Arcy's second wife, Ernestine 'Nina' Nutting, and D'Arcy's five children from his first marriage to Elena: William, Lionel, Violet, Gertrude and Ethel. He had quite a time locating addresses but thought he had directed the invitations correctly.

It took some time for the responses to arrive. From Fisher's family, son Cecil and his three sisters had all replied that they would be delighted to attend. There was no response from D'Arcy's three daughters. William wrote a brief note in reply. 'My father's treatment of my mother Elena was increasingly outrageous veering in the end towards violence. Since I would have nothing good to say about D'Arcy I shall not be attending. However, I do thank you for your kind invitation. William D'Arcy.' Lionel wrote a single paragraph to say that he would attend. D'Arcy's second wife Ernestine said she would be delighted to be there.

Gertrude wrote a warm letter from Baghdad. She gave permission for Richmond to read out an extract on the night. Richmond's own wife Elsa and sister Mary would both attend. The rest of the guest list would be a few interested friends, some from the university history department. The Master asked politely if he could join the celebrations. Winston had of course been asked but regretted he could not come, replying: 'A wonderful, joyous, belligerent, talkative and intelligent friend and colleague. If I might quote Shakespeare: "He was a man, take him for all in all, I shall not look upon his like again." Sadly, I am sure that that is true.'

On the day of the celebrations it was a chilly autumn evening, with cheeks kissed by icy winds and stoles retrieved from the wardrobe. The college, perched on the bank of the river Cam, looked at peace; somehow carrying lightly the nearly 700 years since it had been formed by the bishop of Norwich, Bishop Bateman. His mission was to replenish the supply of clergymen trained in the common law, decimated like the rest of the country by the Black Death. The candles were lit, the chandeliers aglow, and the fifty or so guests sat up close to the high table, under the flinty gaze of

Sir Nathaniel Lloyd, master of the college until he retired in 1737. The walls of the hall were covered by portraits of college celebrities, mostly stern lawyers, all male, peering out from under ill-fitting wigs.

Richmond, dressed in his admiral's uniform with an impressive array of medals, opened the evening by thanking the Master and welcoming the guests, particularly family. He acknowledged it was Trafalgar Day, and an appropriate day to pay tribute to the navy for ensuring that for the 100 years since, Britain had ruled the waves. Turning to Fisher, he re-emphasised what an unwavering commitment he had devoted to the transition of the navy from a nineteenth-century anachronism to a twentieth-century fighting force.

He went on: 'Fisher never commanded a fleet in a major battle, but sea battles are not just won at sea. To win you need a lot more than that and that's what Fisher understood. You need ships that are faster, have better guns, stronger armour, better systems, and most of all a better-trained crew. Vitally, you need the best people, regardless of birth or social status, in command. All that Fisher knew, and he also knew that submarines, mines, torpedoes, airplanes and electronics were here to stay and had permanently altered the power equation. Thank God he did.' There was a round of applause.

Richmond continued. 'His most courageous and difficult decision was the switch of the entire fleet to oil and this he could not have done without the contribution of William Knox D'Arcy and Gertrude Bell, the latter with mixed feelings. She disliked oil but she understood the cause. So that is why we have all three families represented here today. As you all know, Gertrude is in Baghdad busy creating a whole new Arab country but her half-sisters, one of whom is my wife, are here and Gertrude also sent us a letter. I will just read out the most significant part but before I do, I cannot resist a quote from the Old Testament, Isaiah 54:10, which I think, now the war is over, Jacky might have liked.

"'For the mountains may depart, and the hills be removed, but my steadfast love shall not depart from you, and my covenant of peace shall not be removed.'"

'Now, Gertrude's letter.' He unfolded the letter and held it up to read.

"'I became very fond of Jacky Fisher the more I got to know him. So exuberant and very, very smart. Direct but never rude. You could on no account say anything to him that was not quite accurate. He would certainly pick it up. He seemed to retain everything he had ever heard. He would liven things up by peppering his comments with something pithy from the Old Testament. Of course, I also have to acknowledge, he was also a very, very good dancer. I wish all his family well and hope that each of us will ensure that his memory, his great contribution, continues to be honoured.'"

The next speaker was Fisher's son Cecil Vavasseur. He waved his cigar about to emphasise what excellent company Fisher could be whenever he was at home, but stressed that behind this extravagant man was a stoic mother and wife. Kitty had always been there, with her ability to quietly handle Fisher's undoubted eccentricities.

Cecil went on to tell how D'Arcy had visited Kilverstone and he and Jacky had gone pheasant shooting. 'Fortunately, they were both terrible shots. They blazed away at anything that moved but managed to miss most of the time. In between, the noise was appalling. Both of them talked incessantly at the top of their voices. The dogs barked and the beaters provided a continuing backdrop. Servants kept arriving and departing with champagne and a continuing supply of food, all a gift from D'Arcy. His chauffeur had it driven onto the property in his Rolls Royce. All in all, an excellent time indeed. I am proud to have had him as a father.'

The next to speak was D'Arcy's son, Lionel. He looked rather dishevelled, and nervously kept running his fingers through his unruly locks. He had D'Arcy's looks. Heavily bult, a little overweight, the trousers of his hired evening dress ill-fitting and needing the occasional hitch. 'I know I am the only one of the children here tonight. I felt I should attend but I must say parenting was not D'Arcy's strong suit and, as my brother wrote, his behaviour towards our mother became increasingly unbearable for her and for us to watch. I think he preferred racehorses and hounds before children. However, this is about oil and for his persistence I believe we all need to give thanks. If he "saved" the navy, then praise is deserved, although of course he never bothered to visit Persia and honesty requires me to observe that his motivation would sadly have been money before country. All in all, he was certainly a great character and a prodigious entertainer and, as I said, we should all give thanks for his persistence in staying the course in Persia when all others were wanting to give up. For oil he will always be remembered.'

Richmond had asked D'Arcy's second wife Nina if she wanted to speak but she had declined. She had arrived looking ravishing in a black Chanel dress, an ermine stole, her quadruple string of pearls and outrageously high heels. She sat listening to Lionel with her head on one side and just a hint of a smile.

Richmond asked her again if she wanted to say anything. She shook her head but then replied, 'I'm sorry about his treatment of Elena but I must defend him. He was such tremendous fun when he was in the mood, which was quite often. I was with him when he received the news of the oil strike. It is the only time I have seen him lost for words. Needless to say, he quickly recovered, and the next few days were frantic and an absolute cascade of champagne. Such tremendous fun!'

Richmond thanked all those who had spoken or written. He continued: 'I hope today has reminded all of us of the contributions that Gertrude Bell and William D'Arcy made to allow Fisher to persuade the government and the navy that the switch should be made to oil. I ask you to stand, to charge your glasses and to give a toast to Gertrude Bell, to William Knox D'Arcy and of course to Jacky Fisher. May we not forget the great contribution that their efforts made to the winning of this most difficult war.' There was a round of 'Hear, hear' and a clinking of glasses and the guests resumed their seats. Richmond went on to announce that the university's Haydn Quartet would now play a short interlude for them. He was sure everyone would find it quite enchanting.

The guests sat silently, 'enchanted' as Richmond had said, as the music drifted above them into the darkness, drifting up into the great chandeliers, vanishing into the black beams of the ancient, cantilevered ceiling. How Fisher would have liked it.

~

Gertrude Bell was found dead in her bed in Baghdad on the morning of 12 July 1926 by her maid, Marie. On the table beside the bed was a partly empty bottle of pills. Her death certificate gave the cause of death as 'Dial poisoning'. Dial was a common preparation used as a sedative, which later was discontinued as having been frequently used in suicides. The night before Gertrude had asked Marie not to disturb her, and had sent a note to her friend, the King's advisor Ken Cornwallis, to look after her dog if 'anything happened to her'. Gertrude had for some time been having health issues not assisted by her incessant smoking of foul-smelling cigarettes. She was looking increasingly old beyond her years, her skin showing signs of her exposure to the Mesopotamian deserts, notwithstanding her use of her kaffiyeh.

In addition, she had been forced to recognise that the family fortune was significantly diminished, and she could no longer afford to do whatever pleased her. To add to her woes, her much loved half-brother Hugo had recently died of typhoid.

On her desk was a book of Persian poetry. A page was marked by a beautifully illustrated Persian bookmark. On it were written the words of a Hafiz poem.

> *Ah! When he found it easy to depart,*
> *He left the harder pilgrimage to me!*
> *Oh, camel driver, though the cordage start,*
> *For God's sake help me lift my fallen load,*
> *And Pity be my comrade on the road!*

～

Like those with doubts about the death of the great love of her life, Dick Doughty-Wylie, some of the community in Baghdad wondered: could this have been suicide?

Gertrude was buried in the British cemetery in Baghdad's Bab-al-Sharji district. Her funeral was an event of great significance. Large crowds of the local people attended, including colleagues and British dignitaries. Her coffin was draped with the Union Jack and the flag of Iraq. The Iraqi army lined the street. On foot followed the High Commissioner, the Prime Minister, the Regent and an endless procession of officials. From the desert came sheiks alerted by some desert transmission of the news of her death. Among the tribes were the Howeitat and Dulaim. As her coffin was carried to the cemetery, it was reported that King Faisal watched from his private balcony.

Tributes poured in. The Colonial Secretary in the House of Commons, Leo Amery; Sir Valentine Chirol in *The Times*; Leonard Woolley of the British Museum; her friend Professor Salomon Reinach in Paris; and a powerful column in *The Times of India*. In the museum a room was dedicated – 'The Gertrude Bell Room' – and Sir Henry Dobbs, the High Commissioner, commissioned a brass plaque. The plaque in many ways encapsulates the reason for such an extravagant response to her death. It reads:

> *GERTRUDE BELL*
> *Whose memory the Arabs will ever hold*
> *in reverence and affection*
> *Created this museum in 1923*
> *Being then Honorary Director of Antiquities for the Iraq*
> *With wonderful knowledge and devotion*
> *She assembled the most precious objects in it*
> *And through the heat of the summer*
> *Worked on them until the day of her death*
> *On 12th July 1926.*
> *King Faisal and the Government of Iraq*
> *In gratitude for her great deeds in this country*
> *Have ordered the principal wing shall bear her name*
> *And with their permission*
> *Her friends have erected this Tablet.*

The response to her death was extraordinary. King George V wrote to her parents saying, 'The nation will with us mourn the loss.'

T. E. Lawrence had been in many ways the closest as a kindred spirit. They made each other laugh, mocking the establishment. Gertrude had been astounded but full of admiration when she heard that Lawrence, in 1918, standing before King George V in Buckingham Palace surrounded by flunkies, had responded to the King's revelation that he had been summoned to the palace to be knighted, by politely refusing and walking out. Who else would ever do such a thing?

Lawrence wrote a typically enigmatic letter to Hugh from India. Totally disillusioned that the promises the British government had made to the Arabs would not be fulfilled, he had decided to 'disappear' himself. He joined the RAF as Aircraftsman Shaw, in a nod to his friend George Bernard Shaw, and wangled a posting to Karachi. He wrote of Gertrude: 'The Iraq State is a fine monument, even if it only lasts a few more years.' He continued: 'I don't think I ever met anyone more entirely civilised, in the sense of the width of her intellectual sympathy.' He finished his letter, 'Her loss must be nearly unbearable, but I'm so grateful to you for giving so much of her personality to the world.'

Perhaps it was her stepmother Florence who best summed her up. 'In truth, the real basis of Gertrude's nature was her capacity for deep emotion. Great joys came into her life, and, also, great sorrows. How could it be otherwise, with a temperament so avid of experience? Her ardent and magnetic personality drew the lives of others into hers as she passed along.'

~❧

T.E. Lawrence, by now Aircraftsman Shaw, died 19 May 1935. His motorcycle clipped the back of a cyclist while riding to Bovington Camp, where he was stationed. He died after six days in a coma. Winston Churchill wrote, 'I deem him one of the greatest beings alive in our time. I do not see his like elsewhere. I fear whatever our need, we shall never see his like again.'

ACKNOWLEDGEMENTS

The production of this book has been a somewhat solitary affair, but it absolutely would not have happened without the input and encouragement of my publisher Jane Curry of Ventura Press and the extraordinary commitment to editing and content of Catherine McCredie and Amanda Hemmings, not to mention Jane herself. For any errors still within the text I can only blame myself.

Thanks also to Deborah Parry, who patiently designed the book's intriguing cover. I should also thank Gemma Ryan, an experienced writer and editor, without whose initial encouragement the initial outline would not even have reached Jane. Much thanks too to (Admiral) Chris Oxenbould for his considered comments on naval matters. I should also pay tribute to family encouragement and thank my wife Gail, who has put up with endless grumbling and muttering and the occasional lapses of good manners – for which, apologies.